THE
SKYSCRAPER
KILLERS

I. JAMES BERTOLINA

ISBN (paperback): 978-1-7321409-2-9
ISBN (ebook): 978-1-7321409-3-6

Library of Congress Control Number: 2024901369

Published in the United States of America by
East Third Street Press, LLC
1850 East 3rd Street, Suite 310
Charlotte, NC 28204

Book Cover by Ebook Launch
Interior Design and Formatting by Damonza

First edition, 2024

Reader Praise for I. James Bertolina's *Green Zone Jack*

"I recommend this book to anyone who wants to read a fast-paced
mystery… a great way to spend an evening curled up by the fire."
- Power Librarian Book Reviews

"This story is on the same stage as books written by Thor,
Wright and Clancy… a marvelous ride… My first by this
author but I am eagerly awaiting his next effort!"
- Kathi Defranc, Goodreads

"This story reeks of the dangerous, lawless Old West,
but on steroids, in the modern day Middle East… if
you want a great thriller filled with adventure and quick
pacing, this book is for you. A great ride and read!"
- The Fictional Housewife

"There's a lot of suspense, all of the expected twists,
some unexpected twists, and a few moments that just
reach out and slap you in the face. This was a great
read that I sat down and finished in one sitting."
-Raymond Weiand, Amazon

"Full of action, suspense and intrigue. This is the first book
I have read of Bertolina's but can't wait to read another."
- coyotecactus, Amazon

"This is a fabulous thriller."
- Jim Craig, Amazon

"This timely and relevant tale was a very enjoyable read.
Looking forward to reading more of this author's work."
- Thomas Rutherford, Amazon

ACKNOWLEDGEMENTS

The author would like to thank the following people for their invaluable help in bringing this novel to fruition:

Wendy B.R., beta reader

Tony C., the Italian beta reader

Harry T., beta reader

Jeff D., beta reader

Steve H., environmental engineer

Russ A., architect

Bill. P., attorney

Shannon R., editor, The Editorial Department

Julie M., editor, The Editorial Department

Ross B., The Editorial Department

Leigh W., editor

Jane R., author support, Ryder Author Resources

CHAPTER 1

"Are you in or out?" Dom tried the door handle again when his reclamation project didn't respond to his knock.

Her apartment door opened to a soaked sports magazine on the linoleum floor under an upended fifth of Russian vodka.

"I slipped," she said. In gray warm-up pants, white tube socks, and a bulky red sweatshirt, Angie Crete sat curled up on a love seat in front of a picture window. Her shoulder-length black hair hung damp from a shower. Flurries swirled around Uptown's snow globe towers behind her.

"Bad hangover?" he said.

"I've had worse."

"You aren't ready."

"Some other time might be better," she said.

He wouldn't accept any more of her excuses why she couldn't leave the apartment. Here was her last chance if she wanted his help to reengage with life. "No more tomorrows. I'll be out front."

❧

Dom waited in the Porsche. If she failed to show, he'd call her Coast Guard superior, John Brody, and tell him to find someone else to help her.

On the next block, a crane hoisted brick pallets off a flatbed truck at a hotel construction site. Rick Braun's trumpet started in on "Can You Feel It." When the song ended, he would drive away and not look back.

Six minutes later the song faded and still no Angie. He glanced toward the entrance and saw her there, motionless. "Come on, open it," he said.

She stared at him through the snow. Just when the thought came to him that she couldn't muster up the courage, she materialized on the sidewalk dressed in cream jeans, beige down jacket, and chestnut Ugg boots, her damp hair banded in a ponytail. John Brody might be right: she was too tough to let what happened in the South China Sea ruin her life.

Without a word she slid beside him. He drove into a blizzard gust.

CHAPTER 2

THEY TOOK THE last available booth in The Roost, a Central Avenue diner surrounded by new condo and apartment buildings. Construction workers, lawyers, bankers, and students filled the place for the city's best coffee and breakfast.

Angie yawned and rubbed one of her bloodshot green eyes.

"Need aspirin?" Dom said.

She shook her head. "Coffee does the trick," she said.

He mouthed *coffee* to a waitress who glanced their way from the counter.

"We're here for?" she said.

"To meet someone," Dom said.

"And why do I need to meet your someone?"

"Tell me afterward."

She wore a maroon turtleneck sweater under the down jacket she removed. "Brody didn't tell me how a former Coast Guard sniper ends up in Charlotte," she said.

"I figured he gave you the rundown."

"He said years before his appointment to vice admiral he served with you."

"After my sniper days, we were investigators in the Great Lakes Ninth District Intelligence Branch," he said.

The waitress set their coffees down. Given the size of her lip ring, Dom wondered how she ate.

"He also mentioned you considered the priesthood," Angie said.

"Monk, not priest. Never made the leap."

"What held you back at the cliff?"

"A conflict of interest."

"Who has conflicts with monks?"

"Nine-eleven occurred during my Formation Process. I couldn't square vengeance with monastic life."

"You changed curricula from monk school to sniper school?"

"I was handy with a rifle thanks to a father who made sure all his boys knew how to shoot."

Their waitress passed with an armload of dirty dishes.

"Can I have a bran muffin?" Angie said.

"Want it warmed?"

Angie shook her head and emptied three sugar packets into her over-creamed coffee. "How did you end up in North Carolina?"

"A lucrative niche," Dom said.

"Your website says Mundy and Associates' specialty is corporate intelligence and investigations."

"We have more work than we can handle."

She gulped her coffee then added two more sugars. "Wheel around in a Porsche 911 Turbo S Cabriolet with five-hundred-plus horses, I say you've recovered from the vow of poverty."

"You know your cars."

"I'm from Big Lick, fifty miles east of here. In high school I kept the books for my uncle's import car repair garage."

"Why Charlotte over Big Lick?" he said.

Brody had shared with him the reason for her Charlotte medical leave, but he wanted her version. If she talked about what happened, maybe some of the pain would dissipate.

"John figured a bigger city might be the right place for a break. Translation: damaged goods aren't welcome in the Coast Guard Investigative Services," she said.

"He stopped by my office on his way to visit relatives in Cashiers and asked if I could use, on a temporary basis, one of his best investigators who needed time off after an operation went bad," Dom said. "He mentioned your struggles and the blame you still carry around for what happened."

She drank more coffee. "One KIA and one MIA, yeah, I take the blame. They were my responsibility."

"Here she is," he said. Dom slid out and went to the frail woman who surveyed the crowd from the hostess stand.

"Mrs. Giron, Dominick Mundy," he said.

He showed Mrs. Giron to their booth. "Angie Crete, meet Mrs. Ruby Giron."

"Hello, Mrs. Giron," Angie said.

"Everyone calls me Ms. Ruby," she said. She held a plastic grocery bag full of papers. One of her scuffed pink boots was frayed at the toe. When Dom offered to take her coat, she shook her head and sat across from Angie. The bag went next to her in the seat. She removed the scarf from her gray-streaked light-brown hair.

Dom pulled a chair from a nearby table. "Would you like coffee?" he said.

"I'm fine," she said. Ms. Ruby spoke with the same dignity Dom heard when he'd first talked with her on the telephone. He saw a lifetime of hardship on her ruddy, corrugated face. Her wide-set sad eyes took both of them in.

"Who are you?" Ms. Ruby said.

"Angie Crete."

"Mr. Mundy already said your name. Why are you here?"

"She works with me," Dom said.

"Is she any good?" Ms. Ruby said.

The waitress set the muffin on a plate next to Angie's coffee cup.

"I don't have all the answers," Angie said.

"Answers are what I need. If y'all can't give them to me, I'll find someone who can," Ms. Ruby said.

Angie peeled off the wrapper and plopped a wedge into her mouth followed by a swirl of coffee.

"Her son was murdered," Dom said.

From the bag Ms. Ruby withdrew several eight-and-a-half-by-eleven color photographs of a well-dressed man strung by the neck to what appeared to be a bridge girder. "The police haven't found who killed my boy," she said.

"Where'd you get these?" Dom said.

"My attorney, Julian Ybarra, who I told I wanted copies of Palmer's last pictures. He said he knew someone who might be able to help."

"Why Julian Ybarra?" Dom said. He knew Ybarra's reputation. Speed-dial lawyer for every dope peddler in the city, who never missed a prime-time news hour opportunity to preach police incompetence.

"Julian's the only lawyer who offered to help my neighbor get her daughter out of the penitentiary."

"When were these taken?" Dom said. He passed Angie the photographs.

"Seven months ago, after a jogger found Palmer in Freedom Park at one thirty in the morning July Fourth. I've sent letter requests to Chief Zorkaid for more police officers to be put on his case. Only response has been form letters." She gave Dom the chief's CMPD reply envelope. Angie lined up the pictures next to her muffin.

Dom removed the letter. Chief Zorkaid conveyed his condolences and relayed that his investigators would contact her if they received any new information. He handed the letter and envelope to Angie. The waitress refilled their coffees. Angie scanned the chief's reply, then went back to the photos and munched on another chunk of muffin.

"After his father died of a sudden heart attack, Palmer bought a mountain bike to ride to and from his East Boulevard office. He inherited high cholesterol from his father's side of the family and realized if he didn't take better care of himself, he'd suffer the same fate. From where he lived in Cherry, he could be at his desk in less than twenty minutes. They found his bike in Sugar Creek." She pointed to the photograph of a half-submerged mountain bike.

Angie tapped more sugar packets into her coffee and studied a close-up of the rope around Palmer's neck. "He commuted home after midnight?" she said.

"Palmer took pride in his work and put in long hours," Ms. Ruby said.

"How did he make his living?" Dom said.

"He was a trained environmental engineer. Many of those Uptown skyscrapers wouldn't be there without my Palmer's help. He was a good son and smart, too. Received a full academic scholarship from Carnegie Mellon and graduated in the top two percent of his class."

"Do the police have any suspects?" Angie said.

"They have nobody." She set the bag in the middle of the table. "Here's all I have. Newspaper clippings, notes from Julian, a disc with contents from Palmer's computer, and keys to his office and house. If more detectives worked his case, the killer would be in jail already."

Angie leafed through several paper-clipped pieces of paper.

"Julian told me he never heard of Mundy and Associates and recommended his own investigator," Ms. Ruby said. "Mr. Mundy, the only reason I'm here is Mr. Hillstead. He told me you were the only investigator he'd use. Will you help me, or are you too busy like the police?"

Dom gestured toward the bag. "Can we keep these?"

"They're copies. The originals never leave my house."

Angie read a sticky note attached to one of the papers. "Who's Karen Robles?" she said.

"Palmer's office manager, a wonderful lady he hired the first week he went into business for himself."

Ms. Ruby fished a tissue from her pocketbook and patted away tears. "My boy had a big heart. He didn't deserve what happened to him."

"We'll get back with you," Dom said.

"If YOU don't, I'll speak with Julian's investigator."

CHAPTER 3

Dom idled the Porsche in a parking lot behind The Roost.

"Did she mean Carter Hillstead?" Angie said.

"The one and only," Dom said.

"How would she know a billionaire?"

"Her husband worked as Carter's personal driver."

Goose-down snowflakes melted on the hood.

"And why are you a military defense conglomerate's go-to investigator?"

"From time to time Carter brings me on for sensitive projects. He knows a local murder's not my specialty but trusts what I have to say. When he asked, I told him we'd look into Palmer's case."

"I'm sure CMPD has competent homicide detectives."

"A fresh set of eyes might help Ms. Ruby."

A backhoe driver lowered stabilizer legs at a nearby brewery construction site.

"Does she need false hope?" Angie said.

"Hope never hurt anyone."

"She's already been hurt once."

"Is Ms. Ruby who you're concerned about?" he said.

Out her side window Angie followed cases of beer being wheeled through a restaurant's kitchen delivery door.

"At the current moment I might not be your best choice."

"Tell me about the Spratly Islands," he said.

"I failed people I was responsible for."

"Brody's version is six pirates were killed in a shoot-out," Dom said.

The backhoe's bucket started to rise.

"Did he tell you one of mine was killed too? And I was only fifteen feet away when sex trafficker Qi's men snatched Sandi?"

"A fifteen-foot gap between boats in motion no one could clear. He also said a grenade explosion blew a Philippines National Police Maritime Group commander into the water with you.

"I can't get Sandi's screams out of my head."

"*Being* a Coast Guard officer, she knew the risks," he said.

Angie turned toward him with tears in her eyes. "And how about her five- and eight-year-old daughters? Or her husband, who calls me every month to see if we've heard any word? Do I tell him if she isn't already dead, Sandi's been sold to the highest bidder?"

"When the time's right, you'll know what to say."

A brick wall collapsed in a wave from the bucket's nudge.

"The Coast Guard psychiatrist said I've been traumatized," she said.

"Have you?"

"No way."

A Porta-John vacuum truck pulled to a stop behind the backhoe.

"Then why do you stay cooped up in your apartment?"

"I'm not anxious when I'm by myself."

You won't find any answers locked in your Uptown apartment building, he thought.

"Here's the deal, you can join me and help find Ms. Ruby

some closure, or on the way back to your place we'll swing by an ABC store and pick up another Russian."

"A diplomat who drives a Porsche."

"A twenty-dollar bottle of vodka answers a lot of questions," he said.

The beer delivery driver wheeled back for another load.

"I'm full of answers. It's the questions I can't stand," she said.

"You remind me of my soon-to-be ex-wife. Answers are your strong suit."

"You're married?"

"On my way to past-tense status."

"I'm not sure I like the comparison."

"Let's check out that bridge," he said.

CHAPTER 4

DOM AIMED HIS flashlight at the rust-smeared girder under the Freedom Park bridge. "The rope was looped there," he said.

"Not rope, bungee cord." She held up a picture from Ms. Ruby's bag, of Palmer's head inches below the fourth girder. A bungee cord coiled around his neck was secured to the girder.

"Check out the knot?" Dom said.

"A timber hitch," she said.

"Cars, now knots, I'm impressed."

"My brother learned knots as a Boy Scout."

Traffic thumped over expansion joints above them.

"Why would Palmer's killer use one of those?"

"They're a quick tie and secure," she said.

"Our killer's a Boy Scout?" Dom said.

"Or maybe a lineman or an arborist, they both use timber hitches," she said.

He swung the light toward the cement embankment. "Have you seen any background information in the bag about Palmer?" Dom said.

"He and his brother were raised in Albany, New York. After Carnegie Mellon, Palmer relocated to Charlotte for a chemical company job. A number of years later he set up his own shop,

Giron Environmental Partners. Mother and father came down to escape New York's winters."

"How about the brother?" Dom ran his light up and down the embankment.

"Nickolas. Owns and operates an Asheville landscape business. Palmer was single and lived alone."

"Show me the body shots?" he said.

He used the overcast light slanting under the bridge to look at the pictures she handed him.

Palmer's close-cropped chocolate hair and trimmed goatee were peppered with silver. His mouth and one eye, the one not swollen shut, were open. Electrical tape bound his hands behind his back. A dinner-plate-size pee stain spread out on his cuffed khaki pants. The gray suit coat hung open and his red bow tie was skewed. Two buttons were popped off the middle of his light-pink shirt. Half-eye readers with only one lens dangled from a leather lanyard. Above the brown wing tips were cream socks with triangle designs. A quarter-inch-wide rubber band encircled his right ankle.

"The rubber band kept his pant leg out of the bike chain," Angie said.

"He's a big guy, look how close his shoes are to the sidewalk," Dom said.

She scanned one of the bag papers. "Two hundred five pounds, six two and three quarters."

"Might take more than one person to hoist him up there," Dom said.

From another page she read, "A primary care doctor out for a jog almost ran into the body because the bridge lights were out from being vandalized."

"The doctor won't run under any more bridges in the middle of the night," he said.

"Palmer's bike rested near the stone bridge," she said.

In another picture she handed him, part of the chrome handlebars and half the front tire protruded above the water line several yards upstream near a pedestrian stone bridge. One side of the creek was covered with barren bushes, the other with grass encased in shallow snow. There, stone stairs led up to the medical center's campus. A tree limb now snagged on ice where the bike was found. He tapped the picture's handlebars. "A bungee cord," he said.

"Bungees would secure his briefcase. These notes say whoever killed him used one of his own cords," she said.

"The bike's twenty yards upstream. Was he attacked at the stone bridge and brought under here?" He gave her back the picture.

"Investigators believe the attack occurred up at the street. They found drag marks in the grass."

"Let's take a look."

They scaled the embankment next to the bridge and came out at an urgent care facility where new accumulation covered the lot.

"Crime scene investigators found his glasses lens under those rhododendrons," she said.

A row of rhododendrons blocked Morehead Street's sidewalk. Their branches sagged under snow.

"He biked the same route I would. East Boulevard to Latta Park to Romany, then Harding Place toward East Morehead Street." He motioned toward the intersection light. "Once I'm on South Kings Drive, Baldwin Avenue and the house in Cherry are only a few minutes away."

"Whoever attacked him used those bushes for cover," she said.

"With the light up here, maybe someone saw what happened," Dom said.

Light poles lined the streets.

"I haven't seen any mention of witnesses," she said.

Dom looked up at dozens of apartment windows along the opposite side of Morehead Street. How many sets of eyes saw Palmer ambushed and dragged under the bridge before they turned away, not wanting to get involved? His cell phone pinged with the number of Winnie Aviles, his assistant.

On the drive here he'd asked Angie to dial the number on the sticky note for Karen Robles, Palmer's office manager. The call went to her full voicemail. Dom rang Winnie to track down Karen's current place of employment.

"An easy find with all her Instagram activity," Winnie said. "I'll text you her address." Winnie clicked off and her text arrived with an address off Statesville Road.

"Have time for another stop?" he said.

Angie glanced at her watch like she was expected somewhere. "I have a shrink appointment at one thirty."

"You'll be on time."

He saw her hesitation. "I still don't know how my dead weight will be of help to you," she said.

"I'll be the judge of any weight problems."

CHAPTER 5

"How long have you been married?" Angie said.

"Five years. One great year followed by four below-average years." He followed tire tracks along a metal building-lined street with the address on Winnie's text. The gravid sky appeared ready to dump another several inches of forecasted snow.

"What's her name?"

"Rachel Ketton."

"She kept her name?"

"Rachel weighed out the pros and cons of what a name change could do for her consulting-career advancement. Mundy lost out to the corporate ladder."

"Brand protection."

"Rachel's all about brand management."

They left the Porsche on the street and popped along salt on the shoveled walkway. The company's name *Silo Adhesives* scrawled around a cylindrical monument sign near the entrance. Dom opened the lobby door to the smell of burned rubber. He pressed an interior service-door call button beside the sign reading *Appointments Only. NO EXCEPTIONS!* A guy in a laurel-green, long-sleeve shirt with a clipboard answered. "Who are you here for?" His name tag read *Wayne*.

"Karen Robles," Dom said.

"What time's your appointment?"

"No appointment, we were in the area," Dom said.

Wayne indicated the *Appointments Only* plaque with an annoyed look. "No exceptions," he said.

"We're here on a personal matter," Dom said.

Wayne paused long enough to make sure they understood how perturbed he felt. "Wait there," he said.

The door closed.

"Could you work with such a smell?" Angie said.

"Depends how bad I needed the job," Dom said.

She read a framed wall article beside youth girls' field hockey award plaques. "Silo's the largest bumper-sticker-glue manufacturer in the country."

"Your smell is money being made," he said.

Wayne returned and behind him sat a woman in a wheelchair.

Karen fingered Dom's card while they sat around the warehouse breakroom table. "Why do you want to know about Palmer?" she said.

A roll of paper towels stood next to an open doughnut box with a solitary strawberry shortcake éclair left inside.

"His mother's not satisfied with whoever killed him still out there," Dom said.

She ripped off a paper towel to wipe her runny nose. "Police are clueless. Palmer was his mother's life. He talked to her every day, sometimes twice. His murder devastated her."

"How long did you work together?" Dom said.

"Almost a year, and I felt grateful he hired me after the car accident." She bumped the chair's armrest with her elbow. "He was the best employer ever."

"You worked at his East Boulevard office?" he said.

"A house he converted into an office building. When he brought me on he added a ramp to the front steps." She sneezed into her paper towel and pulled off another one.

"Tell us about his work," Dom said.

"He was an environmental engineer who made a name for himself with commercial property people. Never turned a job away. I told him to hire another engineer, but he didn't want to lose the personal touch his clients expected from him."

"What service did he provide?" Angie said.

"People hired him to give his opinion on the environmental situation with commercial property. They might bring him on before a property sale or a development got underway."

"Do you remember jobs he may have been involved with around the time of his murder?" Dom said.

"He kept his jobs-in-progress files in a certain drawer of his desk. I recall a Sunset Road apartment complex; a Gaffney, South Carolina, frozen chicken warehouse; an Uptown developer's mountain resort; and something to do with Irwin Creek."

Angie typed notes on her smartphone.

"And if he found problems, what then?" Dom said.

"He'd offer work-arounds and solutions."

"These problems expensive?" Angie said.

"More times than not they were manageable, but every so many jobs he'd have a cleanup with an open-checkbook price tag. Palmer understood the impact he could have on the financial futures of people he was involved with. Some of his clients were saddled with personal guarantees on loans they took out to fund their projects. Those personals could lead to financial ruin if their transaction went off the rails."

She hacked several times. "Palmer brought more to the table than some engineers who never offer up cost-effective fixes. He told me once the last thing a client needed was an overeducated engineer with a high opinion of themselves and no people skills."

"Tell us about these people who hired him?" Dom said.

"Developers, property owners, and many lenders who fork over big money to fund commercial transactions. All of them knew Palmer was meticulous with his phase ones and wouldn't be intimidated by state regulators and their byzantine rules."

"Phase ones?" Angie said.

A warehouse worker came in and retrieved the doughnut box.

"Initial site evaluation reports he put together to alert everyone involved if the transaction could move forward. He never sugarcoated what he found because he knew more than one shifty competitor who would attempt to generate future income with scare tactics about possible problems down the road with their site."

"How many people made money off these transactions?" Dom said.

"Bankers of course are at the front of the line, followed by vendors like Palmer and the surveyor. If a real estate broker's involved, they'll want their cut, and attorneys are on the clock all the way to the finish line."

"These reports of his pricey?" Dom said.

"Phase ones ran between one and two grand. Additional work would run up the cost up."

He was in the opinion business, and like any guy with opinions, not everyone would agree with him.

"How about client trouble?" Dom said.

"Who would want to kill him?" Karen said.

"Being vise-gripped with personal guarantees might affect how you react to an environmental engineer's negative conclusion," Dom said.

"There might have been raised tempers once in a while but

never any threats. Believe me when I say egos on some of these people were hard to take." She rolled to the sink, filled up a glass of water, and rolled back.

"Anyone in his personal life we need to know about?" Angie said.

"JoJo Cifuentes, his AutoCAD-operator girlfriend. He told me a week before he died they hit a rough patch."

"He share why?" Dom said.

"She reverted to her party-girl lifestyle. When they first met, she dealt with a drug problem. I told him he was too busy to take on someone else's problems."

"JoJo back on drugs?" Dom said.

"No idea. Her cousin, Chico Vega, and his delinquent crew were the problem. She spent too much time with them." She drank some water and put the cup back in her chair's cup holder.

"How long have you worked here?" Dom said.

"I came on a few weeks after his murder. My neighbor mentioned his nephew needed someone to help with social media marketing. The job doesn't compare to being with Palmer. Here I collect a paycheck. With Palmer, I worked with a dear friend."

She pulled out her cell phone and tapped open her photo folder. "Here's my favorite picture and the last one I took of him in his office. The week before Easter he threw a surprise birthday party for me and invited all the tenants." Palmer stood in front of bookshelves at his desk with an infectious smile in a pair of jumbo clown sunglasses and a glitter party crown.

"Can you text me the picture?" Angie said.

"Sure, what's your number?"

❦

Dom removed snow dust with the wipers.

"She'd nominate Palmer for boss of the year," Angie said.

"JoJo sounds like a handful," Dom said.

"From her tone, I'd say Karen wasn't her biggest fan," Angie said.

"Isn't your appointment Uptown?"

"In one of those office buildings."

He wanted to keep her away from her building she hadn't come out of for three weeks. "If you're up for another stop, afterward I'd like to drop in on JoJo," he said.

"Why wouldn't I be?" she said.

"You might need a break."

"Don't kid-glove me, Dom."

OK, he'd push their schedule. Maybe she could use a page turn. "I have another stop to make first," he said.

CHAPTER 6

Dom settled the Porsche next to shoveled mounds of snow in front of his L-shaped building. The Monroe Road property was once a retail center one of the previous owners converted into offices. When they entered the reception area, Winnie looked up from her computer screen. She'd kept her dark blonde dyed hair short after the last round of chemo.

Dom introduced Angie.

"Jock's in," Winnie said.

"He make any headway with Johannsen?" Dom said.

"He only yelled once."

"Tell him I'll be there in a few minutes." Dom gestured down the hall. "Let me show you the place."

They passed a conference room where a slender older man with tight silver hair stood on a stepladder. He spackled a sheet rock crack above a window with a rear courtyard view of a tiny house in a snow-veiled stone garden.

"Who's Jock?" Angie said.

"Among his other duties, my part-time bookkeeper."

"And Johannsen he yelled at?" she said.

"A Stockholm bank chairman who brought us on to find out who embezzled money from his US branch office. We found out his son, the branch's manager, financed his mistress with depositors' money. Now he's under the impression we should agree to a lower fee because his boy was involved."

Dom opened a door to an office with a desk telephone, metal file cabinets, a couch, and a bathroom with a shower. "Here's an office you can use."

"I prefer my apartment," she said.

He ignored the apartment reference. "The couch is a pull-out bed. Your neighbors in the next two offices are former Mexican marines who operate a dignitary protection firm."

"Mexican marines in Charlotte?"

"They like the weather and the airport over New York or Washington."

"Today's weather notwithstanding," she said.

A man with slicked-back silver hair walked up to Winnie's desk.

"Franco."

Dom motioned for him. Franco pulled off his leather gloves and came their way, a beige silk scarf tucked around the collar of his camel overcoat. "My wardrobe isn't prepared for Siberia," Franco said.

"I told Franco, Paris receives more snow than Charlotte," Dom said to Angie.

At a few inches over six feet, his urbane comportment went with the distinguished French accent.

"Meet Angie Crete, a Coast Guard investigator who'll be in the spare office."

"I will?" Angie said.

"Franco Babineaux, the pleasure's mine." He shook her hand with both of his.

"I'm only here on a temporary basis," she said.

"She's here to assist me with a job," Dom said.

"Perhaps, when you have time, you can tell me all about the Coast Guard," Franco said. "I reside around the corner."

He withdrew his cell phone, glanced at the screen, and indicated he needed to take the call. He answered in French and went toward his office.

"French film star looks," Angie said.

"Franco has a colorful past. An architect by trade, he saved the lives of France's president and her family while they vacationed in Martinique. He went to the island to lift jewels from the hotel room of a wealthy Lebanese couple two floors below the president's penthouse suite. Instead of jewels he found military-grade explosives connected to a timer. He cleared the hotel when he pulled the fire alarm. He's our resident cat burglar with a lucky streak."

"I can't wait to hear the lucky part," she said.

"After his fence turned him in, a grateful president offered him a choice. Prison… or, with his unique skills as an architect and cat burglar, work for her on special assignments from time to time. He's here on loan to Homeland Security."

An Asian guy the size of a sumo wrestler filled the exit door when he came in from the rear courtyard.

"Moved in?" Dom said.

"Except for the internet," he said.

"Deuce, Angie Crete," Dom said.

The big man gave her a modest head bow. Half of one pinkie finger was gone and tattoos appeared above his plaid shirt collar.

"Deuce has moved into our rear building," Dom said.

Deuce sauntered into the lobby and out the front door.

"What kind of name is Deuce?" Angie said.

"Takeo Kouda's his name. We call him Deuce because he's the size of two people."

"Those are yakuza tattoos," Angie said.

"Like Franco, he caught a break and left Japan after he saved the life of his boss's daughter and was granted his request to leave."

"He choose Charlotte for the weather too?" She pulled out and checked one of the desk drawers.

"Went to San Francisco's Japantown to live with a relative in the bank-security business who I worked a job with a few years ago. She called me to see if I knew of anyone who needed an extra hand."

"He works for you?"

"I keep him busy."

"How many employees do you have?"

"Deuce, Jock, Winnie, and Hector, in the conference room on the ladder."

"He another master criminal too?"

"Hector de Losa from Miami, thanks to the Mariel boatlift. A gunrunner recruited by Cuba's DGI, directorate general of intelligence, to run guns back to the island from South Florida. He's here thanks to a referral from the United States attorney for the Southern District of Florida."

They went back toward Winnie, where Dom opened a door near the reception desk. "Here's the smaller of our two conference rooms. Feel free to use the computer. Why don't you pull together a list of Palmer's clients from the bag? We might have time to visit one or two after your one-thirty appointment."

He left for Jock's office before she could protest to tell him she wanted to go back to her apartment.

Ninety minutes later Dom found her in the conference room. An empty to-go box from Winnie's take-out lunch order and papers from the bag were strewn across the ten-seat table. "You've been busy," he said.

She pointed to numbers she circled with an orange marker on the white board. "Palmer's financial affairs appear to be in order. He left a thirty-eight-thousand-dollar balance in his business checking account and fifteen grand in his personal checking account. His IRAs totaled ninety-two K. His business line of credit was never touched and he carried no balance on both his credit cards."

"Any real estate debt?"

"The Cherry house mortgage balance was two hundred sixteen grand with another forty-two on the home equity line." She looked at a note. "East Boulevard was four hundred three thousand. He never missed a payment."

"Some might consider six hundred thousand enough motivation to keep late office hours," he said.

She went back to another group of orange-circled numbers. "His one-man environmental business generated, on average, between two and a half to three hundred thousand each of the last three years. Take out Karen's salary, expenses, and payroll taxes and he made a decent living."

Dom saw the time. "If we leave now, you'll be early."

CHAPTER 7

Dom found an Uptown fire lane to pull into and let her out for her doctor's appointment. "After you're through, we'll see if JoJo can work us in," he said. He watched her disappear around a corner and hoped her doctor could help with the pain she carried.

On Church Street he found an open metered space and went into a nearby coffee shop. He ordered his usual black coffee and speed-dialed Winnie.

"You're sure you can fritter away time on a local murder the police can handle?" she said.

"I told Carter we'd take a look and get back to him in a few days."

"By 'a few' do you mean two or three?"

"The shop's in your capable hands, Winnie."

"To my point, you have real clients who pay the bills they—"

"Only a couple of days. Now let's have the rundown."

She ruffled papers. "You remember Felix Lytton?"

"Chief corporate security officer for FFM Industries. LAPD SWAT commander in a prior life."

"He wants to talk with you about the CEO candidate he's about to hire for their Eastern European axle manufacturer."

"Text me his number."

"Your laid-off Japanese gangster has moved in."

"Retired, and help Deuce with whatever he needs. Make sure he doesn't have any internet connection problems."

"What's up with only half a finger?"

"*Yubitsume*, finger shortening, how yakuza atone for mistakes."

"Don't get any ideas if I screw up," she said.

"Only for typos. Any calls for the driver position?" After multiple client requests, he'd decided to hire a driver with evasive driving skills. Someone he could partner up with Deuce for executive and dignitary protection work.

"Only one candidate with two prior DUIs who I told we filled the position."

Twenty minutes later, Angie waited on the sidewalk where he'd let her out. When she climbed in, he could tell from her swollen eyes a river of tears flowed. "Take me back to my place," she said.

"I don't know if—"

"Now," she said.

A dimple on her right cheek appeared when her temper flared. "You're sure?"

She stared straight ahead. "I need more time," she said.

"More time by yourself is not what you need."

"I plan to call John and tell him I want my job back."

No way Brody would bring her back. She'd only been in Charlotte for a few weeks. The Porsche's tires grooved along metal streetcar tracks outside the Transportation Center. He came to a stop at a light up the block from her apartment building.

"When can I swing by to pick you up?"

She climbed out without a word.

CHAPTER 8

Dom's Chicago flight from five days of meetings arrived two hours late thanks to snowstorm delays. One consolation for his travel hassles was a lucrative new insurance conglomerate assignment. Brake lights from Billy Graham Parkway's stalled early evening traffic winked on and off for miles. His taxi driver signaled to an empty exit ramp.

"We go around," she said. Those were her first words since "hello" back at the airport arrival area. The Italian accent went with her laminated driver identification card, Pia Roma. Past the bumper-to-bumper logjam he saw the impassable snowbound ramp.

"I prefer we don't get stuck in snow," he said.

She held up a space between her thumb and forefinger. "*Piccolo neve*, no worry."

His first impression of her tight curly dark hair had been retired grandmother behind a taxi wheel for some extra money. His opinion changed once he slid the minivan's door shut. Pia high-beamed SUV drivers and airport shuttle buses out of the way and wedged through luggage-burdened travelers like a maul. She nosed the minivan into a space between a black Lincoln Town Car limo and a lime Volkswagen Beetle.

Dom's cell phone vibrated. He felt relief when he read

Winnie's text: *Angie's in the spare office.* Neither of them had been able to contact her after she left the Porsche for her apartment before his trip. Winnie even struck out when she went to her apartment building.

Pia cut a channel up the ramp like a Russian icebreaker.

Winnie picked up on his first ring. "Don't get your hopes up. She's out cold on the pull-out bed. A First Ward gin-mill bartender called before lunch to say Coast Guard took a swing at one of his regulars, then passed out in the men's room. Her only possession was your business card. I sent Deuce to retrieve her."

"Don't let her leave," Dom said.

"In her condition, trust me, she'll be here. Do we bill her for the seventy-two-dollar bar tab?"

"We can handle a bar tab."

He saw another call come in and signed off. They crested the ramp under a yellow light and began a wide arc toward a four-lane bridge back across the parkway.

"How's my investigator?" John Brody said.

"One day at a time, John," Dom said. Angie's commander didn't need to know she was comatose at 4:45 p.m. Up ahead he could make out a snowplow attached to a fire-engine-red tractor being hauled on a wrecker service flatbed truck.

"Has she made any progress?" John said.

"She's a competent investigator who asks the right questions," Dom said.

"Not what I asked, Dom."

"You'll have to speak with her." He wouldn't share his reservations that the downward spiral would continue unabated if she didn't put forth more effort.

"Venture an opinion."

The wrecker tobogganed with too much speed toward the bridge.

"She needs more time," Dom said.

"Has she made her doctor appointments?"

"Like clockwork," Dom said.

He doubted she'd kept the last one while he was out of town.

"I'm still convinced she only needed a change of scenery," John said.

Dom muffled the phone against his jacket. The snowplow looked big enough to handle a stadium lot. "Do you see the wrecker?" he said.

Pia ignored him and eased toward the hard shoulder to create more space.

"What wrecker?" John Brody said.

"I'm in a taxi," Dom said. "Angie wants her job back."

"I told her we'd reevaluate in six months," John said.

Dom's Italian was rusty but he thought he heard Pia call the wrecker driver *idiota* under her breath.

"Do you have an update on the South China Sea pirates?" Dom said.

"They disappeared up the Yangtze after the Chinese took two into custody off a stolen yacht."

The wrecker driver's lumberjack beard was visible while he struggled to arrest his fishtail. The plow's edge loomed toward them and a guillotine image popped into Dom's head. He snapped his seat belt into place.

"Stolen yacht?" Dom said.

"The owner was a German industrialist found dead in Ma-Kung Harbor along with a male crew member. His wife and two female crew haven't been heard from."

Pia tapped the gas, spun the wheel, and worked the emergency brake like a hand-crank water-well handle. The minivan's rear end whip-hinged out away from the wrecker's grill. She twirled the wheel and they slingshot off the bridge before the plow crunched into the concrete barrier. A smirk appeared on her face when she saw his white knuckles on the headrest.

"Have Angie call me," John said.

He clicked off.

∾

"Eighteen dollars and thirty-six cents," Pia said. The minivan idled in front of his building.

"Quite the wheel work," he said.

She waved him off. "Easy drive," she said.

He included a business card with the fare and tip. "Give me a call if you ever consider a job change."

CHAPTER 9

"How many?" Dom said. He stood with Deuce inside the spare office.

"Barkeep mentioned eight mezcal tumblers," Deuce said.

Angie sat on the pull-out bed. She looked like she'd slept in her jeans and sweater. A white band held her hair back.

"Sorry I missed your fiesta," Dom said.

She flipped her palms open in a *what?* motion.

"Eight shots are a nice run… in basketball," Dom said.

"No way eight," she said.

Dom sat in the desk chair.

"Barkeep said eight," Deuce said. He filled the doorway.

"He's a liar," she said.

Deuce frowned and left.

"John Brody called," Dom said.

"Did you tell him I'm ready to get back to work?"

"I said you need more time, but I'm not sure time is all you need."

"Can we not make a federal case out of one happy hour?" she said. "My doctor says I'm a work in progress." She slid off the headband and ran her fingers through her hair.

"Why didn't you respond to our texts and calls? And why haven't you set up voicemail on your cell phone?"

"Forgot I turned my phone volume down when I went to my shrink's office. Voicemail, I haven't gotten around to."

He rolled closer to her. "Your disrespect came full circle when Winnie went to your apartment. She heard music inside, but you never opened the door. You may have noticed we're busy around here and don't have time for ungrateful people we can't communicate with because they're too irresponsible to set up voicemail or return calls and text messages."

"I never said I wasn't grateful," she said.

"I made a promise to Carter Hillstead and Palmer's mother I intend to keep." He stood and went to the door. "No hard feelings if you want to leave. I'll let John know another nursemaid might be a better fit."

"Have you ever lost anyone on an operation, let alone two?"

He wasn't sure if he saw shame or embarrassment in her eyes.

"I'm not the problem," Dom said.

"Look… I… I'm sorry. After I left you I wasn't sure what to do, stay or get back to Virginia. I even thought I could look for Sandi and checked flights to the Philippines. Yesterday morning I made up my mind to help you with Ms. Ruby, then go back to Portsmouth. After lunch her husband called me. He wept when he said he didn't know if he could raise their girls by himself."

"And your response was eight mezcals?" Dom said.

"I figured, what's wrong with one? Take the edge off, help me through a low spot."

"Another in your list of bad decisions."

She wobbled up and disappeared into the bathroom.

When Winnie had phoned him while he was in Chicago to say Angie holed inside her apartment and never came to the door when she knocked, he'd been ready to cut her loose. No one blows his people off. Then he thought of Trappist monk Thomas Merton: "Our whole life is a meditation of our last decision—the only decision that matters." He decided to give Angie another chance. Now she had to make a decision.

She returned pale from being sick.

"How about we start over?" he said. "Stay here for a few nights. Deuce can drive you back to your place to pack a bag, then we'll track down a few of Palmer's clients after we drop in on JoJo," he said.

Her eyes welled up. "I'll see what client information I can find in Ms. Ruby's bag," she said.

"After you apologize to Winnie."

CHAPTER 10

After a sun-drenched Sunday, dusk ushered in lower temperatures. Chimney smoke filled the air while Dom gathered another armload of wood from his old pickup truck. He set pieces one at a time on an iron rack.

"I heard your chain saw," Sister Maria Concetta Pucci said. Dwarfed in her oversize Charlotte Checkers hockey jacket, the diminutive Norbertine nun stood framed in the cloister's kitchen doorway. The smell of fresh baked bread the Sisters sold to area food service establishments blended with the smoke.

"You've gone through the wood, Sister," Dom said.

"We used all the fireplaces when our furnace went fritzy last week."

"I'll check it for you."

"The part was on the repairman's truck."

He made a mental note to have space heaters delivered.

"You'll never run out of wood," he said. An endless supply of old-growth trees stood on the cloister's sixteen woodland acres a car dealer had donated to the Sisters, situated a half mile from Mountain Island Lake. After Dom's separation from Rachel, Winnie had arranged a one-year lease for the carriage house on the back of the property.

He indicated her jacket with the last piece of wood. "Your team lost last night," he said.

"They can't find a 'W' since they called up Zimnyakov."

"How about his replacement?"

"The Canadian Phillippe LeBoutellier's still too young. With his size we can only hope he'll be good one day. Do we still need a roofer?"

She handed him a leather firewood sling.

"You won't have any more roof trouble." He'd repaired the leaks caused when the previous tenant removed their satellite dish.

"We don't mind the need for repair people when their services are required."

"You're covered, Sister."

He filled the sling with the last of the truck's wood.

"You'll let us know if more water comes in." She tapped her duck boots on the snow. "Business good, I trust?"

"We're busy," Dom said.

"Some of the Sisters believe you're in the bad-behavior disaster relief business."

"They're not far off the mark."

"You remind Sister Janssen of Joe Mannix. His television show may be before your time."

"Joe was way cooler than I am."

She took the full sling. "We always appreciate the firewood."

"Any more furnace troubles, call me," he said. "What kind of bread today?"

"A German zwieback. I'll have Sister Morales wrap a loaf for you."

CHAPTER 11

Eight fifteen sharp the next morning, Angie exited Dom's building dressed for the eleven degrees in a knee-length down coat, knit cap, and UGG boots.

"How's the pull-out?" he said.

"What would you say if I asked to stay in your building for a while?"

"You can stay for however long you like," he said.

She handed him a slip of paper. "JoJo's work address."

Wind howled out of the alley next to JoJo's low-rise prewar building close to Uptown where her employer, Tabberson and Associates, occupied the second floor. He watched Angie hesitate at the elevator's open doors.

"We can take the steps," Dom said.

She shook her head and took two slow steps inside. The cab smelled of fresh doughnuts from the box a guy they rode up with carried. Angie exited before the doors were all the way open. A woman with a poster board presentation case waited at a wood-frame glass aviary stocked with hyper finches. She asked the guy with the box if he brought sprinkles.

"The last one. The rest are cream-filled with brown sugar glaze."

Dom went to the receptionist, who spoke into her headset and used a pencil's eraser to dial an extension. "The ad agency people are ready."

Dom handed her his card. "Is JoJo in?" he said.

She read his card, then pulled up an office employee calendar on her computer screen. "I don't see you have an appointment, Mr. Mundy."

"Tell her we're here about Palmer Giron."

Dom rejoined Angie and could hear the receptionist respond to JoJo's questions. He figured she could see them through the glass doors behind the reception desk.

"No, they're the ad agency people, the other two. He's rangy with long hair. I have calls to take."

"Rangy's a first," Angie said.

"Better than reedy," he said.

She leafed through Tabberson's glossy brochure.

A woman in her late twenties with spiky moussed-up short indigo hair pushed through the glass doors. Her muscular frame strained against a white blouse. The receptionist gave her Dom's card. "I'm JoJo Cifuentes," she said.

Palmer may have fallen for the husky voice.

"We'd like a few minutes to speak with you about Palmer Giron," he said.

"I already told the police all I know."

At five foot six Angie had an inch on her.

"Can we talk somewhere?" Dom said.

She hesitated and looked at his card, then glanced at her watch. "Give me ten minutes to finish up a meeting. I'll meet you in the restaurant across the street."

∾

Bashara's occupied a parking deck's street-level retail space. The cramped quarters smelled of fresh baklava. A lute soloist played from the ceiling speakers. They sat at the only available table near the front window with a view of snowcapped dinosaurs in a children's park.

JoJo was a natural beauty who Dom thought didn't need the winged eyeliner under her almond eyes.

"Someone better look into his case because the police haven't done their job," she said.

"Do they think you were involved?" he said.

"I couldn't tell you what they believe."

"We spoke with Karen Robles earlier," Dom said.

"She wasn't a fan of our relationship." A L-O-V-E tattoo spanned across the knuckles of her left hand.

"Palmer often ride home late at night?" Dom said.

"He kept long hours. If the weather cooperated, he'd bike. After a heart attack took his father, he started to get serious about his extra weight." Her bottom lip trembled. "You know he was an environmental engineer?"

"We do and we're curious about the people who hired him," Angie said.

"Most were commercial real estate people, and let me tell you, they're not always the easiest to get along with."

Another comment about difficult clients, Dom thought.

"We understand Palmer was in high demand," Angie said.

She tapped nutmeg onto her latte macchiato. "I joked he dug expensive holes for a living." She gestured out the window. "Many of those buildings were his projects."

"Anything unusual about his work?" Dom said.

"How do you mean, unusual?"

"Client trouble, for starters," Dom said.

"A crisis was always happening. Difficult clients"—she

motioned out the window again—"like skyscraper owners, went hand in hand with his business. He had the gift of being able to placate them when problems arose."

"How'd he manage the stress?" Angie said.

"He kept his emotions to himself. Too close if you want my opinion." She pulled a pack of L&Ms from her smartphone zipper case and rapped out a cigarette.

"Difficult customers can be unpredictable. Maybe a work crisis escalated around the time of his murder?" Dom said.

"He was preoccupied, in one of his quiet moods."

"These mood swings a regular occurrence?" Dom said.

"Every once in a while he'd withdraw from me when work pressure got to him. But for the most part, he was even-keeled, never much drama. I think clients appreciated his steady hand. Given the enormous financial pressures some of them dealt with, they didn't need theatrics from an engineer who poked around in dirt."

"He share what might've been on his mind?" Angie said.

"I assumed a mountain job he spent many hours on for Augie Pepitone. He picked up the work after he assisted Augie with One Pepitone Center, his wooden office tower." She stood her cigarette up on one end.

"You two together for a while?" Dom said.

"Almost eighteen months."

"His even keel extend to your relationship?" Angie said.

JoJo shrugged. "Every couple goes through ups and downs."

"How down were the downs?" Angie said.

"They never lasted long. Several weeks before his murder, we'd taken some time apart but bounced back."

"The intermission your idea or his?" Dom said.

"His."

"What seemed to be the problem?" Dom said.

She sat back and opened her hands. "I like to let loose once in a while."

Karen Robles had told them about JoJo and Palmer's rough patch and her cousin Chico Vega being the problem.

"You're a party girl," he said.

"I said once in a while, not all the time. We were solid at the time of his death."

"These once-in-a-while good times include drugs?" Angie said.

Dom looked at Angie. She'd found her groove again.

The cigarette fell. JoJo shifted her eyes between them. "I realized I needed to make changes if I wanted to keep Palmer in my life. I cleaned up my act."

"Drugs part of Palmer's life too?" Dom said.

"In his past, with emphasis on past. After his time at New Dawn, he stopped."

New Dawn. Palmer went to rehab? Why didn't Karen or his mother mention a New Dawn stay?

"Tell us why Chico Vega was a source of friction," Dom said.

"Palmer thought I'd be better off if I socialized with people I come in contact with at work."

"Cousin Chico's not an office worker?" Angie said.

"He owns a car lot." She stirred with her finger.

"You two live together?" Dom said.

"We kept separate places. My condo's in Pineville and he lived in Cherry. Have you spoken to his brother Nickolas?"

"Not yet," Dom said.

"They weren't close. His parents tried several times to get them to reconcile." She licked her finger.

"Why the estrangement?" Dom said.

"After his drug use escalated, Nickolas cut Palmer off. In their younger years Palmer was the family star. Lettered in three high school sports. Four colleges were after him to play baseball until he destroyed his knee in the state championship game his senior year. His spiral started with painkillers his orthopedic surgeon prescribed."

"Have you met Nickolas?" Dom said.

"Palmer never made the introductions."

"You aren't aware of anyone who'd want to harm him?" Dom said.

"No one wanted to hurt Palmer. He was the type of person who could talk to anyone. He always had a five in his wallet for panhandlers. He still volunteered one weekend a month at New Dawn." JoJo checked her watch. "I have a video conference call."

CHAPTER 12

Out of the parking deck they took First Street.

"Isn't your office in the opposite direction?"

"A short detour to see if Palmer's drug problems were behind him," Dom said.

Angie opened her Bashara bag and the buttery smell of a za'atar croissant filled the interior. "How does Palmer end up with JoJo Cifuentes?"

"A smoky voice works every time," he said.

"I can see inked-up knuckles in the nightclub business, but on an architectural firm AutoCAD operator?"

"Palmer may have wanted some excitement in his life, a walk on the wild side," Dom said.

She pulled off a piece of the flaky pastry. "JoJo may have been more than he bargained for," she said.

"Track down Nickolas. I want his version of what happened."

Angie looked toward Uptown's wintry structures. "She said Palmer was involved with several of those tall buildings."

"See the twisted one?" Dom said. The structure swiveled into clouds with three rotations. Light from the many windows resembled orange-blue flames.

"Odd shape for an office building."

"Augie Pepitone's One Pepitone Center whose mountain job JoJo thought caused Palmer concern. Augie goes on our talk-to list," Dom said.

She used paper napkins to wipe her powdered-sugared hands. "Who owns the globe tower?" she said.

Across the street from Augie's spiral tower soared a glass-and-steel cylindrical superstructure capped with a geodesic dome. White light radiated through the dome's brilliant imperial-red and navy-blue hexagonal grid struts.

"The building across from Augie's is Tussey Beauty Products' global headquarters."

"The shampoo company?"

"They churn out shampoo by the railcar."

Hazelnut-size snowflakes melted on contact with the windshield.

"Karen and JoJo each mentioned the financial strain people who worked with Palmer operated under. What kind of money would a skyscraper client have on the line?"

"Figure ten to thirty percent of what they borrow for a down payment," he said.

Visibility went down to a few feet when snow blasted off a vacant lot.

"You have to be a risk junkie to play skyscraper monopoly."

"With a high pain threshold for straitjacket loan terms."

"What kind of terms?" Angie said.

"Start with balloon payments where you strike a check for the total loan amount years before the due date. Another are those personal guarantees. Be locked into one of those when the economy goes south and you're in for a world of hurt." A quick downshift maneuvered them around a produce truck. "What would you do if you overleveraged your skyscraper and your anchor tenant goes bankrupt?"

"Throw up a For Sale By Owner sign," she said.

"Your FOSB snags a buyer who brings in Palmer, who puts together a report and finds trouble. How do you save your skyscraper sale and because of the personal guarantee—your house?"

A homeless woman curled under a Masters umbrella at a fire hydrant.

"Plead with Palmer to fix the problem."

"And if he can't or won't?"

"I might need a divorce lawyer when the bank takes the house."

"Not if you have a creative streak."

"Creative how?"

"Whisper in Palmer's ear a chunk of change that might be a one-man environmental shop's lottery ticket."

"I haven't seen any financial shenanigans in his mother's bag," she said.

"There's always clever ways to hide dirty money."

"If he manipulated a report and someone found out, he'd be sued," she said.

"A lawsuit would be the least of his worries if he cratered a skyscraper sale with the wrong people involved."

They came out from under I-277's bridge into a sheet of white.

"From the little we know about him, I don't see Palmer for the wink-wink, nod-nod type," she said.

"Set aside he was an addict, under the right circumstances, a sweet offer can make anyone weak-kneed," Dom said.

"Has a wannabe monk ever been tempted?" she said.

"Not yet."

"Those knees might still give out?"

"I'll let you know if they start to wobble," Dom said.

They passed a strip center with neon signs for a cell phone shop, tattoo parlor, and vape store.

"JoJo said Palmer spent time in a rehab center called New Dawn. Brenda Wick, an ex-con community activist, runs the place," he said.

"What'd she serve time for?" Angie said.

"Manslaughter. Killed her abusive, drug dealer ex-husband with a Phillips-head screwdriver. She lucked out with the jury, who gave her a break after they saw pictures of her swollen eye and broken finger. The case was Julian Ybarra's—Ms. Ruby's lawyer's—first media circus."

"How long was she inside?"

The Porsche's tires dribbled over rough ice.

"Thirteen months in Swannanoa Correctional Center for Women. Six months after she's out, there's another article about how a crew she ran distributed high-grade hash to rich kids in a parking deck. The Phillips screwdriver confrontation had to do with drug profits from the hash operation. Her pastor son put her in charge of a drug-rehabilitation-center outreach ministry affiliated with his church."

Dom showed her to a bow-roofed brick building with *New Dawn* scripted in multicolor, blocky letters along the parapet, above a cityscape of rainbow colors, next to a truck dock door. Under a box elder tree in the side yard, several men stood around a fire.

They entered the building to a woman with too much lipstick and a teardrop tattoo under one eye behind a glass partition, next to a guy with blotchy skin. With a toothy smile she parted the glass. "Welcome to New Dawn," she said.

"Is Brenda Wick available?" Dom said.

"Your name?"

He gave her a business card. "We'd like a few minutes to ask her about Palmer Giron."

She gave the card to the guy, who scanned it with a phlegmy cough. "Some kind of investigator?" he said.

Dom nodded. The guy took the card and disappeared through an interior door.

A framed poster of the Serenity Prayer hung above a well-used leather couch in the reception area. Fanned out on a highboy were several New Dawn pamphlets. Angie handed Dom one and pointed to the cover. "Look who made the front," she said.

On the front panel appeared a black-and-white photograph of several cheerful men and women in a semicircle with arms on each other's shoulders. Third from the left, Palmer Giron.

"Take it," Dom said.

She slid the pamphlet into her coat pocket.

A door next to the window opened.

"Reverend Wick can see you," the guy said.

The aroma of fresh cornbread filled the tiled hallway he led them down.

"Smells like lunch," Dom said.

"You've never eaten here?"

"If the cornbread's any indication, we'll have to stop by," Dom said.

"Cheapest lunch in town."

They went through another door into a shorter hallway and stopped at an open door. Reverend Brenda Wick sat behind a cluttered desk in New Dawn gray cashmere warm-ups. "Thank you, Robert," she said.

Her hair was up in a makeshift bun held in place with a number two pencil. She came around to greet them with a generous smile. An obese woman, Brenda wore fuzzy brown slippers and favored her left hip. "Pardon my appearance. I'm off today but came in to catch up on paperwork."

After her bear-paw handshake, she directed them to have a seat, then hobbled back and eased down with both palms on the desk. "You have questions about Palmer?"

"His mother's troubled by the police investigation," Dom said.

"Whoever killed him is still out there," Brenda said.

"How was he associated with your organization?" Dom said.

"Palmer knew how to speak in front of business groups and was a valued member of our executive community outreach team." Brenda emptied a water bottle into a glass.

"Many executives come through here?" Dom said.

"Nowhere near enough. We're a tough sell to people with addiction problems full of false pride who might own a multimillion-dollar-a-year company or oversee a major corporate division with thousands of employees."

"Your pamphlet says referral only. Who referred Palmer?" Dom said.

"Brother Bondoc 'Rocko' del Rosario, who has been a dear friend of our ministry for many years."

"When Palmer arrived, was he still employed or on his own?" Dom said.

She pulled open a drawer and brought up a jar of powdered instant tea. "A partner in a regional firm. He was handed the thankless job in the last recession to reduce staff. Several people he let go were friends. He drank his way through his extensive French wine collection to deal with the stress. Cocaine came after the wine ran out. The end came when he was caught in a client's conference room with a spoon up to his nose. After he refused all offers of help, the firm terminated him. A fruitless job search escalated his use until Rocko brought him in."

"Escalated how?" Angie said.

"He added methamphetamines to the mix. With hard work and extensive time with our counselors, he came out the other side. I counted on his gift for compassion many times to help families in crisis with reluctant loved ones in need of our program.

We stress the future is always bright with the Lord in your life."
She unscrewed the lid and stirred tea into her glass.

"Did he have a relapse?" Dom said.

"I prefer not to go into particulars."

"We're only interested if he had his addiction under control, Dom said.

She tasted her tea and spooned in more. "He came to me after a setback with Rushers, a crystal methamphetamine we've seen on the street in the last year. Work stress, and someone threatened him when he found a waterway chemical release. I told him to go to the police."

"Did he?" Angie said.

"I don't know. He was murdered soon after he came to me. Who mentioned to you he was a client?"

"JoJo Cifuentes," Dom said.

She gave them a deadpan look. "Palmer knew how I felt about him being with JoJo. Her time here didn't end well. We called law enforcement when she refused to leave after one of my counselors found prescription pills under her mattress. Palmer was the one who calmed her down."

Now why would JoJo not mention her New Dawn stint?

"Any reason she might want to cause him harm?" Angie said.

"JoJo makes poor choices. Her mood swings don't help. To my knowledge she never acted violently toward Palmer."

"These poor choices have a name?" Dom said.

"Her cousin Chico Vega. Keep in mind when you speak with her, veracity is not one of JoJo's strong suits."

"Do you recommend your lunch?" Dom said.

Brenda's smile reappeared. "We're one of Charlotte's best-kept culinary secrets."

⁊

Dom reversed from New Dawn into snow swirls.

"JoJo sounds like a handful," Angie said.

"Palmer may have gotten more excitement than he bargained for." He crossed into First Ward near Uptown on Eighth Street under a snow-sheathed tree canopy. "See if you can pinpoint the waterway he ran into trouble with from Ms. Ruby's bag."

They passed a convertible sports car with a cracked windshield and crushed hood from a downed cherry tree limb.

"Why did JoJo and Karen Robles fail to mention drug problems?" Angie said.

"We'll have to help them with their recall on our next visit."

"Like his girlfriend and secretary, his mother glossed over the rough parts too," Angie said.

CHAPTER 13

THE NEXT DAY, Julius Watkins's French horn played in the background while they drove to the first name on the client list Angie pulled together: Vineyard Enterprises. The I-85 North drive into Cabarrus County took an extra thirty minutes due to icy roads. The brick-facade, prefabricated metal building stood in the shadow of Charlotte Motor Speedway.

A well-groomed, college-aged man in a pink dress shirt and fleece vest walked them back to a spacious office where Heath Vineyard sat behind an antique desk and ran a green highlighter over a document. Dom and Angie settled into uncomfortable chairs from the 1800s.

The long-established real estate man had a manual adding machine between his desk telephone and stacks of legal documents in manila folders. A Clemson engineer's degree surrounded by framed articles of real estate transactions and aerial pictures of mammoth warehouse buildings covered the wall behind him.

Vineyard snapped the highlighter cap back in place. "Palmer Giron made me millions. I never bought a property without his sign-off." Gold monogram cuff links anchored the sleeves of his starchy white shirt where his Clemson tie rested.

Dom indicated toward the wall aerials. "Those are big buildings."

"I only buy property nobody else will touch."

"What's wrong with them?" Dom said.

The way his cheeks and nose came to a point reminded Dom of a miniature dachshund.

"Environmental nightmares with toxic soil or water problems no amount of money will ever fix. The more toxic, the more I like them."

"Why would anyone touch contaminated property?" Angie said.

"Darling, there's substantial money to be made if you can stomach the risk, which I mitigate with insurance, and believe me when I say the insurance isn't cheap."

He pushed back and went to another wall of building pictures and tapped the green highlighter on an immense rooftop next to a river. "I was duck hunting a number of years ago with my Boykins on the Green River and saw a faded For Sale sign covered with kudzu. I discovered a vacant, thirty-five-year-old, half-a-million-square-foot building owned by Polk County. The largest building on their tax rolls. See these ribs?" He moved the highlighter up and down along the exterior walls. "Concrete molded sections form Ts. These type buildings stand forever. Here's the best part: a private hydroelectric power plant eight hundred yards upriver came with the property."

He retook his chair. "High warehouse ceilings and cheap abundant power, two of my must-haves. Lucky for me the property sat vacant for years thanks to environmental challenges caused by a shuttered battery plant on the adjacent parcel. I turned Palmer Giron loose and he came up with work-arounds to placate state environmental bureaucrats. Guess what I paid for the property?"

Dom didn't answer. Angie shrugged a shoulder.

"A buck fifty a foot. The best part: Polk County's economic development people offered up a twenty-five-year property tax abatement. With all these technology companies in need of data centers and server farms in western North Carolina, I figured my timing was perfect. You know what else those companies require?"

"Coffee shops?" Angie said.

"Giant buildings with massive amounts of cheap power. I can't disclose who I leased to, but they signed a twenty-year term and put millions of their own money into the improvements. The property value increased fortyfold on the day they executed the lease. I refinanced and used the windfall to buy three more buildings. Two I sold and paid off the Polk County mortgage with the proceeds. Without Palmer the whole process never happened."

⤙

They overtook a semi on I-85 South through a veil of snow.

"Heath Vineyard goes in the hero-worship column," Dom said.

Angie typed into her cell phone GPS the next address on her list. "If Palmer showered me with dollars from heaven, he'd be my hero too," she said.

"Did you find a key to Palmer's East Boulevard office in Ms. Ruby's bag?"

"East Boulevard and the Cherry house," she said.

"Tomorrow we'll check both of them."

Dom slowed to stay well back from a salt truck.

"I can see why Palmer's job was stressful with guys like Vineyard who bought giant buildings on his recommendation," Angie said.

"They have the chance to bank millions," Dom said.

"What if Palmer slipped up, made a mistake? No one bats a thousand every time out," she said.

"There'd be hell to pay," Dom said.

"Rushers might take the edge off."

An Australian-male GPS voice indicated to go right at the next exit.

"Up next is Manny Appino," Angie said. "A used construction equipment dealer who belongs on the other side of the ledger page from Heath Vineyard. He sent an email threat to Palmer."

"Did you find a chemical release in a waterway near his property?"

"I didn't see one."

The GPS voice directed them toward a dilapidated house behind a vacant retail center.

"You sure we're here? Your GPS friend might be wrong."

"We're here," she said.

Dom found a space devoid of snow under a pine tree. They picked their way between dismembered construction machinery parts toward a single-story house where a zephyr flapped a ripped screen. A side porch sagged under the weight of a car engine suspended between wood sawhorses.

Manny Appino opened the door on Angie's fourth knock with a cell phone up to his ear. About Angie's height, he wore flip-flops, Army green cargo shorts, and a grimy cut-off-sleeve T-shirt with cities and dates from Lynyrd Skynyrd's 1970s Nuthin' Fancy tour. A thicket of black hair covered his neck and arms. He waved them in and continued on the phone with his sandpaper voice about distributor caps. Dom guessed from his bed-head stringy hair they must have roused him from a nap.

Tomato sauce competed with motor oil for the most prominent odor in his junk-strewn converted bedroom office. Dry heat poured from an electric portable garage heater. Outside the only window, under heaps of snow, were butchered motor graders, draglines, wheel tractor-scrapers, even the hulk of an electric rope shovel.

Manny finished up and sat behind his parts-strewn desk while they remained standing on the oil-stained carpet because a grouser bar occupied the only chairs. "First day back from Gaston Memorial after a nasty bout of indigestion. Now what can I sell you today?" Manny said.

"An opinion," Dom said.

"An opinion on what?"

"Palmer Giron."

"Not one of my favorite subjects." He motioned to his paper plate. "You mind?"

"By all means," Dom said.

Next to a trunnion bearing assembly, Manny lifted a half-eaten cheese-and-meatball sub sandwich smothered with red sauce. He talked and chewed at the same time. "After I read they found Giron under a bridge, I figured I wasn't the only one whose deal he torpedoed."

"When did you work with him?' Dom said.

"My banker brought him on eighteen months before someone offed him. I won't ever use them again either." He shook his head every few seconds to flip parted greasy bangs off his smudged glasses. "Thirty years I killed myself in the machine parts business and on the side picked up a few rental houses out of foreclosure. Handled all the property management myself. Fixed roofs, collected rent, even kicked out deadbeat tenants. Guess the number of busted commode calls I received one Christmas?"

They waited for his response.

"Seven, Merry Christmas. I maxed out at one hundred eighty-three houses."

"You need a spreadsheet to keep up with all those toilets," Angie said.

His stubby index finger tapped the side of his head. "All up here. More than half were Section Eight, low-income houses."

When he took another cheek-bulge bite, a quarter-size sauce dollop landed between his gold chain cross and Bangor, Maine, the first tour date stop.

Dom gestured to his shirt.

Manny glanced down, mumbled, and with the sub in one hand used a handful of paper napkins on the sauce. Empty fast-food containers overflowed from a copy paper box he missed when he tossed the balled napkins sideways, the stain now the size of a smeared fifty-cent piece.

"The government reimburses landlords who can put up with all the tenant headaches," he said. "For decades I dealt with their calls about after-midnight loud music or gunshots being fired. Have you ever collected rent from deadbeats with grown children home from the penitentiary who keep their gun collection on the coffee table?" He took a holstered German Luger out of a desk drawer and set it next to the plate. "Greta joined me on every house call."

"How does Palmer figure in?" Dom said.

"In the last real estate run-up an investor approached me with an offer for my houses. I figure, why not sell. The government always has their hand out. The day will come when they'll screw landlords out of their Section Eight money. With the sale money I planned to put together a ten thirty-one exchange. Sell a property and put off the taxman if you buy another property with the sale proceeds in a certain number of days. A legit tax dodge." Manny mopped up sauce on the plate with a piece of bread.

"Taxes owed on a hundred eighty-three houses is a big number," Dom said.

"Big enough to get my attention. I scrambled and put four never-developed floodplain parcels on the west side under contract for a mixed-use development I could exchange into and avoid the taxman. I planned to put up office, retail, and apartments on the same site to spread the risk because bankers like multiple streams of income." He licked the corner of his mouth.

"Can we get back to Palmer?" Dom said.

"My hundred fifty thousand in escrow money went hard with twenty-four days to close when my chirpy banker calls with egg on her face. She forgot to order the phase one environmental study, but she assures me the person they use has no problem with tight schedules." Manny picked his teeth with his pinkie nail, then gulped from a thirty-two-ounce blue Slurpee. "They send over Palmer Giron and never told him I'm under a tight ten thirty-one deadline. He tells me any surprises he uncovers will be a challenge to deal with in the less-than-a-month time frame I'm up against before I have to close."

He picked his cell phone up when a guitar riff sounded.

"Build Masters," he said.

After a short conversation about a fixed-boom tow truck, he wedged the phone into his shirt pocket. "Giron blows two weeks before he hits me up with his first surprise: long-gone asbestos brake pads piled on the property's back corner in the 1930s. Surprise number two: a dry cleaner plume from Tuckaseegee Road. I says, what does a dry cleaner half a mile away have to do with my dirt? His reply, 'You're down gradient.'" He took another Slurpee pull. "Banker of the year informs me they won't close without Giron's thumbs-up, then she adds any surprises his phase one uncovers will be the parcel owner's responsibility. She didn't have a comeback when I says the sellers were two sisters with no money in the same retirement center." He belched. "Long story short, my ten thirty-one times out, the IRS tags my rental house proceeds, and I wish I never heard of Palmer Giron."

"Wouldn't another environmental engineer turn up the same results?" Dom said.

"If they shared bad news, they wouldn't give me excuses why

my ten thirty-one was in trouble. Not Giron, he needed ten days just to put together a proposal for the bank. I find out later the guy has a reputation. A buddy of mine, a guy in my Lions Club who owns more cell towers than anyone else in the state, called Giron a 'deal killer.' I'm a small-time operator who sold a few houses and wanted to turn some floodplain dirt into productive real estate. Instead, I take a gut punch from the IRS."

"Did you have any follow-up contact with Palmer?" Dom said.

"I told him he could pay the medical expenses for the ulcer he gave me. When he started in on the plume again, I hung up."

"And the threat you emailed him around the time he was murdered?" Angie said.

"The financial hit I took thanks to him still burned me. You should've seen the one I deleted. Someone needs to call out these people for the damage they inflict on the real people who pay their salary, risk-takers."

"Change up your diet and those digestion problems might clear up," Dom said.

"I quit booze and cigars," Manny said. "Won't ever give up my meatball subs."

⁂

Dom turned down I-85's ramp where he merged into snowbound traffic. "Bad day when you have to cut a check to the IRS with a string of zeros thanks to an environmental report from Palmer Giron," he said.

"I might be tempted to introduce Greta to the guy responsible," Angie said.

"Manny blames Palmer for his cratered floodplain dreams, but any lender would need an environmental sign-off. His 'I'm a small-time real estate operator' is a hard sell when you dodge taxes with a ten thirty-one exchange," he said.

"Palmer being good at his job didn't endear him to everyone whose property he investigated," she said.

They crawled along the Catawba River bridge behind a luxury RV with Florida plates.

"Think about how he made his living. Snoop around real estate parcels for problems. Half the time he's a hero to the Heath Vineyards of the world and the rest of the time he has people like Manny who wish they never heard of him."

"You know he must have happened onto some nasty situations," Angie said.

"Situations people would want left alone. Check the state engineering licensing board's website for any complaints lodged against Palmer. We might find another Manny Appino," Dom said.

Traffic came to a stop between off-ramps for Freedom Drive and Tuckaseegee Road.

Angie looked out her window toward Uptown where in the distance, a granite cloud ceiling glowed with Tussey Center's globe next to the last flame rotation of Augie's one-of-a-kind lumber building. "I'm curious which of those JoJo meant Palmer was involved with?" she said.

"We know at least one, Augie's One Pepitone Center." He tapped the gas to close the gap with a plumber's van. "Manny's dreams are chump change compared to those trophy buildings."

"Manny aside, my impression of Palmer, he tried to shield his clients from liability problems," she said.

He motioned at the high-rise huddle. "Uptown's full of national landlords who could send Palmer on jobs all over the country if he does right by them in Charlotte."

"You mean if he doesn't deliver Manny Appino-type bad news?"

"I'd be curious if Palmer ever flinched before he picked up the phone to crater a trophy office tower transaction owned by people with skyscrapers in major markets spread across the nation."

"You mean he might've been pliable to deliver positive results?"

"Wouldn't you be if skyscraper money was in play?"

"You're back to those weak knees again," she said.

"The guy was only human."

CHAPTER 14

AFTER HE LET Angie out back at his building, Dom drove into Uptown to Lizzie's Place, a gas-station-turned-saloon near the courthouse owned by retired court reporter Lizzie Mullinax. With dartboards, antique shuffleboard tables, and a stand-up Pac-Man game, Lizzie's place never changed, like her customer mix sprinkled with off-duty cops.

"How's the mountain man?" Voos Lor said.

CMPD's Violent Criminal Apprehension Unit Montagnard commander slid onto the stool next to him.

"Always ready for the next summit," Dom said. Dom held up two fingers when the bartender set a bowl of salted peanuts in front of them.

"Last time we spoke, you were after the Eiger," Voos said. He tossed peanuts into his mouth.

"When the weather didn't cooperate, we tackled Patagonia's Cerro Torre instead."

"How's work?"

"Have more than I can handle. The job offer still stands." He'd asked Voos on more than one occasion to come on board.

"Still enjoy the bad-guy hunt," Voos said. "On the topic of money, isn't a local murder below your pay grade?"

The bartender set two draft beers down.

"Carter Hillstead asked if we could lend a hand," Dom said.

"Why you?"

"We do work for Hillstead Industries. Carter's driver was Palmer Giron's father, whose widow reached out in frustration."

"Tell her to get in line," Voos said. He drank a swirl of his beer.

"Any bites with Carter's reward offer?"

"His fifty thousand brought out a few dozen nutjobs. Waste of our people's time."

"Did Palmer's drug past catch up with him?" Dom said.

"Who told you about his problems?"

"New Dawn's Brenda Wick. We also talked with JoJo Cifuentes and Karen Robles, his office manager."

The smell of bar detergent rose when the bartender washed highball glasses under the bar.

"JoJo let you in on her prescription drug arrest record?"

"The conversation stayed on Palmer," Dom said.

"Those two hooked up at New Dawn, where Giron landed after his drug problem spiraled out of control. Two addicts in a relationship is not a recipe for success," Voos said.

"Brenda Wick shared that Palmer's sobriety ended with a trip-up on Rushers around the time of his murder."

The bartender changed music channels to Kenny Chesney's "She Thinks My Tractor's Sexy" video.

"Hellish new crystal meth we've been introduced to."

"What's your opinion of JoJo?"

"A change-up would've done Palmer good."

"We hear he didn't care for the crowd she ran with," Dom said.

"One of her relatives, Chico Vega, and his northside crew, the Patriots." Voos munched more peanuts followed by another pull on his beer. "We checked both JoJo and Chico. They have solid alibis. Witnesses put them in Jamaica on a Vega family vacation at the time of Palmer's murder."

"Have you looked into a possible work angle? His clients were big-money people with a lot to lose."

"Current and past clients we interviewed all checked out. Most praised the guy."

"Most?" Dom said.

"In Giron's world there's no shortage of irritated high-maintenance property operators. We don't believe he was taken out because a real estate play went south." Voos acknowledged a man and woman, both cops who came up to the bar to order drinks.

"You'd find characters involved with these transactions Palmer wouldn't even be aware of, like silent partners for starters," Dom said. "The wrong people might not appreciate an environmental engineer with an SOS flag who torpedoes their big payday. The killer or killers find out he bikes home, they might arrange a rhododendron rendezvous near a bridge to deliver a message," Dom said.

"We haven't confirmed more than one person was involved."

"With Palmer's size, I don't see one guy takes him out," Dom said.

"Could be another big man jumped him," Voos said.

"Thanks for the help, now we'll focus our search on a few million small guys or one big guy."

"See, I already helped you," Voos said. "You know Nita and her partner are the leads?"

Dom turned the mug on his napkin. After their time together, he'd lost touch with Nita. "She still partnered with Willis?"

"He took a job in Morehead City. Her new partner's retired Marine Corps. Came from their criminal investigation division. When did you see her last?"

"A few years ago."

"You know she's divorced?"

Dom drank the last of his beer. "Won't ever happen, Voos."

"With your divorce I thought…" Voos said.

"… pending divorce," Dom said.

"I figured you'd be on the loose by now." Voos stood.

"Job offer still stands," Dom said.

"You sure you'd want an old guy around?"

"There's more tread on those tires."

The CMPD commander left.

Palmer's professional life was populated with high rollers who gambled fortunes, and in his personal life he had Rushers and a girlfriend with LOVE knuckles. The same question nagged at Dom: What if his two worlds collided?

CHAPTER 15

Dom idled the Porsche with two fresh coffees in front of his building the next morning. Winnie's number flashed on his cell phone.

"I don't know what's wrong with her," she said.

"What's up?"

Angie exited the front door and came toward him.

"Seven fifteen I stroll past the conference room, she's at work with the Giron papers," Winnie said. "Twenty minutes later I look in again and she's on her back on the floor with the lights out. She said the light bothered her eyes."

"Thanks for the update."

Angie slid next to him. "Nasty headache today," she said.

"How about some aspirin?"

"Already took four, they haven't kicked in yet."

"Caffeine might help," he said.

She sipped the coffee and leaned her head back with her eyes closed. "I haven't seen any mention of waterways in Ms. Ruby's bag, but I did speak with his brother Nickolas. He didn't want to talk about Palmer on the phone."

"We'll take a drive to Asheville, see if he's a better talker in person," Dom said.

Her eyes were still closed, the coffee resting on her knee. "No Palmer complaints on the state engineering website. I did find a testy email exchange six weeks before his murder with another environmental engineer. A guy named Jerry Qwain who Palmer reported to the same state board."

"The treacherous world of environmental engineers, who knew?" Dom said.

"Here's his address." She handed him a slip of paper and powered her window down for some fresh air.

Dom looked at the address. "His office is only fifteen minutes from here."

∾

Look-alike one- and two-story brick buildings sprawled across the office condominium development off Pineville Matthews Road.

"How's the head?"

"The caffeine helps," she said.

Qwain Environmental Resources was up a flight of stairs next to a pediatric orthodontist. Dom told the receptionist who answered the call he made from the wall phone, why they were here. Angie examined one of the many wall-mounted fish on the reception area wall. Etched on a plaque below a foot-and-a-half-long behemoth with a black-dot-covered back was *Giant Brown Trout, Rio Grande River, Tierra del Fuego, Argentina 1998.*

"Check out the teeth," Dom said. A basketball-size fish hung on the next wall with what appeared to be human incisors.

"Caught her in Papua New Guinea in 2012 on my last cast, a world record Black Pacu," said a bantamweight guy at the doorway in running shoes, shorts, and a long-sleeve raspberry Charlotte Running Academy shirt. The only hair on his head was a tar-black soul patch.

"Impressive collection," Dom said.

"Fishing gets me out of the office. A month from today I'll be in Ecuador after my first arapaima. Those suckers run a few hundred pounds." Jerry Qwain spoke with the rapid cadence of a horse track announcer. He led them down another fish-filled hallway to his conference room where a swordfish graced an entire wall.

"Water, coffee?" he said.

Dom held up his hand no, Angie shook her head. Pencils and pads were in the center of the round table they sat around.

"Run in the snow?" Dom said.

"When the main roads clear, I'm on go. Marathons are another pastime. Berlin next September will be number sixteen. My PR's four o seven."

"You're quite the runner," Dom said.

"I put the mileage in. You're here about Palmer Giron?" Jerry glanced down at the card Dom gave him.

"His mother brought us on to help find out what happened to him. We've started with his friends and business contacts."

"Palmer and I go back a long way—sorry, went back. We opened our shops six weeks apart and used to refer work back and forth."

"How long were you competitors?" Dom said.

"A number of years until I turned my focus to service station and convenience store operators. I keep them current with compliance requirements."

"Gas stations have been good to you with all the fish and marathons," Dom said.

"My motto's work hard, play harder."

"Why'd Palmer report you to Raleigh?" Angie said.

So much for the headache.

"I'm not sure I get your drift."

"Why did he have a problem with you?" Angie said.

"A client brought me on to head off environmental problems before they put their building up for sale. Easy job I've pulled off a hundred times before. My report came back clean, but when they went under contract the buyer's lender ordered up a new phase one."

"Yours didn't count?" Dom said.

Over Jerry's head a bull dorado stared at him.

"Lenders won't use reports more than several months old. The buyer's bank hired Palmer and he found a fuel tank."

"A tank you missed?" Angie said.

"First and only time I ever overlooked one. I arranged a call with Palmer, the buyer, their banker, and the property owners to review my action plan. Palmer lit a fuse when he started in with nightmare stories about tanks he's seen leach into groundwater. I tried to tamp down everyone's emotions and said we needed to pull the tank before anyone jumped to conclusions. The buyer bailed after the call."

"How irritated was your property-owner client?" Dom said.

Jerry squirmed when he talked. "They fired me and brought Palmer on. Then they sued me for five hundred twenty grand, and my E&O company lawyers negotiated down to three fifty and change. After Palmer turned me in, Raleigh slapped my wrist all because of a garden-variety fuel tank."

"I read the tank measured twelve feet around and contained forty thousand gallons of diesel fuel," Angie said.

"We find them on a regular basis. I didn't appreciate when Palmer blindsided me on my own conference call. Nine out of ten times tanks aren't a big deal. Remove them, cart off a few truckloads of dirt, and everyone's happy."

"Unless you're number ten," Angie said.

Jerry fiddled and tapped a pencil. "Nine to one are pretty good odds," he said.

"What did they find when they pulled the tank?" Dom said.

"No problems. Thanks for nothing, Palmer."

"How about those asbestos floor tiles?" Angie said.

Jerry's Adam's apple bobbed when he swallowed. "Who could find them behind a bathroom's false wall?"

"Palmer did," she said.

"He got lucky."

"These property owner clients with the missed tank, who were they?" Dom said.

"You wouldn't know them," Jerry said.

"Try me," Dom said.

"The Laphoon family."

"Virgil Laphoon?" Dom said.

"A family trust controlled by his children."

"The noncriminal branch of the family tree?" Dom said.

"Don't believe what you read in the papers. Old man Virgil's a sharp business operator, a pioneer in the field of high-risk borrowers."

"He's a loan shark?" Angie said.

Maybe her headache reappeared.

"Virgil never spent a day in jail. The SBI never made a case against him. His boy Emmett's in charge now and his sisters run the commercial property empire. They own millions of debt-free square feet."

"Being dumped for Palmer must have hurt," Angie said.

"I recovered. Through the grapevine I heard Palmer told Emmett I bungled the job because I was preoccupied with my divorce."

"Were you?" Dom said.

"All I'll say is my ex's attorney is nicknamed the strip mine queen. Look, the Laphoons came out all right. They made an additional half million when they sold the tank property eighteen months later."

"Did you talk to Palmer after he filed the complaint?" Dom said.

"Once when I ran into him with his wacko girlfriend in a restaurant after too many margaritas. She coldcocked me when I moved around her to speak with Palmer."

His secretary stuck her head in. "Your meeting's here."

"Good luck on the Amazon," Dom said.

Jerry pointed to the only open space without a mounted fish. "The arapaima's new home."

↬

Sunlight streaked across the fast-food restaurant's drive-through lane.

"Your wife hire the strip mine queen too?" Angie said.

"Her lawyer didn't operate a continuous excavator."

A teenage girl with inch-long gold nails passed Dom an orange juice and water bottle. He handed Angie the juice.

"Why would JoJo hit Jerry?" Angie said.

"Another question we'll add to our JoJo list. Palmer was in way over his head with her," Dom said. He took his change and waited for cars to file out of the parking lot.

"What would your reaction be if Palmer took advantage of your personal situation and walked with a Laphoon-type client and their millions of square feet?" Angie said.

"Depends if I'm in a charitable mood," he said.

"Not me. I hold grudges, a character flaw." She shook and drank her orange juice.

"Jerry should count himself lucky he got off with a wrist slap from the state."

"What do you mean?"

"A bungled job for the Laphoons might not be good for your long-term health," Dom said.

"He said the family came out ahead when they sold the property," she said.

Dom screwed off the water bottle cap. "Virgil's an old-school Cajun racketeer who doesn't lose money. I can guarantee you his girls and Emmett didn't fall far from the tree."

"Law enforcement ever get close to them?"

"Once, before he made the move to Charlotte in the seventies. A bookmaking operation he ran in New Liberia for the Louisiana mob was raided by an anti-organized crime task force. His case was dropped before the trial started when it leaked to the press Virgil acted as the task force commander's bookie. The family empire's now based out of an appliance store off Freedom Drive."

"Virgil behave himself in North Carolina?"

"Charlotte police looked into him years ago after a prominent plastic surgeon was found in the trunk of his Jaguar with a bullet in his head. The good doctor was into Virgil for twenty large for dice game debts. Months later the MD's mistress died from an apparent suicide. In a note she left behind, she confessed to killing the doctor in a jealous rage."

"Virgil seems to have a lucky streak," she said.

They followed an electric car out onto Highway 51.

"Real estate's not the family's only business. They've made a fortune in payday lending. Have you come across any Laphoon reference in Ms. Ruby's bag?"

"Not yet. If I find one, I'll let you know. I came across another project where Palmer ran into problems. He worked for Dever Multifamily, which builds luxury apartments located in a place called Indian Land. The file was light on details," she said.

Dom looked at his watch. Indian Land was beyond Ballantyne. They could be there in ten minutes if traffic cooperated and still make it to Palmer's East Boulevard office building before his twelve-thirty lunch meeting. "Look up their address," he said.

CHAPTER 16

The Porsche carved through Ballantyne's building maze under a sable shelf cloud to Dever Multifamily's snow-scraped entrance. They left the Porsche beside a pond with Canada geese on an ice floe. A woman in black-and-white polka-dot rain boots with a down jacket over her business suit held the door for them.

"Who do you need to see?" she said. Her straight hazel hair matched the color of her cat eye sunglasses.

"Connie McCovey," Angie said.

"You've got her." She looked at her Longines bracelet watch after Dom explained why they were there. "I have a construction site meeting but can free up a few minutes."

On the way back to her office, Connie responded to Angie's question about Dever Multifamily's business with a market director's drippy brochure speech. "Not only did we survive the downturn but we're back to our prerecession volume. We've completed four communities in the last seven months and are ninety-eight percent leased."

Her glass-lined office offered views of more reclined geese on another frozen pond. Clear plastic-encased tombstones of apartment community development announcements lined her credenza like parade ground infantry.

"Why the small building?" Dom said.

In a warehouse below her, office workers constructed what appeared to be a miniature apartment building.

"Our sample product for the once-a-year Dever Academy we put on, for all our trades to see the level of detail we expect."

"Palmer a graduate?" Angie said.

"Our land department used his services." She leafed through phone messages left on her desk.

"When did he come on board?" Dom said.

"We kept him on after we made Augie Pepitone's Campus Living acquisition. Student housing is another line of business we've succeeded in."

"Augie was into dorm rooms?" Dom said.

"Made his fortune with dormitories. Palmer did his environmental work. We asked him to come along when the sale closed. With his input we've passed on hundreds of acres of future development sites. I'll show you."

She led them to an enlarged aerial map on a worktable and drew a circle with her finger around the southeast edge where Mecklenburg met Union County. "We put thirty-six acres near Weddington under contract for one of our exclusive Eagle Run fifty-five-and-over communities. Nine months into our due diligence, Palmer finds groundwater problems he traces back to a nearby industrial plant." Her finger slid several parcels away to a football-field-size roof surrounded by hundreds of parking spaces. Railroad tankers sat on a spur along the building's rear. "The Wesley Chapel number four plant where they ship out shampoo by the trainload."

"Who owns the plant?" Dom said.

"The Tussey family."

"An industrial site can't be good for apartment lease-up," Angie said.

Connie traced along a wooded area. "Topo here hid the plant from where we wanted to build. We were days away from a quarter-of-a-million-dollar binder payment when Palmer uncovered trace amounts of degreaser chemicals in the groundwater. He said the chemicals leached from what he thought might be illegal buried metal drums on the Tusseys' property."

"Did he alert the Tusseys?" Dom said.

"They put their company fixer, Jefferson Wallach, in charge of the situation after Palmer let state environmental people know what he found. Wallach ran circles around those people. All the while shampoo continued to flow."

"How did Palmer address the problem in his report?" Angie said.

"He was murdered before we received it." She put her coat back on. "I wasn't privy to all the details, but I heard Wallach had him in his crosshairs. Needless to say, we moved on to another site."

They came out of Dever's office into gossamer snowflakes, the sun now a dusky globe. Dom powered up the Porsche while Connie's Range Rover Sport drove off.

"How's the head?" Dom said.

Angie wobbled her hand. "I get the impression every time Palmer showed up with his shovel, someone's checkbook was about to take a hit," she said.

"You heard Manny Appino. He was a deal killer," he said.

"You were right when you said problems might appear when Palmer trudged around parcels near his client's property."

"He'd never know what situation he might be walking into," he said.

Geese glided in for a water-ski landing.

"Connie meant the same family who owns the globe-topped building, didn't she?"

"The city only has one first family of the shampoo business, the Tusseys'."

"How can we confirm their fixer went after Palmer?" she said.

"Go to the source. Call the corporate office and find someone we can talk to."

Dom drove toward 521.

"Dever goes in the win column with Heath Vineyard," she said.

"Those buried degreaser drums might put the first family of shampoo in the loser column along with junkyard Manny and Jerry Qwain."

"Manny wouldn't kill Palmer under a bridge. He'd rely on Greta for the job, and Jerry Qwain's not killing anyone with his weapon of choice—his email account."

They came up to 521's light alongside a cream-puff Cadillac SUV with a twentysomething blond driver whose fawn puggle scratched and slobbered on the window.

"Keep on those client files. You might find another Manny with checkbook zeros from on a busted real estate play thanks to our environmental engineer. You bring the East Boulevard key?"

She held up a silver ring and key from her coat pocket.

CHAPTER 17

A WHITEOUT DELAYED their visit to Palmer's office building until the next morning. They parked in a cleared Greek church lot and crunched across East Boulevard's packed snow. Someone cleared off the front walkway and ramp Palmer had installed for Karen Robles's wheelchair. His building, a renovated house turned into office space, sat between a dog spa in another converted house and a vacant lot under a sheet of snow with a developer's quadplex sign.

A woman in tan yoga pants and a Campbell University sweatshirt came down the lobby stairs and noticed they were at the glass entry door. Dom made the introductions and asked to see Palmer's office.

"Speak with Bill Eversole, he looks after the building. His office is down the hall." She started back up the stairs.

A slender man with a sandy, bird-down-rimmed head opened Eversole Insurance Partners' door. Well past retirement age, Bill Eversole appeared to be on the mend from a major illness. The office smelled of Vicks VapoRub and fresh brewed coffee. After Dom explained why they were here, Bill retrieved his keys.

"You keep an eye on the place?" Dom said.

"I was Palmer's first tenant and do what I can for Ms. Ruby."

"How many tenants lease space in the building?" Dom said.

"Five if you include me." He pointed with the key back down the hall from Palmer's door near the front entrance. "Shelly Budd, a psychologist with a practice focused on teenagers, is across from me."

"A woman upstairs let us in," Angie said.

"Melissa Mauk, who runs a concierge business. Helps out overworked families. We also have a textile designer and an internet social media person on the second floor."

Bill flipped to Palmer's office key, unlocked the door, and turned the light on. Windows with closed blinds faced East Boulevard.

"Has anyone been in here?" Dom said.

"The police, after he was killed and again after the break-in."

Dom looked at Angie, who signaled with a slight shake of her head she didn't know about a break-in.

"His mother never mentioned a break-in," Dom said.

"A week after his murder someone broke into the building."

"The security alarm didn't work?" Dom said.

A security company keypad was mounted on a wall in the reception area.

"They came through an upstairs window and bypassed the exit door to the rear staircase with the only sensor up there. The whole episode was strange. We couldn't determine if they took anything. Melissa's framed rare coin collection worth several thousand dollars wasn't even touched. I came in early and went upstairs to check on the float arm in the bathroom I replaced the day before, when I saw the window ajar. Police found Palmer's office was the only room accessed and they couldn't determine what, if anything, was taken. They'd already removed his computer on their first visit."

"Can we see the bathroom?" Dom said.

Bill took them up past a landing with chairs and a table covered with outdated magazines. The bathroom was down the hallway opposite three offices and next to the kitchen break room and exit door that led to outside stairs down to parking behind the building. Melissa, who let them in, sat on a balance ball chair behind her desk in her office. Dom went into the narrow bathroom big enough for one person.

"The window was popped from the outside," Bill said.

Dom slid the flimsy curtain above the toilet to the side and saw four panes of glass and no latch. Paint was cracked and chipped where the window met the sill. Nails now secured the window shut.

"I put the nails in," Bill said

Dom saw the dog spa fifteen yards away. "They use a ladder?" Dom said.

"I overheard a policewoman say the air conditioner's cement pad was a perfect place to anchor one."

Back downstairs Bill left them inside Palmer's office.

"What were they after in here?" Angie said.

"His files will be a start. I'll take the interior room," Dom said.

Angie went to a wide set of file drawers beside a coat closet. He stood in the doorway and scanned the second office. A multicolor polygon mobile hung from the ceiling in front of a single window with a view of the vacant developer lot with the posted quadplex sign. Next to the window was a ride-in-place bike stand and an abdominal wheel on the floor. Palmer's mesh office chair was pushed under his adjustable stand-up desk below a framed poster of a beach sunrise. His uncluttered desk held only a desk telephone and a wire pencil holder. An enlarged tax map was pinned to a wall-mounted corkboard next to his desk.

He took a closer look at the map. Several parcels with tax identification and address numbers abutted a circular street in a

Gaffney, South Carolina, industrial park. Various-size buildings occupied each parcel. Pink highlighter shaded in a number of parcels on either side of a parcel with a circled red X, with *TPP* written in tight neat script inside the parcel.

Dom pulled out the mesh chair and sat. Under the desk sat a pair of little-used fluorescent running shoes. Several computer wires left by the police were still connected to a wall socket. The top left drawer contained pencils and pens in a divider tray, a handheld calculator, and an empty checkbook box with breath mints, aspirin, and dental floss. The next drawer held legal pads, printer cartridges, an unopened ream of copy paper, and a clear plastic sandwich bag with several tea bags, sugar packets, and non-dairy creamers.

Another drawer contained hanging files for his tenants. Dom saw Bill Eversole's folder. Inside were his lease and rental payment history recorded on five-column ledger paper in the same tight script used on the tax parcel map. Bill always paid his rent early.

Inside the right-side drawer were more hanging files for Palmer's jobs-in-progress Karen Robles mentioned. The first file contained a luxury apartment complex off Sunset Road called The View at Sunset, accompanied by legal documents, tax records, and aerials along with close-up pictures of a plant demolished to make way for the apartment buildings. Dom saw close-ups of concrete stains, pavement cracks, discolored steel support beams, and oil-slick runoff.

Documents for the Gaffney, South Carolina, frozen chicken plant for Tenorio Poultry Processors were in the next file. He looked up at the corkboard map. *TPP* would be the handwritten abbreviation for the red circled X on the chicken facility. Paperwork in the final file went into detail about the Uptown lumber skyscraper owner Augie Pepitone's mountain resort, Bufflehead Reserve.

He thought Karen had mentioned four jobs, not three.

Bookshelves lined the wall beside the desk. Engineering and technical reference books stood next to stacks of engineering magazines and Palmer's preferred fiction, Scandinavian crime hardback novels.

He rolled for a closer look at a number of purple Post-it Notes stuck on the shelf below the novels. Notes were jotted on each in the same penmanship used in the job files and on the corkboard chicken-plant parcel. The first read *Steele Creek Road overlay*. The second, *Ronald Shepherdson/vapor intrusion* with a telephone number whose area code he didn't recognize, followed by an empty space, then *ETF bonds*, and in even smaller script on the last note lines from a poem about sadness after the loss of someone.

Angie came in and joined him. "All the drawers out there are old job files." She tossed an inch-thick doorstopper on the desk. "One of his phase one reports."

"Read me those jobs Karen Robles shared with us."

She swiped and tapped open her screen. He pulled out the jobs drawer again and put each file she read off on the desk. "Sunset Road apartments, mountain work for an Uptown developer, a Gaffney, South Carolina, chicken warehouse…"

He held up the Gaffney file and pointed to the corkboard tax map with the circled red X. "TPP is the chicken warehouse."

She went up to the map and read the street name with the colored-in tax parcels. "792 Bombardier Circle."

"Pink are neighbors' tax parcels around his client's property. The same process he undertook for Dever Multifamily, which led to Tussey shampoo plant problems with those buried degreaser drums. Didn't Karen mention another job?"

She looked at her screen. "Irwin Creek."

"I don't see Irwin Creek in here."

"With all his files I can see how one might be misplaced," she said.

"Look how organized he was. Does he look like someone who'd lose a file?"

"JoJo said he worked all the time. Maybe the file went home with him."

"We'll see if Irwin Creek's in the Cherry house."

She looked at the shelf with the purple notes, then pointed to the poem.

"Those are rap song lyrics about a woman who walked out on her lover. Maybe he had JoJo on his mind."

"She must be a heartbreaker. Call contact numbers in these files. I want to know if these customers were in the thumbs-up column."

Angie took down names and phone numbers from each file, then took pictures of the bookshelves, the purple Post-it Notes, and the rest of the office.

On their way out, Bill Eversole called them back to his office. "I forgot to show you these. Palmer's dry cleaner delivery a month after he died." He opened his closet to plastic bags over hangered clothes.

Angie looked through them and pulled out a bag inside a bag with a torn parking receipt.

"The receipt they found in one of his pockets," Bill said.

Dom looked at the receipt from a West Morehead Street parking lot. Angie took a picture and Bill rehung the bag. They left the building and started back toward Monroe Road.

"A week after he's killed, Palmer's office is broken into but it doesn't appear anything was taken. He only kept files in there. Were they after one?"

"Those pink tax-map parcels are neighbor properties he looked into around his chicken processor client property. There might be other owners close to a client's real estate who weren't pleased when Palmer turned up on their property with his shovel."

"The neighboring properties in all those files could be in the hundreds," she said.

"Ask the Tusseys how they felt about Palmer being on their property."

CHAPTER 18

Visibility was down to a few feet by the time they rolled up to the Monroe Road building.

"I have a speech to deliver at a security conference in Lima, Peru, in a few days," Dom said. "Keep at those bag notes while I'm away."

Angie disappeared into the conference room and Winnie handed him his messages. Jock hobbled into Dom's office on his bum knee. In his fifties, the former ninety-six-kilogram Olympic champion weightlifter stood an inch under six feet, with a bald head and full crimson beard laced with silver.

"How's Coast Guard?" he said.

"You two haven't met?" Dom said.

Angie came in with a piece of paper.

"Angie Crete meet Jock McGuire."

"You're the one who yells at Swedes," she said.

"Only when they renege on our fees," Jock said.

"Jock relocated from Ontario, Canada, after his wife informed him she wanted warmer winters in their retirement," Dom said.

"Like today's twenty-eight degrees," she said.

"Sweater weather," Jock said. "I'll have your information by the time you land in Lima. My pleasure, Ms. Crete."

"Tell Winnie Mrs. Giron will be here in a few minutes."

Angie watched Jock hobble out. "What happened to his knee?"

"An injury from his undercover days with Ontario's Iroquois Six Nations Provincial Police."

"He's Indian with a name like Jock McGuire?"

"Half Iroquois, half Scottish. We rolled up an entire heroin network with his help."

"And now he's your bookkeeper?"

"Debits and credits are one of his many skills."

She looked at notes on her paper. "After Jerry Qwain blew the Laphoons' bakery tank job, Emmett Laphoon put Palmer on a thirty-K-a-year retainer."

"Nice payday thanks to Jerry's preoccupation with a strip mine queen."

Winnie buzzed his desk telephone intercom. "We have a taxi driver out here for you," she said.

"I didn't order a taxi," he said.

"She said you gave her your card."

He remembered the grandmother taxi driver from his airport ride who he'd toyed with the idea could be a candidate for the dignitary protection driver position he wanted to pair up with Deuce.

When he went into the lobby he saw Pia Roma, dressed in dark Puma sneakers, beaver-brown slacks, and a white blouse under her waist-cut leather motorcycle jacket. A lilac ribbon entwined her curly hair. Her motorcycle helmet sat on a chair next to her with a pastry box. A motorcycle in today's weather. He liked her even more.

"Hello, Ms. Roma," he said.

Pia handed back his card. "Your offer still on the table?"

"Let's talk," Dom said.

He shepherded her into his office with her box and helmet. "Angie, Ms. Pia Roma."

"Ciao," Pia said.

Dom saw the "are you serious?" look Angie gave him. Pia handed him the pastry box. He lifted the lid to the smell of an Italian bakery.

"Did you bake these?" he said. He handed Angie the box.

"Of course," Pia said.

Angie withdrew a cannoli with chocolate filling.

Dom said, "Ms. Roma—

"Pia please," she said.

"Pia's driving skills impressed me," Dom said.

"Oh my god," Angie said. She'd taken a cannoli bite.

"Where's home?" Dom said.

"Elmores Crossroads," Pia said.

"I'm not familiar with Elmores Crossroads," Dom said.

"On 279 past Cramerton."

"I wouldn't put your accent from Gaston County," he said.

Her smooth Italian cadence could turn a hardware store catalogue into an audiobook bestseller. "Maranello's my true home."

"Northern Italy," Dom said.

"You know my country," Pia said.

"Stayed on the Italian side for a month when we tackled the Matterhorn," Dom said.

Angie said, "Is Marnell—"

"Maranello," Dom said.

"Is Maranello near Milan?" She used a napkin from the box to dab chocolate cream off the corner of her mouth.

"Close to Bologna." Pia said.

"What's Maranello known for?" Angie said.

Pia pinched her fingers and thumb together for emphasis. "*Delizioso* food."

"And a modest car company," Dom said.

Pia smiled.

"Ferrari, where I believe our taxi driver acquired her skills," Dom said.

"For many years I test-drive new models," Pia said.

"How fast have you been?" Angie said.

"Two twenty-three."

"Kilometers per hour?" Angie said.

"Miles per hour, a Ferrari F40 LM, a wonderful creation."

"How do you go from Ferrari to an airport taxi?" Dom said.

"We move to the states for my husband to be closer to his daughter. After he died, I take taxi job to keep my mind busy," Pia said.

"Can you use a gun?" Dom said.

Pia pulled a 9mm Springfield Armory Hellcat from under her jacket and set it next to the pastry box.

"A job applicant who brings a 9mm and cannoli to an interview," Angie said.

"Take her out to Winnie to get the paperwork started."

"You haven't discussed salary," Angie said.

"She'll be satisfied with our offer," Dom said.

"We're in trouble if she brings a pastry box every day," Angie said.

CHAPTER 19

THE NEXT MORNING Angie came into his office and stood with a hand on her hip while he finished up a call about a stolen Paolo Uccello painting with an Interpol art investigator. When he replaced the telephone handset, Deuce towered behind her.

"Babysitter, are you serious?" Angie said.

"You the babysitter type?" Dom said.

"A waste of time," Deuce said.

Dom figured with Deuce close by, she might not have another boozy derailment while he was in Peru. Her eyes drilled into him.

"Bring Franco's SUV around, we'll be out in a minute," Dom said.

The big man left.

"I can take care of myself."

"The bartender who found you in the men's room might have a different opinion."

"You asked Deuce to watch over me?"

"I told you no more dive bar rescue operations. We don't have time around here to soft-pedal someone who doesn't recognize people who care for her. Deuce and Pia will be on a job while I'm away, but I told him to be available if you need him." He saw from her expression she didn't know whether to drop the subject or keep up the pushback.

"Does he live in the back building?" she said.

"He does. Now how about we see if Ms. Ruby's attorney works weekends?"

Her look softened. "Saturday morning, he'll be at the indoor range with a bucket of balls."

❦

Deuce drove along an industrialized section of Old Pineville Road until he came to the law offices of Julian Ybarra sandwiched between a warehouse gun range and a brewery with a Bow Wow welcome banner.

"Does my au pair here know about the armed baker you've hired to partner up with him?" Angie said.

"Pia and Deuce have met," Dom said.

"No troubles if she has skills," Deuce said.

"Trust me, she can drive," Dom said.

Deuce maneuvered the SUV Dom borrowed from Frenchman Franco through an icy entrance of topiary balls and trimmed hedges. Salted wet circles crisped under their tires when they settled next to the only car, a Mercedes-Maybach S600.

"One of those will set you back two hundred grand," Angie said.

"Solicitor must bring in the dough," Deuce said.

A cloud cut exposed a zaffer sky. They crunched along pavestones peppered with more rock salt up to Ybarra's front door. No one answered when Dom rang twice. Overhead awning trim snapped in the wind.

"I saw a back building," Dom said.

They made their way toward a rear warehouse connected to the office building. Dom pulled open the exit door to a sodium vapor glare. Twelve museum-quality cars stood in rows on an epoxy floor. The immaculate space smelled of floor wax, engine oil, and tobacco pipe smoke. Next to a 1974 spaghetti-squash-yellow Lincoln Continental Mark IV a guy leaned under the hood of a 1968 Acapulco Blue Shelby.

"Your taxi driver would go nuts in here," Angie said.

When they approached, the guy glanced up from a tool he tugged on the pristine engine.

"Julian Ybarra around?" Dom said.

He stood out from under the hood. Dom recognized the slicked-back hair and ash-ringed charcoal eyes from the local news. A mechanic's smock replaced the handmade suits he preferred whenever a microphone was stuck in his face outside the courthouse.

"I'm Julian Ybarra," he said. The law school mechanic set what looked like an orthopedic surgeon's wrench next to a sawed-off coffee can on a cerise cloth folded on the Shelby. Dom made the introductions. Julian tossed his gloves on the cloth and retrieved an elephant's foot pipe from the can. "I told Mrs. Giron a corporate investigator is a misuse of her limited resources and time. She should use my investigator, Jethro Contreras." He stirred the pipe bowl with a wooden match.

"We drop the ball, Jethro might still get a call," Dom said. "In your assessment, did Palmer's drug use lead to his murder?"

"I've made no assessments." He flared the match with his thumbnail.

"I figured you for at least a point of view," Dom said.

"Many theories have been floated for why he was killed." An accordion flame danced off the pipe bowl.

"These theories touch on his work?"

"Why would a professional environmental engineer have problems with people he came into contact with?" Julian said.

"Big buildings equal big money could turn into big problems," Angie said.

"Besides a nuisance lawsuit, his livelihood's a dead end," Julian said.

"By nuisance, you mean the Tusseys' Wesley Chapel number four with buried degreaser drums?" Dom said.

The smoke smelled of almonds, raspberries, and burnt oak.

"A complete waste of time."

"Having Jefferson Wallach sicced on you might focus one's attention," Dom said.

"The legal action was resolved and now the family's plant managers are diligent with their chemical disposal."

"Who represented Palmer?" Dom said.

"Lucas Kepley before he died on Stone Mountain, President's Day last year."

From the several times Dom climbed Stone Mountain's granite face he knew a climber had no margin for error.

"Don't overlook the obvious reason Palmer's murder hasn't been solved." Julian puffed up a cloud. "Shoddy police work."

"Nita Lopez is an experienced detective," Dom said.

"With two reprimands for mishandled evidence in her personal file. I've stressed to Mrs. Giron she should request Detective Lopez's removal."

"Cheap shot, scapegoat law enforcement," Angie said.

"I speak from experience when I say don't give the department under arrogant Chief Zorkaid a pass." He fingered his gloves back on, pipe clenched in mouth.

"I'm sure you have ideas how to get the chief's attention," Dom said.

"The media has an insatiable appetite for police ineptitude."

Dom said, "Any other assessments you—"

Ybarra cut him off with the elephant's foot. "None I care to share."

"Where'd you find the Shelby?" Angie said.

"A private California collector." He bared his Wite-Out-painted teeth. "Don't barge in here again on weekends. I keep regular business hours."

&

The temperature had dropped while they were in Julian's auto museum.

"More than a few million worth of cars in there," Angie said.

"Lucrative niche, police incompetence," Deuce said.

"He better have sharp elbows to go after cops," Angie said.

"Sushi chefs can't compete with Julian Ybarra's elbows. Head toward Uptown. I want to make another stop," Dom said.

Their front tires sluiced through icy snow furrows.

CHAPTER 20

A HALF A block from the corner of LaSalle Street and Beatties Ford Road, Dom directed Deuce toward a former lube shop. They found the last space next to a florist delivery van. A flower business occupied one bay, a body-oil emporium a second, and the third bay was converted into a rent-by-the-hour event venue.

Dom knew Brother Bondoc "Rocko" del Rosario, with volunteers from his Tuckaseegee Road Saint Faustus and Companions parish food bank, rented the space the last Saturday of each month. Rocko brought popular chefs in from around the city to coordinate a gourmet lunch buffet for the homeless in the venue space.

They negotiated a herd of grocery carts huddled around the entryway. Each cart overflowed with the detritus of broken lives. A fetor of wet wool, unwashed sour bodies, wood smoke, convenience store wine, and stale vomit hit them when they entered the crowded fifteen-hundred-square-foot space.

At a piano surrounded by tables, Rocko blessed all those gathered. Dom edged against the back wall and stood behind a woman in multiple coats and a sunflower-pattern ripped cloth knotted at the end of her two ponytails. Angie attempted to inch after him until a water buffalo-size guy with knotted curls stepped back into her. Dom saw panic flare in her eyes before she shouldered her way back outside. Thank you, South China Sea pirates, he thought. Deuce went after her.

When Rocko finished, chairs and tables were banged out of a closet and a line formed at the Sterno-flamed chafing dishes. A primary care doctor and nurse waited at a portable curtain booth in the back corner to administer free healthcare. Dom joined Rocko in the serving line after they cleaned beef stroganoff, sautéed green beans, and lemon meringue pie off the floor when a gentleman in a threadbare cantaloupe Nehru jacket passed out and upended his tray. Rocko could keep tabs on his flock from the table they carried their trays to.

"You still hang at Sammy's?" Dom said. Henry Sammy's was the boxing gym Rocko, a onetime super featherweight boxer, frequented to keep in shape.

"I'm lucky if I can work in a few rounds with the young guys once a month."

"You're not too hard on them?"

"I have a few tricks they haven't seen. And you? Still into the Israeli drill?"

"Krav Maga, keeps me limber," Dom said.

A woman with stooped shoulders and platinum hair shuffled close and whispered into Rocko's ear. She untied an electrical cord around her ankle-length down coat patched with duct tape and lifted a Norwich Terrier out of a makeshift inside pocket. Rocko placed his hand on the tiny head and said a silent prayer. With tear tracks on her cheeks, she eased the dog back into the pocket, closed and retied the cord, kissed the top of Rocko's head, and mumbled her way outside.

Dom explained Ms. Ruby's request and what they knew about Palmer. "Brenda Wick told us she accepted him into New Dawn on your recommendation," Dom said.

"I asked Brenda to help a friend in need."

"How'd you know Palmer?"

"He was a regular at our Friday handball games," Rocko said.

Dom speared his fruit cocktail with a plastic spork. "He ever voice any concerns about his work?"

"Palmer never shared much. He took part in our group for a year before I even knew he was an environmental engineer. In three and a half years he never missed one of our four p.m. Friday games until he no-showed two months before his murder. 'Buried under work commitments,' he replied to my email. When he missed the next game, I swung by his office. I could tell he'd lost sleep. He said a project ate into his time."

"He share which one?"

"Work for a mountain resort developer. The same guy who put up the twisted wood tower Uptown."

"Augie Pepitone?"

"Have you seen the thermal spring grotto outside his building?"

"Not yet."

"The Lost Souls Grotto—I've used it for baptisms on occasion. You'll also see his lobby is one of a kind."

The food line now extended out the door. Dom took a pull of Gatorade from his Styrofoam cup.

"Have you heard of JoJo Cifuentes?"

"Not one of Palmer's better choices," Rocko said.

"Brenda indicated people she pals around with were a source of friction with Palmer," Dom said.

"JoJo's step-cousin, Chico Vega, a northside hood, and his Twenty-Eighth Street Patriots, who Ms. Cifuentes should keep her distance from." Rocko salted his coleslaw. "Smooth cat in expensive threads who operates a high-end car lot. Has professional ball players for clients. I hear he dabbles in illegal after-hours liquor houses and drugs."

"A multitasker."

"More go-getter with street smarts."

"Brenda said Palmer relapsed not long before he ended up under the bridge," Dom said.

"His setback came as news to me until she told me at his funeral."

"She mentioned Rushers in the same sentence with relapse."

Rocko motioned around the room. "We first saw their carnage about a year ago. Swept through my people like a synthetic forest fire."

"Any connection between Chico and Rushers?"

"He'd be a good place to start."

"What else about JoJo?"

"She plays hopscotch between pencil pushers Uptown and Chico's crew. Before her Charlotte move, she lived in Durham where her side gig tripped her up. Sold hillbilly heroin on her lunch break behind a fast-food place next to where she worked for an architectural firm."

"Dope with a side of fries," Dom said.

Rocko watched a one-legged woman on crutches at the next table who started an argument about an unoccupied chair with a short, tubby guy who wore an oil-stained homburg.

"JoJo caught a seven-month stretch in North Carolina Correctional Institution for Women after an off-duty cop in the drive-through lane busted her. Her current employer was a volunteer in the prison's remedial reading program. JoJo worked with other inmates in the same program. They struck up a friendship and JoJo ended up with a job offer, where she now works."

JoJo had forgotten to tell them about her state-sponsored vacation.

"If Chico might be into Rushers and JoJo hangs with him, is she a player?"

"What do you see when you look Uptown?"

"Skyscraper light shows," Dom said.

"Think like a criminal, you have product to move," Rocko said.

"Hotels, condos, and office high-rises populated with disposable income," Dom said.

"A concentrated population of prequalified customers with steady paychecks. If I'm Chico Vega, a northside tough with smarts, my market research tells me white-collar types are picky. Prefer their dope come from someone in their peer group. An AutoCAD operator might be the perfect fit," Rocko said. He sprang up to catch the raised crutch. The situation dissipated after he found a place at another table for the guy with the homburg.

A series of questions flipped through Dom's mind. Did Palmer know JoJo spent time in prison? If Chico Vega had ties to Rushers, would he use JoJo for his conduit into Uptown's high earners? If Rushers were JoJo's second job, why would Palmer stay with her, and was she to thank for his Rushers relapse?

Rocko retook his seat. "Hard to believe those two are brother and sister."

"Where's Chico's car lot?"

"Kueentown Motorworks on North Tyron Street. Don't be fooled by his bookish appearance and upscale wardrobe. Behind the facade is a volcanic, hair-trigger temper. He's the only gangster I know who graduated with a degree in accounting. Even looks like a numbers guy."

"Checkbook know-how comes in handy with drugs and liquor house cash flow," Dom said.

"Has the organizational skills to keep his crew in line, too. Rumor on the street, he has a financial backer with juice. A patron saint without the halo," Rocko said.

Dom finished his tilapia and pushed aside the tray. "JoJo gave us the impression she and Palmer were closer than ever."

"I've dealt with enough JoJos to be suspicious. She'll know

more than she's let on. If you're curious about Chico, try pickup basketball games at the midtown YMCA."

❦

Dom climbed back into the SUV. Deuce played a game on his smartphone. Angie didn't say a word in the back with her eyes closed and her head on the headrest.

"You OK?" Dom said.

"I'm fine," she said.

He could see by her drawn mouth she wasn't over the panic from being jammed against the wall.

"Rocko preaches to a full house," Deuce said.

The windshield wipers removed a quarter inch of new snow. Dom felt his phone vibrate and read Winnie's text message. "Mrs. Giron never showed."

Deuce reversed away from the florist van.

"We have one more stop to make," Dom said.

"You and the padre have a history?" Deuce said.

"A friend from my monk days." Dom motioned to make the turn on Statesville Avenue. "I wanted Rocko's take on Palmer after Brenda said she admitted him to New Dawn based on Rocko's word."

Angie lifted her head off the headrest.

"How did he know Palmer?"

"They played in the same handball group."

The volume of snow started to decrease after they made another turn on Norris Avenue.

"Rocko said JoJo served time for dope sales."

"She never mentioned prison," Angie said.

"These acquaintances Palmer struggled with are the Twenty-Eighth Street Patriots, a crew run by JoJo's stepcousin who Brenda Wick and Karen Robles mentioned, Chico Vega. His business interests run the gambit from car sales and illegal liquor houses to dope. Venture a guess who Rocko thinks his pipeline could be into Uptown's drug scene?"

"LOVE knuckles?" Angie said.

"Her résumé fits the job description. Rocko said Chico may be involved with Rushers," Dom said.

"Rocko, Brenda, and Karen are all opinionated about JoJo," Angie said.

"Not good for Palmer if he got caught between her and Chico Vega," Dom said. "You play b-ball?"

"I have a killer skyhook," Deuce said.

"Chico plays pickup hoops."

"I'll need sneakers," Deuce said.

They turned parallel with Sixteenth Street's bridge and bumped across several sets of railroad tracks. Angie listened to her voice messages. They cleared the last set of tracks and Deuce started to cruise east on Parkwood Avenue. "Tussey Beauty Products' corporate communications person left the name of someone we can speak with," she said.

"An intern to an assistant vice president?" Dom said.

"Elizabeth 'Babe' Tussey."

"Now why would the owner of a trophy skyscraper want to meet with us about a dead environmental engineer?" Dom said.

"We should be honored by her presence," Angie said.

"Hold off with autograph requests," Dom said.

CHAPTER 21

"WHERE ARE WE?" Angie said.

"Ms. Ruby never showed. Take the next right," Dom said.

Several houses down Umstead Street, a periwinkle-blue ranch matched Winnie's texted address. Serviceberry trees blocked the neighbor's house and their motor home on jacks under an ice-crusted tarp. Undisturbed snow covered Ms. Ruby's property.

"She might be snowbound," Angie said.

"I'll be back in a few minutes," Dom said.

He forged a path up to the porch where a miniature Elvis statue held half-gallon frozen spring boxwoods on each step. Dom used his boot to brush snow away from the storm door. When he reached for the brass knocker for the third time, the door cracked open and Ms. Ruby appeared in her faded pink terry-cloth bathrobe.

"Couldn't get out, forgot to ring your office," she said.

"Can I come in?"

"Julian Ybarra called in a huff. Saturdays are his car day, and he didn't appreciate the interruption," she said.

"We forgot the camera crew."

She looked past him to the SUV. "They the woman and Chinaman he mentioned?" she said.

"Korean Japanese."

"Take your shoes off," she said.

She let the door go and padded away in flesh-tone compression socks. The eighty-plus-degree house reeked of smoke and cat litter. Dom went along the spiky vinyl runner mat in his socks to the living room. *The Price Is Right* blared from a seventy-inch HD television. Plastic slipcovers enclosed every piece of furniture.

Palmer's mother shooed away a Siamese cat stretched out on her couch spot. The cat waltzed and plopped on the plastic with three other Siamese. A rolled newspaper fire roared in the fireplace. Elvis, in a sequined white pantsuit, smiled down from a framed poster on the mantle. Eight weeks after the holidays her silver Christmas tree still stood in the corner weighed down with Elvis ornaments. Various-size pictures and portraits of the Memphis singer surrounded the television screen. The wall behind her held a Graceland tour map. Dom crinkled down on a wing chair.

Ms. Ruby muted the excited screams of a woman who won a year's supply of laundry detergent. The clicker went on her side table next to a can of Fanta, a stand-up portable telephone, an Elvis Zippo lighter, a pack of Kents, and an ashtray. "Julian urged me not to waste my time with you."

"Keep his telephone number handy. If we have to dig for every aspect of Palmer's life you hold back from us, his investigator Jethro might be a better match."

Another Siamese gnawed on a chicken bone in an open fast-food box under the plexiglass coffee table where Elvis-imprinted bottle caps were encased inside.

"What aspects?"

"For starters, his drug use."

"A misstep he received help for."

"Misstep or steps?"

"I don't count the second time." She crossed her socks next to her sudoku book on the plastic-zipped footstool.

"Why not?"

"He told me he just needed a tune-up and went back to the same people who helped him the first time."

"A tune-up for methamphetamines might be considered an understatement."

"The second go-round was nowhere near the hell he went through the first time."

"How long did he wrestle with his addiction?"

She lit a cigarette and exhaled sideways. "All his troubles started with a baseball foot injury his last year in high school. Doctors sent him home from the hospital with enough painkillers to knock out an elephant."

"When did you know he had a problem?"

"He circled the drain during the Great Recession when the firm he helped start lost a major customer. Palmer got the thankless job to pare down payroll. That's enough pain to make anyone turn to drugs. He let friends go with mortgages and college tuitions to pay. I failed him because I never realized how bad the problem was."

Her lip quivered.

"Don't be too harsh on yourself."

"Harsh? You lose a child twice." She finger-counted. "Once to drugs and then under a bridge."

"Any indication what triggered his relapse?"

"I figured his work again. He was a workaholic, channeled all his insecurities about money into long hours. Sometimes he racked up fifteen-, sixteen-, even seventeen-hour days."

Why money stress when Angie had said his financial affairs were in order?

"From what we've seen, he appeared to be in solid financial shape."

She snapped her fingers. "He feared everything he worked for could be lost in the blink of an eye. The pain and disappointment his father carried after the family moved in with my sister, when the bank took our house in the savings and loan crisis, is a trauma Palmer carried into adulthood."

"Karen Robles didn't mention money trouble," he said.

"She's a sweet lady who looked out for him. If you want to know about his financial situation, try his accountant. She used to be a member of our church before her husband died. Cynthia Padbury—I believe she still goes by Candy. She moved to Lenoir to be closer to her grandchildren."

Ms. Ruby flicked her cigarette in the butt-filled ashtray, a dish formed out of a chunk of glass with Elvis astride a motorcycle engraved on the side. "The only work comment he made to me in the weeks before he died had to do with a difficult client. He said with the kind of money his clients risked, they could scream all day if they wanted to."

"The screamer have a name?"

She shrugged her shoulders no.

"How did the move to your sister's affect Nickolas?" Dom said.

"Palmer was the introspective one who fretted the details. Being an engineer was the perfect career choice for him. Nickolas is younger and goes with the flow."

"We hear they weren't close."

A one-eyed Siamese jumped in her lap.

"Communication between them stopped after Palmer told Nickolas he didn't approve of his first wife. She spent more on shoes than any person I've ever met. Nickolas held down multiple jobs to keep current with all their credit card bills."

"Palmer's drug use wasn't the problem?"

"His brother was the last person who could lecture Palmer. He went through his own version of hell with drugs. I called Nickolas after Palmer's health scare and told him enough was enough. Get in touch with your brother. By then he was divorced and remarried to a wonderful woman with two small children who we adore."

"Health scare?"

The fast-food-box cat tubbed around Dom's legs with a purr.

"Three months before his murder, Palmer was in the hospital with a perforated ulcer. I never bought stomach-lining weakness for the reason his doctors gave. Stress ate a hole in him."

"Have you met JoJo Cifuentes?"

She rubbed behind the cat's ears with both hands, the cigarette between her lips. "While we're on the subject of stress."

"A girlfriend who spent time in prison another one of his missteps?"

"JoJo's an ex-con?" The cat looked at her when she stopped. "You're full of surprises. After huge blow-up fights, they wouldn't speak for days, then I'd hear they were back together like two birds who mate for life."

"These blowups ever turn violent?"

"Her mouth was violent enough."

Another cat walked along the couch behind her head.

"The name Chico Vega mean anything to you?"

"He one of Palmer's clients?"

"JoJo's relative."

"Then I'm sure he's not a candidate for citizen of the year."

"Were you aware of any legal trouble Palmer may have been involved in?"

"A shampoo company caused him to hire a lawyer. They didn't appreciate he exposed them for being polluters." She jabbed out her cigarette and fired up another one. "With all your questions, I'll assume you have no idea who killed him?"

"Too early to say. We have many people we still need to speak with."

A Siamese with a french fry walked on the table toward Dom.

"Julian says he'll wait for the right time to talk with reporters about the police's botched investigation."

"You're his PR goldmine."

"Do you have an opinion?"

"About the police?" Dom said. He set the french-fry cat from his lap down with the one between his legs.

"Yes, because Julian believes they're nowhere," she said.

"I'll tell you when I have one."

"You surprised me. I thought you and your lady friend would put on a show for Mr. Hillstead's sake, then blow me off."

"Not my style, Ms. Ruby."

Elvis's "Love Me Tender" played as her ringtone. Dom heard the caller, a Siamese cat rescue service in need of an emergency home. Ms. Ruby put her hand over the receiver.

"Find my boy's killer."

Deuce had let the SUV run while Dom was inside.

"Ms. Ruby's not a JoJo fan," Dom said. "She said they had a volatile relationship with up-and-down blowups followed by makeups. Palmer never told his mother JoJo served time in prison."

"We're not sure he even knew," Angie said.

"His brother might know if she told him. After Palmer's health problems, they got back together. When I return from Peru, we'll drive to Asheville and catch up with Nickolas."

"What type of health problems?" Angie said.

"An ulcer," Dom said.

"Because of his work or JoJo?" Deuce said.

"Take your pick," Dom said.

CHAPTER 22

DOM EXITED THE jet bridge from his Lima, Peru, flight into a sardine ball of weather-delayed travelers. After he retrieved his bag, he waited in the wet snow for Pia to collect him. He was surprised when Franco's black SUV appeared and Angie powered down her window. "Where's Pia?"

"Last-minute change of plans. Babe Tussey can work us in at five. I took the liberty to say we'd be there," Angie said.

He climbed in and Deuce drove toward Uptown.

"Flight uneventful?" Angie said.

"If you discount the hard landing," Dom said. "Any problems with the job?"

While he was away, Pia drove and Deuce worked personal protection for a billionaire cement magnate who flew in to inspect a Rowan County batch plant. "Simple job," Deuce said.

"And our driver?"

"No daredevil tricks required," Deuce said.

Dom saw a new Wilkinson Boulevard coffee shop. "Pull in, we have time," he said.

Deuce let Angie out to go get in line while they parked.

"How's she been doing?" Dom said.

"Spent all her time in the conference room with Ms. Ruby's

bag notes. Monday, she stayed in there until after midnight. Never complained about the office pull-out bed either."

"She didn't ask to go back to her apartment?"

"Yesterday morning to retrieve a few items." He backed between a Hummer and a Kia.

"How about her doctor appointment?"

"We were there early. Afterward, appeared pretty broken up."

They started up the entrance sidewalk toward a Great Pyrenees the size of a mini polar bear leashed to a bike rack. Inside, a blue-grass singer with electric-orange dreadlocks sat on a barstool near the birch log fire and played her dobro. Angie sat at a table with an expansive view of Uptown's luminous reflection off the cloud-carpeted night sky. She handed Dom his black coffee and pushed Deuce his double expresso. Hot chocolate wafted from a family with children at the next table.

"After Ms. Ruby told you about Palmer's financial insecurities, I went back through his financials again," Angie said. "He never missed a Welker Street or East Boulevard mortgage payment, and the investment and savings accounts were both well funded."

"Did you contact his accountant?" Dom said.

"Candy Padbury, who lives in Hickory, tried her four times with no luck."

"We'll stop by her office on the way back from Nickolas's," Dom said.

"I asked Deuce to take me back to the East Boulevard office to check something out. Look at these." Her phone screen showed Karen Robles's favorite Palmer picture, of him at her birthday cel-ebration in oversize glasses and a party hat. "Check the bookshelf and sticky notes."

Dom saw the purple notes stuck on a shelf beside his desk.

She slid another picture across the screen. "From the day Bill Eversole let us in his office."

He saw the space before the last note with Tupac's lyrics. Karen's party photo didn't show a space. "One of the notes is missing," he said.

"Deuce drove me back to the East Boulevard building to check if it slipped behind his desk. The note's gone, it's not in his office." Back to the birthday party picture, she enhanced the notes with a finger spread.

Dom saw on the missing note in neat Palmer penmanship *irwin coldpepper? cv??*

"I couldn't find an Irwin Coldpepper anywhere near Charlotte on the internet."

"They could be separate people," Dom said. "Or waterways. Karen Robles mentioned an Irwin Creek job, and Brenda Wick told us Palmer was threatened on a waterway after he found a chemical release. The waterway problem she cited for his stress-related Rushers setback. You haven't seen Irwin or Coldpepper referenced in Ms. Ruby's bag?"

"No, and I've been through her notes multiple times. I think Irwin must be Irwin Creek. How many Irwins can there be?" She used a straw to stir her drink's cake batter froth.

"Then who or what are *cv* and Coldpepper?" Dom said

"I didn't see any Coldpeppers or *cv*s in her bag either."

Deuce waved to the toddler at the next table who sipped hot chocolate and couldn't take her eyes off him.

"See what Karen has to say about the Irwin Creek job. Maybe she can flush out what Palmer was up to. She may have some ideas about *cv* and Coldpepper too," Dom said.

"You could be on the wrong track. They aren't related to business," Deuce said.

"We'll keep all options open," Dom said. "Text me those pictures." He knew of one *cv* Palmer's girlfriend might be able to verify: Chico Vega.

Angie tapped her phone and hit send, then licked whipped cream off her straw. "I checked the job your monk friend said was behind Palmer's missed handball games, Augie Pepitone's Bufflehead Reserve. Palmer almost cratered the six-hundred-acre development when he stumbled into a rout of noonday globes behind Augie's showcase gorge waterfall."

"Are they plants?" Dom said.

"Snails, and I mean a lot of them."

"Rout?" Deuce said. His lopped-off pinkie finger stuck out while he held the expresso's tiny handle pinched between his index finger and thick thumb.

"Weird name for a bunch of snails. A zoology professor at Banner Elk's Lees-McRae College heard about the find and called the US Fish and Wildlife Service."

"Why all the commotion over some snails?" Dom said.

"Noonday globes have never been found outside the Nantahala Gorge two hundred miles to the southwest. Work screeched to a halt while the property was combed for any sign of another rout. Six more routs were found, each larger than the next. Augie hired private security to keep all the snail lovers off his property."

"Rout might be an accurate description for what Palmer did to Augie's pro forma," Dom said.

A teenage boy and girl strode past the window with a brindle Akita puppy.

"Augie Pepitone could be the problem customer Palmer's mother mentioned," Angie said.

"How would you react if snails invaded your resort?" Deuce said.

"After I fired the person who found them, I might look for the nearest wailing wall," Angie said.

"Any mention if Augie cut Palmer loose?" Dom said.

"I didn't see one."

"We'll hear Augie's take on his routed high-country dreams when we visit One Pepitone Place," Dom said.

"Palmer and Augie shared something else in common. Tussey family legal dustups. Palmer, for the degreaser problems he stirred up at the shampoo plant, and Augie, for his contorted skyscraper." Angie glanced at her cell phone time. "We can talk about an article I found on the way."

Deuce sipped down the last of his expresso.

✌

Uptown's skyscraper brilliance exploded into view when they sped out from under I-77's bridge. In the high-rise cluster, One Pepitone Place radiated orange-tinged blue, with upper double-helix floors obscured by a solitary cloud. Across the street, Tussey Center soared like a beacon to the rent-check gods. Backlit against an early evening star-filled sky, the brilliant globe of white, navy blue, and imperial red beamed above the setback floors and crown.

"Augie holds the tallest building record by ten feet. Venture a guess who crossed the line behind him?" Angie said.

"Do I smell shampoo?" Dom said.

"A business article I found referenced the first salvo of Augie and Babe's skyscraper battle, which occurred when Augie released renderings for his building at a news conference a few weeks before Babe topped out Tussey Center."

Deuce accelerated and cut across several lanes to make South College Street's exit.

"Skyscraper wars aren't for the faint of heart," Dom said.

"Augie brought in architect Mandisa Hardenberg who's designed cloud busters in Beijing, London, and Dubai. One Pepitone Place was her first United States commission."

"Why her?" Dom said. He looked at the timber tower where cantilevered floors swept its central core.

"She's the star architect of the moment. Augie's news conference received global attention when Hardenberg announced lumber would be a substantial component of the tower's construction."

"The windows her idea too?" Dom said. A simulated flame radiated around One Pepitone Place from orange, blue-tinted windows.

"Hardenberg accepted the commission with one condition: she wanted Augie's tower to be included in her exclusive Blaze trophy skyscraper collection."

"Blaze like fire?" Deuce said.

"All her Blaze buildings are outfitted with Flares by Hardenberg, the patented glass curtain wall systems she invented to project flames above the skylines of her award-winning buildings," she said.

"Simulated fire from a wood building—someone has a sense of humor," Dom said.

Construction cones funneled South Mint Street traffic into a single lane.

"Augie announced at his news conference he'd put up enough floors to win Uptown's tallest-building title. How does Babe react? She war-rooms her architecture firm to find a way her superstructure can retain the tallest-building title. Their solution: a globe with Tussey Beauty Products' signature colors and enough height to overtake Augie."

"Looks like a snow cone," Deuce said.

"No one figured a globe would make the stiletto tower resemble a snow cone. Her corporate headquarters now bears the nickname 'The Snow Cone Building.'"

A worker with a hard hat and fluorescent vest held up a stop sign.

"Augie a good loser?" Dom said.

"The day Babe flipped her globe lights on for the first time,

Augie announces in the media he's ordered enough lumber to nail-gun eight more stories up to take back the height title. To add insult to injury, he poaches an anchor tenant she was about to sign and absconds with her head leasing agent," she said.

"Who's the tenant?" Dom said.

"Roo Woo, the phone game app. Do you play?"

"I don't waste time on telephone games," Dom said.

The road worker rotated his stop sign to slow. They started to move with traffic into Uptown.

"I play," Deuce said.

Dom looked at him.

"What's your screen name?" Angie said.

"Sobo," Deuce said.

"How many floors did Roo Woo lease in Augie's building?" Dom said.

"A block of twenty-two."

"For a silly game?" Dom said.

"A silly game with tens of millions of users," she said.

They crossed over South Davidson Street.

"If Augie took a twenty-floor tenant from Babe, he put the hurt on Tussey Center," Dom said.

"Four hundred fifty-thousand square feet of hurt," Angie said.

"Any idea what Tussey Center rents for?" Dom said.

Deuce's eyes were on the rearview mirror.

"Babe's brochure quotes thirty-two dollars per square foot."

"Pull up your calculator and multiply four hundred fifty-thou-sand by thirty-two."

She speed-typed on her smartphone screen. "Fourteen million eight hundred thousand."

"Times seven."

"Why seven?" she said.

"Seven-year lease terms are not uncommon."

She typed again.

"The parking garage." Dom said.

He pointed up ahead to Tussey Center's midblock below-level parking entrance.

Deuce looked behind them in the driver's side mirror.

"Ninety-eight million and change," she said.

"With year-over-year escalations the number will grow north of a hundred million, which is the rental-income hit Babe Tussey took thanks to Augie Pepitone."

"She started legal action against him when her leasing agent walked across the street to join up with the enemy. Babe contends the agent took Roo Woo with her. A quotable gal named Mercer Worthey who said she made the move because Mr. Pepitone put more chips on the table. I'd be curious how many chips jingle down to a real estate agent off a hundred-million-dollar lease," she said.

"Figure a few percentage points," Dom said

"A few points on a hundred million is a bag of jingle."

Deuce slow-rolled past the garage, his eyes back to the rear-view mirror.

"You missed the turn," Dom said.

The big man indicated with his chin behind them. "Picked up a friend."

Dom looked into the passenger door mirror. A Triple Nickel Challenger pulled up behind them.

"The Challenger?"

"Joined the party when we exited the freeway," Deuce said.

"Make the block," Dom said.

They passed a tan-uniformed Tussey Center guard with a look-alike highway patrol hat and stubby white nightstick at the loading dock entrance. After a right at the light, they were alongside One Tussey Center's upscale steak house.

In his mirror Dom watched the Challenger turn after them.

"Why would we have a tail?" Angie said.

Dom kept his eyes on the mirror. "Good question," he said.

Deuce waited at the next turn behind a UPS truck. When the light changed, he followed the truck and turned again. Across from Tussey Center's lobby entrance stood One Pepitone Place. Steam billowed out into the street from Augie's geothermal hot spring Lost Souls Grotto inside the dramatic U-shaped drive.

"Don't stop," Dom said.

He opened the door, jumped out, and used a bus stop shelter for cover. The SUV's rear lights disappeared when Deuce went right at the next cross-street light. Guards at Babe Tussey's security desk were visible through the lobby windows. The Challenger came toward the bus stop and disappeared into the grotto steam. When the Triple Nickel emerged, Dom was out in the street before the driver realized he was there. He grabbed the passenger door, but it was locked. Darkened windows obscured the driver's face but not his beefy hands on the wheel and the turquoise index-finger ring. The driver lurched into the opposite lane. Dom jumped out of the way when the back end swerved and sprayed him with snow. He glimpsed the knit skullcap on the driver's head before he rooster-tailed back into the grotto steam. "G" was the only letter on the North Carolina tag Dom could make out. The Triple Nickel's lights disappeared in a blur under an elevated crosswalk.

Deuce came back around and collected him.

"Any luck with the driver?' Angie said.

"Only a 'G' on his plates."

"You're helpful," Angie said.

"Next time I'll ask for a photo ID."

CHAPTER 23

A CONVENTION IN Tussey Center's exhibit hall forced them to circle several levels down before Deuce found an open space. When the parking garage elevator doors opened, Angie stepped aside to let them go in first. Dom saw her apprehension.

"We can take the stairs," he said.

She shook her head and came in close behind him to stand facing toward the doors when they came back together.

"Palmer's connected to two prominent Uptown building owners. Sued by one, unleashed a snail invasion on the other," Dom said.

Angie didn't reply at his attempt to distract her.

The doors parted to a massive wall canvas of conquistadors separated by a river from a massed army of native warriors. A metal bust of renowned artist Diego Rivera rested on a plinth below the artwork. They crossed through the cavernous airy lobby of natural light, ivory wood, and ruby-veined marble floors toward the security guard desk. One guard stood with a clipboard and, like the loading dock guard, a white nightstick hung from his belt.

Dom thought white clubs were a bit much for a trophy skyscraper. A twerpy, ponytailed guard with a back-of-the-hand spiderweb tattoo put down the desk telephone receiver. He looked at Deuce and made a moo goo gai pan delivery wisecrack to his clipboard partner.

They were issued name tags after a call upstairs to confirm their meeting with Babe Tussey. Ponytail put on a patrol hat and escorted them to the elevator bank. Dom saw his name tag read Officer Earl Jessup and motioned to the nightstick.

"Why the wood?"

"The boss isn't a gun lover," Earl said.

His sharp twang reminded Dom of counties along western North Carolina's Tennessee border. "Ever come in handy?" Dom said.

"Once, when I caught a scumbag with a stolen phone in the parking garage. Stopped his lip with one whack." Earl pressed the private elevator call button, stepped around Deuce, and went back to the guard desk.

Dom looked at Angie when the doors parted to a tighter cab than the parking garage elevator. "You OK?" he said.

She gave a quick nod and squeezed in behind Deuce. The doors were almost closed when she hand-swiped them open and stepped back out. "Give me a moment," she said.

Dom and Deuce waited near Rivera's bust while she went to Earl, who pointed to the restroom sign.

"Trauma mind games?" Deuce said.

"She's been through the ringer," Dom said.

Dom looked out the lobby's several revolving doors to across the street and noticed Babe's skyscraper sat on a slight incline above the Lost Souls Grotto and Augie's valet-manned One Pepitone Place grand entrance.

A few minutes later she rejoined them. "Since I've been back, cramped spaces can be a problem," she said.

"We can reschedule?" Dom said.

"No, let's go." Back inside the cab, Angie grabbed the metal-edge doorframe when they hurtled skyward.

Dom made another attempt to distract her. "From the little I've heard about the shampoo fortune, Great-Grandfather Percy Tussey started with a concoction he brewed on the family's Wingate farm. When did Babe step into the top job?"

"She quit law school to take the reins after Uncle Weldon plowed his glider into a north Georgia mountain. On her watch, revenues doubled. She handed off the job to a cousin when she decided to focus on the family's real estate portfolio. Babe has a reputation for being competitive. Translation: she hates to lose and never met a lawsuit she didn't like."

The elevator swooshed to a stop and opened to a square-headed, buzz-cut guard at a desk. "Mrs. Tussey will be available in a few minutes," he said.

They waited at a group of leather chairs near the floor-to-ceiling windows. A river of car lights inched through the glass walls far below.

"I couldn't work up here," she said.

"Heights a problem?" Dom said.

"Only when I have to look down," she said.

Deuce pointed across the street to Augie's corkscrew tower roof. "Pepitone flies in style," he said.

A black Sikorsky S-92 executive helicopter sat on a helipad. *Pepitone* with a paladin logo appeared in script along the tail boom.

"Tussey Center is equipped with two helipads," Angie said. "Augie's being feted at a sold-out black tie awards banquet next week where he's to receive a national building award."

"Might be an opportune time to catch him with his guard down. Gauge his reaction to Palmer's snail fiasco," Dom said.

"Did you miss I said sold out?" Angie said.

"Winnie enjoys a challenge."

The guard with his white nightstick came their way. "Mrs. Tussey will see you now," he said.

They followed him down another hallway into a spacious office whose centerpiece was a model of every building inside Uptown's 277 freeway loop. A well-stocked bar ran along one wall, and a treadmill next to a stationary bike faced windows south toward suburban lights and South Park's distant buildings. The guard pressed a call button on yet another elevator. When the doors opened, Dom knew no way all three of them could squeeze in.

"We'll see you back at the SUV," Dom said.

Deuce nodded.

Dom rested his hand on Angie's shoulder after the doors closed. Seconds later, they stepped out into the humid smell of tropical vegetation, roses, potting soil, and the sound of a waterfall. A weak sun filtered through the glass dome. Pea gravel covered a path toward a trimmed Bermuda grass square bordered by dense foliage.

Babe Tussey, a slender woman with khakis tucked into rubber garden boots, stood near rows of rose bushes whose blooms could double for grapefruit. In a long-sleeve saffron Oxford shirt and veiled beekeeper's hat, she moved a smoker under a wood frame screen coated with bees.

"I could be in trouble if I get stung," Angie said.

Babe fed the screen back into the hive and replaced the lid. The smoker went on the worktable. She pulled off her veil and hat, and a shock of white hair flowed onto her shoulders.

For Dom, fashion model first came to mind before corporate firebrand.

"I'm Babe Tussey. Please." The accent pure southern silk. She motioned to chairs at a garden table.

The square-headed guard came out of the elevator with lemonade and glasses on a sterling silver tray.

"Thank you, Hubie," Babe said.

He set the tray on the table and retreated back to the elevator. His high-gloss boots ground into the gravel.

"Nice touch, an office building conservatory," Dom said.

"I needed somewhere to grow my roses," Babe said. She hung the hat and veil on the chair next to her.

"You have quite the green thumb," Dom said.

She filled their glasses with lemonade and offered a plate of wedged lemons. "We grow our own lemons too," she said.

Angie dodged her head when a bee buzzed past her ear.

"Don't worry, my bees don't sting." Babe shooed one away from the pitcher. "You're my first private investigator visit. How can I help you?"

"We'd like to discuss Palmer Giron and the Wesley Chapel number four plant," Dom said.

"Unfortunate how the whole episode unfolded."

"Because he caught you?" Angie said.

Babe leveled her eyes at Angie. "No one caught anyone, young lady," she said, emphasis on *caught*.

"Buried degreaser drums were put there by someone else?" Angie said.

The elevator rides or bees must have her on edge.

"Are you here to level accusations?"

"We're not here to accuse anyone," Dom said. He looked at Angie. "On behalf of Mrs. Giron, we're in touch with people her son came into contact with."

"Our number four problems were caused by a general contractor we hired to retrofit the plant. Their subcontracted plumber misread plans and buried an industrial mixer's regulator valve."

"The plumber did it?" Angie said.

"How would our safety staff know about a buried defective valve?"

Angie used a lemon spear to flick a bee off her lemonade.

"A bum valve, not leaky drums, was the problem?" Dom said.

"Your source needs to get their facts straight. Our attorney negotiated settlements with the GC and the plumber's insurance carrier to pay for the cleanup."

"Jefferson Wallach your negotiator?" Dom said.

"Mr. Wallach's been our legal counsel for many years."

"We understand Palmer was on his radar?" Dom said.

Babe topped off her lemonade. Angie waved another bee away from her lemon wedge.

"Fanatics at the Clean Water Action Committee were in possession of a topography map Palmer put together for a developer who planned to build an apartment complex not far from our plant. We found the map on one of C-WAC's people who trespassed on our property."

"And you believe Palmer gave them the map?" Dom said.

"Who else would?"

"Confidential information given to an outside party doesn't square with what we know about Palmer and how he conducted his business," Dom said.

"Are you aware we employed him at one time? The site where we sit once housed a prewar building we demolished to make way for Tussey Center. Excavators uncovered roof timbers from a horse-rendering barn. We discovered contaminated soil below the kill room."

Babe reached over and picked a bee off Dom's glass. "The national company that performed all our environmental work missed the kill room soil. We brought on Palmer for a second opinion. He impressed my real estate staff, who decided to send more work his way."

"The topo map couldn't have helped the relationship," Dom said.

"Situations can become confused," Babe said.

"Jefferson help Palmer with his confusion?" Angie said.

Several bees swarmed from bucket blooms behind Babe.

"We believe then and now Palmer gave C-WAC the topography map." She sawed a lemon into wedges with a serrated knife. "He made a nice living off the work we sent his way for many years. I'd hoped our business relationship would not have ended on a sour note. Let me show you something."

She stood and they followed her along the path into the dense green growth past kumquats, miniature banana trees, and tomatoes the size of softballs. Dom happened to glance off to the right and saw a greenhouse's gabled glass inside an impregnable stand of bamboo plants.

"What's in the greenhouse?" Dom said.

"A conservatory for endangered plant species," Babe said.

Where the vegetation stopped at the six-sided panes of glass, she pointed beyond a plain of snow and a rented helicopter lashed to one of her two helipads. "See the cleared piece of dirt?"

Dom saw far below through cloud mist a vacant rectangle among a boomtown of apartment buildings, restaurants, bars, and office towers.

"I have those thirteen acres under contract for my Mother Lode Heights project. When the project's completed, we'll have a million two square feet of office space, another one fifty K of retail, and eight hundred doors of multifamily."

"Mother Lode is a good name for all the money you'll make," Dom said.

"We're close to the Gold District, where miners flocked to Charlotte in the 1800s before they went to California, after a farmer found gold nuggets on his farm near where the stadium now sits. Shafts from their abandoned mines can still be found along West Morehead Street."

Through the clouds Dom could make out the low-slung buildings and acres of gravel parking around the seventy-five-thousand-seat stadium where football players made their mother lode on top of dank shafts where another generation of dreamers hacked their way toward glory.

"We lined up Palmer to take care of the project's environmental work when we found his topo map in possession of those C-WAC trespassers. We let him go and brought on another engineer."

"Who caught the job?" Dom said.

"Jerry Qwain of Qwain Environmental Resources, who completed the work a few months before Palmer's death."

"Ouch, it stung me," Angie said. She swatted a bee off her arm.

"I guess my bees don't like you, Ms. Crete."

Two fast elevator rides and they were back in the lobby. Angie bought some Benadryl for the bee sting from Tussey Center's sundries shop.

"If Palmer was involved with Babe's Mother Lode, why would he give Dever's topo map to these Clean Water Action Committee people?" Dom said.

"Doesn't sound like him to hand off confidential information," Angie said.

"You going to be OK?" Dom said.

She nodded. "Babe blames a plumber for number four's troubles." She swayed her hand. "Take your pick, overlooked valve or Palmer's buried drums?"

He didn't want to put her through another cramped elevator ride when he saw people stacked back from the parking garage elevators.

"Let's walk. Deuce can pick us up out front."

Earl smiled and tapped his hat brim when they passed the guard's desk. A twenty-degree wind greeted them outside the revolving door and blew the Lost Souls Grotto steam back toward One Pepitone Place. They walked toward an ice-skating rink and boutique hotel Babe was putting up next to her skyscraper.

Industrial space heaters warmed bystanders who watched skaters wobble and spin around the rink.

"How's the sting?"

She showed him the welt on her forearm. "The Benadryl helped. Bees in a skyscraper, are you kidding me?" she said.

"Add those C-WAC people to our go-see list," he said.

Angie huddled into her coat against the cold. "Of all the environmental engineers to choose from, she picks Jerry Qwain?"

"Jerry might figure Babe's fair game after the Laphoons dumped him for a missed bakery fuel tank and went with Palmer."

An attractive brunette in an Armani overcoat snowplowed to a stop in front of them. "Hello, Dominick," she said.

"Rachel, I didn't see you out there," Dom said.

"I'm with Pierre," she said. Her hand followed a bent guy who wove through skaters with hands on his lower back.

"Angie Crete, Rachel Ketton," Dom said.

Rachel extended her leather-gloved hand. "Still Rachel Ketton Mundy until Dominick finds time to sign the divorce papers," she said.

Angie gave Dom a look. Deuce tapped the SUV horn from the curb.

"Give me a minute," Dom said.

Angie said goodbye and left.

"Isn't she youngish for you?" Rachel said. His statuesque wife watched Angie go to the SUV. Well, wife until he signed off on the divorce papers, still in the same place on his desk where he put them two months ago.

"We're together on a job," he said.

"In Charlotte for an international guy like you? Business

must be slow." Rachel wielded comments like a pikeman from the Middle Ages.

"A cold case."

"I thought corporate work was the golden goose," she said. Rachel knew all about golden geese. She'd blown enough of them out of the sky. Her ability to bring new clients into the fold of her international consulting firm employer propelled her to partner faster than anyone in the firm's history.

"A client favor," he said.

"Angie Crete part of the favor?"

"An investigator with chops. How's Hans Christian Andersen?" Pierre whisked between teenage girls, launched into a lutz, and landed next to a senior citizen who looked like he might sprawl forward.

"He's been offered a major promotion in Boston."

"Boston's ripe with skating opportunities."

"He wants me to say yes to the move, which is hard with our unsigned paperwork."

For years she'd wanted to move out of Charlotte to one of her firm's big-market offices. Her reason, more wine-and-dine client opportunities.

"I haven't gotten to them."

"Our run's over, Dom. Time to move on."

Her boyfriend glided by in a forward sizzle. Dom didn't understand her attraction to him. Was it that the guy could skate, or because he was a player in the bathroom fixture industry?

"You're sure he's who you want to be with?"

"Pierre makes me laugh."

"I can remember when we used to laugh."

"Let's not, OK? He has to decide by the fifteenth of next month. Get the papers back to me." She skated away. Dom could list many excuses why their marriage petered out, from her corporate ambition and desire to leave Charlotte to his travel. What brought them down in the end was a lack of will to fight for each other, and he now understood another reason: he wasn't a comedian. He watched them skate hand in hand and knew the inspiration or new idea he'd hoped for to save their marriage didn't matter anymore.

⁕

Deuce started along Monroe Road when Angie broke the silence from the back seat. "Who skates in Armani?"

"Rachel has certain style expectations," Dom said.

"You still love her?" she said.

"We were lucky to have one great year."

"Why the paperwork holdup?" Angie opened her smartphone screen.

"Avoided them because I hoped we could work through our problems."

"Don't tell me about avoidance genes. We all have them." She showed him the picture of Palmer's dry cleaner receipt found in his pocket. "Look at the date."

Dom saw Palmer was in the West Morehead Street parking lot in June before his murder.

"Babe told us Jerry Qwain finished up the Mother Lode job a few months before Palmer died. June on the receipt puts Palmer not far from the Mother Lode after Jerry completed his work. Why's Palmer on West Morehead Street if he no longer worked for Babe?"

"Sporting event at the stadium," Deuce said.

"Stadium was empty. He was there on a Tuesday morning."

"Might be at a meeting in one of those office buildings along West Morehead," Dom said.

"Odd he'd pay for parking when they all have their own free lots."

CHAPTER 24

Angie was already in the conference room when Dom came through the front door at seven forty-five. She was there with Pia and a sfogliatella from another of her pastry boxes. Pia pushed the box Dom's way. He considered the powdered sugar pastries.

"You ever go low fat?" he said.

"Food, like life, should be enjoyed," Pia said.

"When do you leave?" Dom said.

"Ten forty-five," Pia said.

"Where are you off to?" Angie said.

Dom lifted one of the delicacies from the box.

"Washington, DC," Pia said.

"Winnie located a low-mileage Range Rover with the security specifications I want in a vehicle for the executive and dignitary protection work Pia and Deuce will handle. Liechtenstein's embassy staff intends to unload it. She'll fly up, and if the vehicle checks out, drive back," Dom said.

"Every ding and scratch means discount," Angie said.

"They'll cry diplomatic immunity," Pia said.

"Let's not cause an international incident over a used Range Rover," Dom said. He ate a piece of the flaky sugar-coated pastry filled with almond paste.

"I'll be back before Ms. Medfeathers's flight arrives," Pia said.

"Who's she?" Angie said.

"Alondra Medfeathers, aka Hipsta Shee," Dom said.

"The singer?"

"You're a hip-hopper?" he said.

"Her sophomore album, *Angel Pleaze*, garnered four Grammy awards," Angie said.

"The head of her security team and I go way back. He called and asked if I knew a driver and someone who could work security for his singer's sold-out Uptown show."

"I should be on my way," Pia said. She collected her phone and left.

"Where's Deuce?" Dom said.

"Went to gas up Franco's SUV," Angie said.

Dom looked at Angie's whiteboard scribbles, Ms. Ruby's bag notes on the table, and New Dawn's pamphlet. They were still no closer to Palmer's killer than the first day they met Ms. Ruby in the diner.

Deuce came in and looked at the open pastry box.

"Have one, gift from Pia," Angie said. She turned her laptop to show a picture of Augie Pepitone's company website home page. "Since we plan to ambush Augie at his banquet about Palmer's snail invasion, I thought we might want to know more about The Pepitone Group Companies. Mr. Pepitone takes puffery to new heights. He devotes an entire page on his website to his Buncombe County hardscrabble youth. Of course, his bankruptcies aren't mentioned."

"He's gone down more than once?" Dom said.

Powdered sugar covered Deuce's fingers.

"The guy's an inflatable bounce-back clown. His first crash and burn was a savings and loan he founded taken down by soured commercial real estate loans. The second came after a Y2K technology start-up he poured money into flamed out. He won the lottery with the student housing business Dever Multifamily paid him a fortune for."

"Third time's a charm," Deuce said. He licked his fingers.

"Here's how guys like Augie operate. He moves one of his daughters into her college musty dorm building when the light bulb goes off for his next untapped market, well-maintained, amenity-rich, off-campus quarters baby boomers will pay up for their kids to live in. Augie put his dorm properties next to colleges and universities in thirty-eight states before Dever knocked on his door. He deposited generational money when their check cleared."

"How many generations?" Deuce said. His pastry was already gone.

"A hundred twenty million worth."

"How does Augie settle on a lumber store skyscraper with all the business possibilities a nine-figure check presents?" Dom said.

"He's bought into green construction for the future of sky-scrapers. Makes the decision to use lumber for the small carbon footprint. If One Pepitone Place succeeds, he plans to duplicate the process in center city markets around the country."

"Unless tenants have a problem being in a wooden structure," Dom said.

"The app game company Roo Woo and their few hundred employees left Tussey Center behind to sign a long-term lease in his lumber wonder," Angie said.

"And if a wing nut with matches comes on the property?" Deuce said.

"Augie installed a state-of-the-art sprinkler system," she said.

"He's a good salesman if he convinced his financial backers a twisted wood tower can compete with steel-and-glass high-rises," Dom said.

She shuffled through her papers. "Here's a piece from a commercial real estate finance magazine."

Dom saw the highlighted headline: *Pepitone Secures Permanent Financing for Timber, LEED Platinum-Certified Skyscraper.*

"What's LEED?" Dom said.

"A designation given to buildings if they have minimal impact on the environment. Not many buildings meet the stringent requirements."

"Someone overlooked a Sherwood Forest being buck-sawed to produce enough board feet to put up a skyscraper," Dom said.

"His sold-out event is being sponsored by an organization that recognizes the most innovative building in the country each year. Augie's teed up to receive the top award."

Deuce lifted out another sfogliatella.

"Wouldn't the smell from one burned coffee pot start an exit stampede?" Dom said.

"One Pepitone Place's marketing material goes into great length about the structure's life-safety systems," she said.

"Translation: he upped the rent," Dom said.

She looked at her notepad. "His rental rate's the highest in the state. The beekeeper's tower across the street came in second by three dollars per square foot."

"Was Palmer involved with Augie's tower?" Deuce said.

"Performed the environmental work before Augie sent him to his mountain resort where he made snail history."

They got up to leave.

"I also gave Karen Robles a call," Angie said. "She said she has no idea what Palmer was up to on Irwin Creek."

"What about Coldpepper and the missing note with *cv?*" Dom said.

"She apologized and said, 'I can't help with those either.'"

CHAPTER 25

They left the empty pastry box and drove to Palmer's house in Cherry, a historic neighborhood close to Uptown being transformed by gentrification. Raw wind made their walk down Welker Street feel several degrees colder than the morning's thirty-degree high.

Dom looked through naked branches of a rare basswood tree to the cloud-streaked sky, where hope and all-being-right-with-the-world reigned. In front of Palmer's midblock, white Cape Cod, he thought of Ms. Ruby and the world she lived in where right didn't exist anymore.

An umber-painted iron fence enclosed the tidy front yard and sun reflected off the snow-frozen St. Augustine grass. Box-sash window shutters matched the fence's color. A thorny-olive evergreen hedge ran on either side of the fluted, column entryway and a cucumber magnolia stood guard at the entrance to the side yard.

Angie tried Ms. Ruby's key in the wooden front door's lock. "Doesn't fit," she said.

"Let's go around back," Dom said.

A frozen bark walkway filed between the house's edge and a wide magnolia's waxy leaves into the shaded side yard with deeper snow and an eight-foot wood privacy fence. A metal extension ladder lay on the ground against the house foundation behind an air conditioner compressor.

Dom noticed fresh footprints around the compressor. "Someone's been here," he said.

The same privacy fence enclosed the postage-stamp rear yard. Roll-out garbage cans stood behind another thorny-olive hedge beside the stand-alone one-car garage.

"Must be a neighbor's car. Palmer drove a Volvo wagon," Angie said.

An Alabaster Silver Honda Brio was parked in the alley outside the open fence gate.

Deuce opened the garage door to the cream 1994 Volvo wagon.

Algae-streaked pots with frozen ferns stood on the snow-draped rear steps. A gas grill and outdoor furniture with large cushions were inside the screened-in porch. The key worked and Dom stepped inside the mudroom and punched in the security code Angie read from a piece of paper Ms. Ruby had supplied.

"Palmer's mother said she only emptied the refrigerator. Otherwise, the house won't be touched until his killer's found," he said.

A pair of cowboy boots stood next to the door under a raincoat on a hook. Clothes were still in the dryer. The modest kitchen had a table and chairs against glider windows. A birds-in-flight mobile dangled above the table. Clear spice jars lined the black-and-white tile counter next to an espresso maker. "Serious cook with one of those," Deuce said.

The stainless steel oven looked like a piece of equipment out of an institutional kitchen. Chairs circled a round table in his hardwood floor dining room. A Picasso bust rested in the center of the table. Sliding glass doors led to a wide-screen TV room with shelves of hardback cookbooks and, similar to his office, several hardback Scandinavian murder mysteries. Throw pillows embroidered with an image of Scotty, Carnegie Mellon's mascot, were tossed on a leather couch.

"Does the place have a basement?" Dom said.

Deuce opened the only door down a center hallway. "Bathroom," he said.

Dom passed ocean sunset photographs on the way upstairs. From the second-floor landing he saw bedrooms, a bathroom, and a closed door on the front side of the house.

"Check the door," Dom said.

Deuce went to the closed door at the end of the hall.

Angie went into one of the bedrooms. Inside the other stale bedroom, Dom saw two made-up single beds with a desk and chair.

"In here," Deuce said.

Dom joined him in the front room, a converted office with a view of the front yard. Contents from open file cabinet drawers littered the carpeted floor. Reference books, three-ring binders, and a number of phase one reports were piled in a heap. A smashed desk lamp with a ripped-out cord rested under the picture window.

"Someone's been up here besides the police," Angie said.

Dom saw cables connected to the wall socket under Palmer's desk. As with his office, the police would have his CPU. Dom went into the alcove and looked down to the side yard. Metallic marks were on the exterior windowsill along with chipped paint where a tool was used to jimmy open the crescent latch from the outside.

"Whoever came up here used the ladder behind the compressor to bypass the alarm," Dom said.

"A second-floor window like East Boulevard's break-in," Angie said.

Deuce slid back a multifold closet door. "Check out the visitor," he said.

Dom came back and saw the blood-splattered Charlotte Running Academy jacket, running shoes, and warm-up pants on the diminutive Jerry Qwain, who dangled by the desk lamp cord from the closet rod. Four inches above his head, a timber hitch, the same knot used on Palmer.

CHAPTER 26

THIRTY MINUTES AFTER Angie called 911, yellow crime scene tape was being strung around the Cape Cod and police cruisers crowded Welker Street. After he questioned Dom, a Lieutenant Waguespack instructed him to wait on the sidewalk for detectives to arrive.

Moisture-rich clouds trundled overhead by the time a black, unmarked Jeep Cherokee pulled to a stop in front of a fourplex across from Palmer's house. Nita Lopez came out from behind the wheel and her partner exited from the passenger side. Her partner, who Voos mentioned was ex-Marine, appeared to be in his early thirties and still kept his raccoon cut high and tight. Nita motioned her partner toward a police commander at his cruiser.

"Wait here," Dom said to Angie and Deuce. He walked toward Nita in her CMPD jacket.

"Voos said I might run into you," she said.

"My preference would've been without a dead body," Dom said.

She was five six and a quarter with shoulder-length pulled-back dark hair and dusky determined eyes Dom knew all too well. "What've you gotten yourself into, Dominick?"

"A not-quite-cold case," Dom said.

She fingered on a pair of gloves and motioned toward Angie and Deuce. "Who's she?"

"Angie Crete."

"You find her on a college campus?"

"Coast Guard investigator on medical leave. A temporary pinch hitter in my rotation."

"Does your ambitious Aphrodite have an opinion about the Coast Guard?"

"Rachel's opinion is, my opinion no longer matters."

"Trouble in paradise?"

A CMPD crime lab van pulled behind the Jeep.

"Consider paradise lost. I meant to call when I heard you made detective."

"We're even. I started to dial your number on more than one occasion," she said.

Technicians removed equipment from the van's side door and started toward the house.

"Sorry about your orthodontist."

"Don't be, he wanted nine-to-five hours," she said.

"From a homicide detective… *right*," he said.

"Curious neck art on the sumo wrestler."

"A requirement of his former employer."

One of her fellow officers asked over her radio if the crime scene photographer had arrived.

"You sure about former?" she said.

"One of the few yakuza with a successful exit plan."

"Coast Guard and an Asian gangster, only you could come up with such a combination." She looked at the house. "How'd they get in?"

"A ladder to the upstairs office bypassed the security system. We stayed close to the side yard fence. Have your people check the two sets of footprints around the air compressor. One pair belongs to the dead guy, Jerry Qwain. I believe you'll find the Honda Brio in the alley to be his."

"You knew him?"

"Met him once."

"I can't wait to hear. Stick around," she said. Nita went through the gate with her partner.

Deuce retrieved the SUV after Dom told him they would sit inside rather than shiver on the sidewalk.

"You two seem to know each other," Angie said.

"We go back a ways," Dom said.

"How far back?" Angie said.

"Before Rachel."

Deuce looked at Dom with a grin through the rearview mirror. A cop with a camera walked onto the property and disappeared behind the magnolia after Nita spoke with him and pointed to the side yard.

"Second-story work was a risky side gig for running man," Deuce said.

"Did his killer come in on Jerry while he was up there?" Angie said.

"Maybe Qwain came in on the killer?" Deuce said.

"Or Jerry climbed up with his killer," Dom said.

"They knew each other?" she said.

Nita stepped onto the front porch and spoke with another policewoman.

"Who would know what to look for in an environmental engineer's office?" Dom said.

"Another environmental engineer," Angie said.

"So, you take Jerry up the ladder to help you find what you're after," Dom said.

"Then kill him?" Deuce said.

Nita came back out into the front yard.

"A dead Jerry can't talk about what they found," Dom said.

"Our drop-in visit to his office may have prompted him to be up there with someone who knows how to tie a timber hitch," Angie said.

Nita waved Dom's way. He climbed back out and joined her. "Palmer's mother give you the house key?" Nita said.

"And security code."

"What else did she give you?"

"Printouts from his computer and her attorney's name, Julian Ybarra."

"Ybarra's a complication we don't need," Nita said.

"Playing up an incompetent police angle's good for business," Dom said.

Another detective motioned for Nita. After they spoke she came back to Dom. "You're right about the Brio."

"Educated guess," Dom said.

"How far along with your look for Carter are you?"

"We've talked with a few of Palmer's friends and business contacts."

"I'll stop by your office. Can't wait to hear about your detective work," she said.

✌

Deuce pulled out of Welker onto Baxter Street toward Uptown. Dom thought about their conversation with Jerry Qwain in his fish-lined conference room when Jerry said he wasn't in contact with Palmer since the Mexican restaurant where JoJo went off on him. *Then why are you in Palmer's home office?*

Deuce took the left on East Independence Boulevard where Dom told him to turn. An American and a North Carolina state flag snapped in the wind on poles at Memorial Stadium's entrance.

"I guess we now focus on Palmer's work, not his personal life," Angie said.

"Both are still in play," Dom said. "Nita said they ID'd the Brio for Jerry's car," Dom said.

"Palmer's been dead for months. Why's Jerry in Palmer's house now?" Angie said.

"Jerry or someone with him was motivated to find a file in one of Palmer's offices," Dom said.

"We know of one missing file, an Irwin Creek job," Angie said.

"I'll ask Nita if she has the file when we get together," Dom said.

"A get-together," Angie said.

"She wants to know what we have," Dom said.

"Don't hold back with all the leads we've generated," Angie said.

Central Piedmont Community College's buildings lined the boulevard.

"What's a common theme with Palmer's work?" Dom said.

"He gave his opinion on soil content," Angie said.

"Besides his opinion," Dom said.

"Beaucoup money in play," Deuce said.

"If he conveyed bad news, someone's money train might go off the rails," Angie said.

Across from CPCC's bookstore they pulled behind a pea-green Toyota Tacoma plastered with dog waste removal business decals.

"Bad news could be turned into good news with the right incentive," Dom said.

"I still don't believe Palmer was the persuadable type," Angie said.

"A Jang Bong would change his mind," Deuce said.

"Jang what?" Angie said.

"A martial arts wooden staff," Dom said.

Angie looked at Deuce while they waited for a light to change. "You used those on people?" she said.

Deuce shrugged. "Only to emphasize a point," he said.

They left CPCC's campus and accelerated up John Belk Freeway's ramp. Sunlight streaked through fractured clouds above Uptown's building mass.

"How would we know if Palmer received pressure to change what he found?" she said.

"A start could be jobs with unusual delays. Do we know how long he needed to write up one of his reports?" Dom said.

"Three to five weeks. I can put together timelines for projects we know he worked on," she said.

Deuce sped up over I-77's bridge.

"We only have Jerry's word for what happened between him and Palmer once the Laphoons' job went south," she said.

"Not if the guy we're about to speak with is in," Dom said.

Angie read a text message she received. "You're right about Winnie's talent for sold-out events. She scored tickets to Augie's awards banquet. Formal wear required."

"Pack a tux?" Dom said to Deuce.

Deuce's blank stare gave Dom his answer.

"We'll find you one," Dom said.

"The band starts at seven," Angie said.

CHAPTER 27

ANGIE ENDED A call while they accelerated through snow-dust sparkles at the bottom of Freedom Drive's ramp. They passed repurposed warehouse buildings, fast-food joints, auto collision shops, tattoo parlors, and vacant lots.

"How large a portfolio did Jerry say the Laphoons assembled?" Dom said.

"Millions of square feet," Angie said.

"Losing their business would be a painful cash flow hit when they fired Jerry and brought on Giron Environmental Partners," Dom said.

"A few million reasons to off Palmer," Angie said.

"No way a guy Jerry's size took out Giron," Deuce said.

Dom motioned for him to make the Camp Greene Street turn.

"Jerry could if he had backup with him," Angie said.

"The same backup who joined him on Welker Street," Dom said.

"Jerry's bakery-fuel-tank miss for the Laphoons happened three years before Palmer died. Why the wait to take Palmer out?" Angie said.

"Turn up there," Dom said. "Because I think Jerry and Palmer butted heads on another job."

"But Jerry told us he wasn't in contact with Palmer since the run-in with JoJo at the restaurant," Angie said.

"We know one situation he left out: Babe Tussey's Mother Lode Gold District development where she sacked Palmer for Jerry thanks to his number four plant accusations. Karen Robles or JoJo will know if any other recent problems existed between these two engineers," Dom said.

They bounced on to an appliance store's parking lot. Above the showroom, splayed in fire-red letters on a billboard's yellow background was ZZZZ APPLIANCES…NO MONEY DOWN…60 MONTHS 0% FINANCING…WE MAKE LOANS…NO CREDIT…NO PROBLEMS!!!

"Who needs white goods?" Deuce said.

"Welcome to Virgil Laphoon's original location," Dom said. "Cut through to the next lot."

They maneuvered between mounded snow and concrete wheel stops onto salted asphalt acres at a former church. A street pole sign advertised Camp Greene Yoga.

"Virgil's gone from appliances to yoga?" Angie said.

"His boy Emmett has diversified the brand," Dom said.

"In a church?" Deuce said. He avoided the rear end of a cream Tahoe.

"Smart real estate play—scoop up down-on-their-luck church properties for pennies on the dollar," Dom said.

People in yoga gear streamed from the narthex. Steam trailed from their sweat-plastered hair. Dom doubted any of these suburbanites realized Camp Greene Yoga was not here for their enjoyment without the fortune Virgil made from loan-sharking, prostitution, and gambling.

"A place of worship should never be used for exercise," Deuce said.

"I hear hot yoga's a religious experience," Angie said.

They pulled into a space alongside a BMW Roadster convertible. The SUV's front end faced toward Camp Greene Street.

The church interior smelled of perspiration, diffused lavender, and coffee. Sunlight streamed through stained-glass windows. A group of women congregated at a juice bar next to a retail shop stocked with yoga products. A glass partition separated a young man and woman at the welcome desk from a mirror-lined studio with rows of sweat-soaked yogis planted on their shoulders with their legs and toes aimed toward the ceiling.

Dom approached the woman and motioned to the toe pointers. "Looks uncomfortable."

"They're our new instructors being trained," she said.

"How hot's the room?" he said.

"Only one hundred eight," she said. Scripted in pink across her armless warm-up top, *Camp Greene Yoga*.

"Emmett Laphoon in?"

She turned back to a guy who licked and stuffed envelopes at a stand-up table. "Is Mr. Laphoon here today?"

Between licks, "He came in thirty minutes ago."

The leg forest behind her lowered. One woman close to the window looked to Dom like she might pass out. The reception girl used the house telephone to make a call.

The person on the other end fired off questions she relayed. "Who are you?" "What do you want?" "Why do you need to speak with him?"

She conveyed Dom's answers, waited, then replaced the receiver. "Follow me." They went through double carved-oak doors into the main worship area with stationary bikes in place of pews. "Spin and CrossFit are new additions to our Camp Greene brand."

Several men and women performed burpees under the choir loft.

"How many Camp Greene locations up and running?" Dom said.

"Fifty-four in six states. By December thirty-first, eight more states will be awarded franchise territories," she said.

"All in houses of worship?" Deuce said.

"Vacant church buildings are everywhere," she said.

They moved between hip-high wooden boxes, coiled ropes the size of cruise ship mooring lines, stacks of free weights, and a pair of hundred-pound tractor tires. She led them past a floor fan with enough size to power an Everglades airboat, up stage stairs to a curtained doorway, and down a flight of narrow stairs to a wood-paneled hallway lined with a hundred forty years of pastor pictures. At the end of the hall, she went into a door to the boiler room. "Through there," she said and left them.

The smell of oil and stale cigarette smoke permeated the space. Dom led the way between discarded pews and a steam-ship-size mounted boiler into an area with a ceiling high enough to accommodate the basketball backboard and hoop secured to the cinder-block wall. A free-throw line was painted on the concrete floor. Several basketballs were scattered around the makeshift half-court. A Charlotte Hornets NBA banner covered with signatures hung over the closed roll-up dock door behind the backboard.

A futuristic motorcycle stood in front of Emmett Laphoon while he sat in his Charlotte Hornets warm-ups and unlaced high-tops crossed on his metal desk. He laughed while he leaned back in his chair on a call with his cell phone hunched between his shoulder and meaty cheek and spun a basketball on his middle finger like a globe on a chubby pedestal. "I says, why didn't you?" Emmett said.

He tapped the ball to keep the spin up. At the angle he sat, he didn't realize they were at the bike. On the wall behind him Dom saw a framed photograph next to an electrical box where Emmett stood a foot shorter than Hornets players gathered around him. "Right, like the other one… slow down. Tell nickels and dimes he has our best number. Trust me, he'll come back."

Dom saw display easels with aerial photographs of abandoned church properties for future Camp Greene Yoga locations. Saint Catherine's Lutheran Church, Pueblo, Colorado; Jersey Avenue AME, Virginia Beach, Virginia; and Corktown All Souls Episcopal, Detroit, Michigan.

"He has a problem, tell the reverend we walk." With the ball still in motion, Emmett tossed the cell phone on the desk and pulled his feet down. When he realized they were there, the ball slipped off his finger and bounced once on the desk into Deuce's hands. Deuce shifted and drained a perfect twenty-foot skyhook, his shirt pulled up to expose his artistic ink.

Emmett eyed Deuce, awed by either the intricate tattoos or the agility of a guy his size. "My semipro team needs a big man who can shoot," Emmett said.

"Nice ride," Angie said. Her hand rested on the motorcycle's handlebar.

"Confederate B120 Wraith," Emmett said.

"Tops out at… eighty… eighty-five grand?" she said.

"Ninety-two fifty," Emmett said. His double chin disappeared when he sat forward. "My girl said you wanna talk about Palmer Giron."

"He worked for you?" Dom said.

"Took over for another guy."

"Jerry Qwain?" Dom said.

"Yeah, him."

"Jerry's convinced Palmer stole your business," Dom said.

"He's delusional."

A yodel sounded from his cell phone. He glanced at the caller ID and left it unanswered.

"Was Jerry fired?" Dom said.

"My sisters made the call to let him go."

"His delusion include a fuel tank?" Angie said.

"He missed a diesel tank you could find with a hand spade."

"We heard he was preoccupied with his divorce," Dom said.

"Three things you never want to get Qwain cranked up on: marathons, fishing, or his divorce." Emmett lounged back in his chair.

"The six-figure check Jerry's insurance company mailed your way didn't hurt," Angie said.

"Aggravation pay. Look, we paid him a nice chunk of change for years and cut him way too much slack after both his rehabs. The illegal liquor house raid was the last straw."

"Jerry didn't mention a liquor house," Dom said.

"Being popped with dope in an illegal liquor house doesn't look good on your résumé."

"When did you bring Palmer on?" Dom said.

"After the tank screwup. My sister Roselle covers property management and liked how Giron handled himself. My other sister who does all the legal legwork concurred, so they let Jerry go."

"What's your role in the family business?" Dom said.

"Finance and acquisitions."

Dom waved toward the churches. "You have Camp Greene Yoga on a roll."

Emmett lifted a box full of property fliers from the floor and dumped them on the desk. "These are only a few of the available church properties we receive every month."

"Camp Greene Yoga kept Palmer busy," Dom said.

"He could juggle several jobs at once, another reason we used him."

"Were you a satisfied customer?" Angie said.

"For every stumbling block, he found a fix. We like problem-solvers."

Frank Sinatra started up again. Emmett checked the screen and silenced the call.

"Palmer a customer, too, for your other line of business?" Dom said.

"No idea if he was into yoga or appliances."

"How about if he needed a bridge loan with a yard a day in interest?" Dom said.

Emmett dead-eyed the three of them. "Don't come in here and bust me up over interest rates. Behind every Uptown door you'll find a rate-jack-up banker."

"But your kneecaps stay intact when you borrow money from bankers in wing tips," Dom said.

"Since when don't deadbeats need a nudge from time to time? To answer your question, Palmer never asked for money. We hated to lose him. A good environmental man's hard to come by." Emmett twirled his cell phone.

"Jerry Qwain's dead. We found him in Palmer's home office yesterday," Dom said.

"Now why would he be in Palmer's house?"

"We hoped you could enlighten us," Dom said.

"Qwain might still be alive if he'd stayed out of illegal liquor houses," Emmett said. Frank Sinatra started to croon.

✺

"Look who's back," Deuce said.

Sun reflected off the appliance store's wet lot and the Triple Nickel's tinted windows. Deuce rolled the SUV forward. When they closed half the distance, a linen truck with a driver distracted on her phone pulled off Camp Greene and cut them off. After Deuce horned her out of the way, the Challenger was gone.

"We've attracted a fan club," Angie said.

Dom got back in the SUV with a bag of tacos from a food truck outside a hardware store around the corner from the Laphoons' yoga house of worship.

"What do you know about these illegal liquor houses?" Angie said.

"Operators set up unlicensed after-hours booze joints in residential neighborhoods and operate tax-free until neighbors complain."

Angie unwrapped her shrimp taco. "How would an engineer like Jerry Qwain with a suburban office condo even know where to find an underground liquor house?"

Dom used a tortilla chip to scoop up guacamole. "A couple of rehab stints will round out your education. Give Brenda Wick a call. See if Jerry was one of her customers," he said.

"We're still back to why Jerry tossed Palmer's office," she said.

Deuce pulled a wad of napkins out of a paper bag. "I might want to know why JoJo coldcocked running man," he said.

CHAPTER 28

N ine forty-five Tuesday morning, Winnie walked Nita Lopez into Dom's office.

"Can you bring us coffees with sugar on the side?" He remembered Nita always tapped in four packets. Nita joined him at his side table.

"No marine today?" he said.

"He's focused on business like me."

"Good to see you too, Nita."

"Our shared history isn't why I'm here."

He could always tell when Nita was on the job. Her demeanor changed, the hard edge on full display. You'd never know from the look she loved to dance, and kiss, and take you in with those angelic eyes when the lights went down.

"You're a homicide detective on point. I wouldn't assume otherwise."

She draped her coat over a chair and sat across from him. "Tell me what you know about Jerry Qwain," she said.

"An environmental engineer who bagged trophy fish and marathons and sent an email threat to Palmer. We visited him to ask why Palmer put his name in front of the state license board."

"Who told you Palmer reported him to state regulators?"

Winnie came back, set the tray down, and left.

"A nugget Angie uncovered. Jerry mentioned before he focused on gas stations, he and Palmer were competitors on good terms until they fell out over a property one of Jerry's clients owned."

"Which client?"

"The Laphoon family. Palmer found a fuel tank and asbestos tiles Jerry missed on one of their properties. Jerry put the blame on being preoccupied with his expensive divorce. Palmer ended up with the Laphoons' business and reported Jerry to Raleigh. Jerry assured us their differences were in the past."

"I guess he was wrong. Emmett and his sisters run the show now Virgil's retired," Nita said. She tore and tapped in four sugars.

"We stopped by Emmett's yoga place. You can put the Laphoons in Palmer's fan club."

"We're aware he worked for them. The family is not on our radar for his murder. Who else have you contacted?"

"A Cabarrus County warehouse investor Palmer made millions for and a pull-apart construction equipment dealer across the Catawba River. Another guy who email-threatened Palmer because his environmental report cratered his payday real estate play."

"Manny Appino's harmless."

"Unless he shows up to collect rent with his Luger, Greta."

She made a note in her pad and added another sugar. "Palmer died under a bridge, not from being shot," she said.

"With a timber hitch above his head like Jerry Qwain."

"You're a knot expert?"

"I told you Angie was good. She thinks our killer could be a tree person or lineman because they use timber hitches, maybe even a Boy Scout. Whoever hit Palmer's East Boulevard office building came through a second-floor window similar to how Jerry accessed Welker Street. Do you have Jerry for the East Boulevard break-in too?" Dom said.

Her cell phone rang. She checked the screen, then put the phone down. "We have no evidence he played a role in East Boulevard."

"We couldn't find an Irwin Creek job file from Palmer's office."

She jotted down Irwin Creek. "What's your interest with that job?"

"We heard he may have worked on the waterway and wanted to see who hired him." He left out Irwin Creek could be the source for the stress Palmer was under. "While you're at it, look for any references to Coldpepper and *cv*. They may be clients who also need to be checked on."

She made another note. "Who else have you spoken with?" she said.

"Karen Robles, JoJo Cifuentes, and Babe Tussey."

"His office manager and lady friend, you're on a good run. How does Babe Tussey make your sleuthhound list?"

"Her overactive legal team sued Palmer."

Nita jotted "Tussey lawsuit" and flipped the pad closed. "She's a prominent builder who raises tens of thousands for the department with her annual hunt club turkey shoot. You might want to focus your attention elsewhere."

Winnie appeared again in the doorway. "The courier's here."

Dom got up and handed Winnie a red folder from his desk that she took out with her.

"Paperwork for another lucrative assignment?" she said.

"Rachel's signed divorce papers."

"I'm sorry, Dom."

"Way overdue. They've been on my desk for weeks."

She stood and slipped her coat back on. "You still have the same cell number?"

"I do," Dom said.

"I almost deleted it," Nita said.

"I'm glad you didn't."

"Give me a call if you and Coast Guard have any revelations," she said.

CHAPTER 29

Wednesday before lunch, Deuce wound the SUV through mountain roads south of Asheville.

"Hipsta concert go off without any hiccups?" Angie said.

"Hiccup free," Deuce said.

Dom was satisfied with how Alondra Medfeathers', aka Hipsta Shee's, job played out Friday night. Deuce only dealt with one inebriated groupie who rushed the superstar singer when she walked toward the Range Rover after the show.

"Her management company asked our dynamic duo to work another show," Dom said.

"Who's up next?" Angie said.

"Wyatt Lake."

"Hipster to country western, you're on a Grammy roll," she said.

They crested a rise to a snowscape valley under heavy clouds.

"Where are you with Palmer's job timelines?" Dom said.

"He needed on average three and a half weeks to write up a phase one report. If he uncovered contamination problems, the job lasted longer. Other than the histograms, scatter plots, pie charts, test-site aerial maps, and lists of chemicals I've never heard of, I haven't come across anything out of the ordinary."

Half-buried tree-staked saplings bordered the entrance road to Giron Landscape and Design across from a herd of Suri alpacas gathered around hay racks. They parked at the main building. An employee with a snow shovel directed them to Nickolas around back at the road salt shed.

Palmer's brother climbed down in his coveralls and heavy work boots from his front loader, annoyed at the interruption. Dom noticed his brown beard and hair were darker than his brother's and he was thicker through the chest. When he removed his sunglasses, the Giron wide-set eyes resemblance was clear. His annoyance dissipated at the mention of Palmer. "Inside might be better," he said.

Wind chimes rippled on the front porch. Inside, the toasty store smelled of rustic wood sprinkled with cinnamon. George Strait's "The Seashores of Old Mexico" played in the background and a cast iron stove provided heat. Silver buckets of taffy, caramel squares, and peppermint balls stood on the cash register counter.

Nickolas led them past a display of wren, bluebird, and fly-catcher bird boxes and through racks of garden books and seed packets. A mature Hamilton hound on a pillow bed wore a clear recovery cone. Inside Nickolas's office, he offered them waters, then they settled into chairs by double glass doors. A woman cast a fly rod on the stream behind his store.

"Dad worked for Carter Hillstead up to the day of his heart attack." A lighter tan circled his eyes from outside work with sunglasses.

"Your mother mentioned for a time you two weren't close," Dom said.

"She share any other family secrets?"

"A first wife was behind the rift."

"I didn't listen when Palmer told me to walk away. Shelly

ended up being a total waste of three years. After Mother called about Palmer's hospital stay, I reached out to him."

The hound with the cone wandered in and sniffed their shoes.

"She said you went through your own drug struggle like your brother," Dom said.

"Cleaned up and remarried now. Palmer and I were in a better place when he died. Tell me you've spoken to his girlfriend."

"JoJo Cifuentes, why?" Dom said.

Deuce reached down and scratched behind the hound's clear cone.

"Besides being an ex-con, the people she associates with leave a lot to be desired."

"You knew she did a stint in prison?" Angie said.

"Palmer said she made a mistake and he didn't care to hear from me he should find someone else."

"These 'associates' Chico Vega?" Dom said.

"A hood who Palmer should've known was trouble." He drank from his water bottle. "I never understood his JoJo infatuation. She was a fire-torch juggling act where a bad burn is always a possibility."

The hound stretched and rested her cone on Deuce's sizable shoe.

"Here's what happened the last time I saw JoJo. I'm in Charlotte with the family at Mother's for a few days Memorial Day weekend before Palmer's murder. At three thirty Sunday morning he calls my cell, concerned JoJo stormed out after one of their many flare-ups and won't return his calls or texts. He's worried with her drug history what she might do and wants me to join him while he looks for her."

The rough patch Karen Robles had mentioned to them.

"He said he knew where she might be. We end up behind the airport after four in the morning at a packed ranch house being used for an illegal after-hours booze house. The kitchen's a bar, the master bedroom's a betting parlor, and the dining room's a mosh pit."

Another Hamilton waltzed in and plopped down with her head on Deuce's other foot.

"We find JoJo in the basement at a blackjack table. Guess who turns into a mean drunk when Palmer asks her to leave? Several lowlifes press in, who Palmer tells me afterward were associates of her cousin Chico Vega, who owns the house. I don't help the situation when I back off a guy with a gold mohawk. The guy pulls a knife and JoJo starts to scream. The room goes quiet when Chico, who looks like an actuarial science major, steps forward. The blade disappears and he informs JoJo her evening's over."

The hound with the cone leaped into Deuce's lap.

"Then a shrimpy, shiny-head guy with Chico said he knows Palmer from business."

Shrimpy could be one way to describe Jerry Qwain, who Emmett Laphoon said frequented illegal liquor houses.

"He have one of these?" Dom pressed his thumb to his chin to mimic Jerry's soul patch.

"A black one the size of a postage stamp. How'd you know?"

"His name's Jerry Qwain. We found him dead in Palmer's house last week," Dom said.

"In Palmer's house?"

"We believe he was after one of your brother's work files."

"You're sure Jerry's with Chico?" Angie said.

Nickolas unscrewed his water to take a drink. "I saw them together at the blackjack table with JoJo. Jerry's lubricated like a barfly and comes in close to Palmer and starts in about some environmental job."

"He say which one?" Dom said.

"I can't recall."

"Did he make a reference to bakery fuel tanks?" Angie said.

"He didn't mention bakeries, but I won't forget what happened when he said, 'These Uptown people are serious.' He gives Chico an elbow and says, 'Tell him,' like they were in on a secret. The look on Jerry's face flashed from stupid drunk to big mistake when he realized what he'd done. No one elbows Chico Vega."

"Jerry say who these serious people might be?" Dom said.

"He didn't elaborate. We ushered JoJo outside where she was sick. She snored in the back seat all the way to her condo."

"Can you recall the liquor house's street name?" Dom said.

"No, but we turned near a temple onto a dead-end street."

CHAPTER 30

Sleet became snow on I-40 past the Blueridge Mountain Parkway.

"Jerry Qwain's with Chico Vega?" Angie said.

"Emmett Laphoon has Jerry for an illegal liquor house regular," Dom said.

"But with Chico?" she said.

"Hoods need environmental engineers too," Deuce said.

"I doubt Chico Vega's concerned with dry cleaner plumes," Dom said.

Traffic slowed to a crawl.

"When Jerry made the 'serious Uptown people' reference he could mean any one of a number of people who play skyscraper games in the Central Business District," Angie said.

"We stick with what we know. Palmer uncovered Augie's mountain snail invasion, and degreaser drums cost him the Mother Lode," Dom said.

They passed exits for Swannanoa and Black Mountain.

"If your friend Rocko's right, JoJo might be tied into Chico's drug trade. Why would Palmer stay with her?" Angie said.

"Blinded by love," Deuce said.

"Or like Brenda Wick said, he was a Good Samaritan," Dom said.

They inched past highway patrol flashing lights at an accident where an empty school bus had skidded into a saltbox house being towed on a house mover's rig.

"Palmer may have run into problems if he found himself between Chico and his Uptown earner JoJo," Dom said.

"I'd pay the boyfriend a visit," Deuce said.

"With one of those martial art staffs for emphasis?" Angie said.

"Only to eliminate any confusion about my Uptown sky-scraper trade," Deuce said.

Angie's GPS took them along Hickory's First Avenue Southwest toward Cynthia "Candy" Padbury's tax service. They drove by multiple fast-food restaurants, a log cabin with a Land for Sale sign, furniture showrooms, and a doc-in-a-box urgent care.

Dozens of empty parking spaces surrounded Candy's A-frame that Dom figured were from a previous owner's car dealership. They pulled up next to a midnight-black aluminum Prius. Deuce stayed in the SUV.

Through the glass door Dom saw a woman strapped by her ankles to an inversion table rotated upside down with her head inches off the floor. She looked up with a surprised expression when he rapped on the glass. The table hinged upright, she unbuckled, stepped into moccasins, and came toward them. All of five feet and well past retirement age, she wore yoga pants and a zipped-up NC State sweatshirt.

She let them in after Dom made the introductions. Her office was infused with the scent of lilac, watermelon, and hazelnut from candles on a side table tray. Dom pointed at her mesh-and-aluminum inversion table.

"Those contraptions work?"

"Keeps my lower back limber," she said.

They sat in armchairs while Candy settled into a kneeling chair, the view behind her a forest incline being lashed with snow.

"My husband and I knew the Girons from our church. Wonderful people who've been through hell. Palmer remained a client long after I relocated up here to be closer to my grandchildren and daughter when my husband passed away."

"We understand Karen Robles managed his office," Dom said.

"A godsend after his previous bookkeeper embezzled from him." She fed pages into a side drawer.

"His mother mentioned her boy stressed about finances," Dom said.

"You'd be stressed too if you were clipped for twenty-seven grand. His kleptomaniac was clever and only hit him for a few hundred dollars with fake invoices every month until she slipped up with the wrong suite number for a company I do taxes for. I can still see the shocked look on his face when I told him and his lady friend what I found."

"JoJo Cifuentes?" Angie said.

"Lovely girl."

A sweetgum tree limb covered with spiky brown fruit stalks cracked and crashed to the forest floor.

"The ex-bookkeeper go to jail?" Dom said.

"Palmer wouldn't press charges. I couldn't believe he forgave her."

Good Samaritan, Dom thought.

"Besides his taxes, did you know much about the nuts and bolts of his business?" Dom said.

"Enough to know he saved people large sums of money." She now alphabetized large white tax envelopes in her lap.

"We found a file missing from his office. An Irwin Creek job," Dom said.

"I remember Irwin Creek."

Angie looked at Dom.

"When I drove down to tell him about his bent bookkeeper, JoJo was there on the stationary bike and Palmer was at an enlarged tax map on his wall with a highlighter he colored tax parcels with. I asked him what the colors meant, he said for an Irwin Creek project where he thought chemicals may have been released."

Dom remembered the corkboard tax map and the colored parcels around the Gaffney chicken warehouse.

"I delivered the stolen-twenty-grand bad news and left."

"How did he react?" Angie said.

"Didn't believe me until I pulled out the phony invoices. Typical Palmer, his first concern wasn't the money lifted from his checkbook but what would happen to the divorced bookkeeper's ten-year-old twins. Through another business-owner client I work for, we found Karen Robles, a retired IRS auditor."

CHAPTER 31

THE SLEET AND snow cleared by the time they drove along Highway 321's warehouse buildings, cow pastures, and churches.

"Did you find enlarged tax maps folded in any of the file drawers you checked?" Dom said.

"I didn't see any," Angie said.

"Karen might know where he stored them," Dom said.

Clipboard Wayne opened the glue factory's lobby door again. "Karen's not here," he said, his wintergreen breath mint no match for the onion breath.

"Is she off today?" Dom said.

His saggy eyes never left Deuce, who filled the doorway over Dom's shoulder. "Try Mikey's Place."

Mikey's Place occupied a former auto parts store set back from Clanton Road behind a snowbank close to South Boulevard. A fluorescent Play Anytime sign flickered against the arcade's blackened windows.

Dom's eyes adjusted to the low-light interior while he scanned the afternoon's fish-game-obsessed clientele. Prince's "Darling Nikki" played in the background. Someone at a nearby game table applied their spicy perfume with a garden hose.

Deuce tapped his shoulder. "In the corner," he said.

Dom saw the wheelchair and walked to Karen's side of the room. An aquatic game lit her face while she rapid-tapped a luminous sand dollar button and at the same time brushed an incandescent joystick ball to manipulate her starfish into position to attack a high-value corn-flour whale.

"Go baby," the woman to her right said. Three empty high-energy cans sat next to her octopus control stick.

Karen's starfish sailed between ocean mountain peaks and obliterated the whale.

❧

The storeroom had just enough room for the four of them to pack in among the discarded fish games, soft drink cases, and janitorial supplies.

"Why did you leave off Palmer's rehab from our last visit?"

She squared up and folded a tissue. "He dealt with the problem and sought help. I figured you already knew from his mother."

"Don't hold back any information. What you share could be helpful," Dom said.

"You're here to call me on the carpet?"

"Palmer's accountant Candy said he was lucky to find you," Dom said.

"Falsified invoice suite numbers can be tricky." She almost sneezed. "I saw the news about Jerry Qwain in Palmer's house."

"Deuce found him when he opened the accordion closet door," Dom said.

"He and Palmer weren't friends," Karen said.

Dom sat on a stack of soft drink cases.

"We know about the fuel tank and asbestos floor tiles Jerry overlooked and Palmer found," Angie said.

"Their relationship never recovered," Karen said. "A few weeks before Palmer's found in Freedom Park, Jerry called the office. I recall because Palmer took his mother to her periodontist appointment. Jerry wanted to know if he had some involvement in a waterway job, and I asked him who he was to have interest in Palmer's work."

"How'd he react?" Dom said.

"He slipped into jerk mode, starts to question me like I'm a clueless temp. I hung up on him."

Deuce talked to a surprised arcade worker who opened the door. He handed her a case of paper napkins and closed the door.

"Could he have meant the Irwin Creek job you mentioned on our last visit?" Dom said.

"Jerry didn't share a name."

"We ask because we didn't see Irwin Creek in his job file drawer," Dom said.

"Maybe the file went to his home office?" Angie said.

"Palmer took paperwork back and forth between his offices because he liked to work when he couldn't sleep. But the actual job files never left East Boulevard."

"When we found Jerry, we also found Palmer's office pulled apart like Jerry went to search for one of those files," Dom said.

"How would he even know Palmer had an office in his house?" Angie said.

Karen was quiet while she folded more tissues out of her plastic packet. "Before I hung up, I told him we had no waterway information here or on Welker Street."

"By here you mean the East Boulevard office building?" Dom said.

"Yes."

"Waterway was all you remember from the call?" Angie said.

"And his bad attitude."

"How did Palmer react when you told him Jerry called?" Dom said.

"He shook his head and said he'd ring him back."

"Show her the chicken warehouse tax map," Dom said.

Angie opened pictures on her phone and held up the screen with the colored parcels around the Gaffney warehouse.

"We stopped by Candy's office. She said when she delivered the crooked bookkeeper news to Palmer, she noticed a tax map on his corkboard of Irwin Creek with colored tax parcels like the chicken warehouse," Dom said.

"He always pinned maps to his corkboard. He liked to see the lay of the land around properties he was hired to work on."

"Did you read the sticky notes on his bookshelf?" Angie said.

"He jotted notes often and stuck them there."

"Written on one were *cv*, Coldpepper, and Irwin. Does Coldpepper ring a bell?" Dom said.

"Never heard of them," she said.

"*cv* could be Chico Vega," Dom said.

"JoJo's relative?"

"His initials fit," Dom said.

"The weekend Nickolas visited his mother was the only time Palmer mentioned he met JoJo's cousin. He said he didn't want her spending time with someone like Chico."

"We didn't find any tax maps in either of Palmer's offices," Angie said.

"Did you check down the hall past Bill Eversole's office in the old bathroom space? Palmer kept his mobile plan files down there because they took up too much room for his office."

⌘

No one came to the East Boulevard door when Dom knocked and pressed the chime. They were about to go around back when the same woman who let them in last time came through the kitchen door from the parking area.

"Hello again, but I don't have keys to any of the offices," she said.

"We need access to the old bathroom down the hall," Dom said.

"You're in luck, no key required." She left them and climbed the stairs.

The no-longer-used bathroom was across from the kitchen at the back of the first floor. Three mobile files with twenty compartments each had been moved into the space, rolled tax maps in each compartment. Dom slid one out to Angie and one to Deuce.

"Look for Irwin Creek," he said.

Inside the bathroom he unfurled one tax parcel map after the other, each with colors around a particular property. None were for Irwin Creek.

"Here's your Coldpepper," Deuce said.

Angie stood examining the plan Deuce spread on the kitchen table. Dom came over and saw *Coldpepper?* circled in pencil with an arrow pointed to another circle of an entire Uptown block— the one where Tussey Center stood. "Coldpepper is connected to Babe's skyscraper location?" Angie said.

Dom saw another arrow to a smaller circled X across from Tussey Center in the middle of Augie Pepitone's U-shaped entrance drive. "His interest ran onto Augie's property too."

CHAPTER 32

Dom waited in his tuxedo on One Pepitone Place's plaza, protected from the wind by the underground parking garage's elevator and exit stairway structure. He could smell the street vendor's fresh pretzels.

He scanned up the length of Augie's cantilevered tower and saw the genius of the Blaze windows his architect installed. A flame mingled with stars in the clear, crisp night sky.

CMPD officers with orange-glow flashlights managed limousines, town cars, and luxury SUVs stacked back from One Pepitone Place's grand two-lane U-shaped entrance drive. Their chauffeurs waited to wheel up to the skyscraper's valets. Uniformed doormen ushered banquet attendees through the massive timber entrance doors.

On a slight incline up from Augie's entrance were Tussey Center, the ice rink, and the hotel construction site. Babe's globe burned like a lighthouse beacon.

Steam rose from the Lost Souls Grotto inside the U. Shells used to construct the grotto around the geothermal hot spring sparkled in hardscape lighting. The grotto was where Palmer had affixed the X and circled the tax map with Coldpepper arrowed toward Tussey Center. What about the grotto piqued his interest?

A brass band with a saxophone, trombone, multiple trumpets, and a guy on an upturned pickle pail for drums braved the cold to entertain onlookers. Dom rubbed and blew into his hands when a frigid gust raced between high-rise condominiums like a mountain-gap wind.

Rocko said Palmer was preoccupied with Augie's mountain resort job. If they could corral Augie long enough tonight, Dom could clear up what Palmer's snail find meant to Bufflehead Reserve. They knew Palmer had already lost one Uptown customer and job, Babe Tussey's Mother Lode. He wouldn't want to be cut loose from another one.

Miniature snow funnels veered into couples when they emerged in evening wear from the garage structure. The street musicians started up. A news helicopter whirled sideways around One Pepitone Place.

Jerry Qwain was another poster boy for question marks. Was his killer with him when he climbed into Palmer's office, or was Jerry already inside and the killer surprised him? Why, months after Palmer's death, would he hit Welker Street? Was it because they dropped in to ask a few questions related to Palmer? If these two engineers were in the middle of another client dispute, a list of Jerry's clients could provide some answers.

Angie and Deuce came toward him across the marble plaza.

He also planned to ask JoJo why Jerry would be inside an illegal liquor house with her cousin.

Angie looked wonderful in her black coat and elegant full-length blush dress Winnie borrowed from a relative's trendy women's boutique. A wave of fury cut through him when he thought about the South China Sea pirates—what they put her through and how she struggled with the aftermath.

"I'm not a fan of heels," she said. Her breath came out in white wisps.

They walked from the gift shop inside Augie's below-level medieval warfare museum where they went to find a quick fix for the popped-off top button of Deuce's one-size-too-small big-and-tall-shop tuxedo rental.

"Any luck?' Dom said.

"We used a Seven Dwarfs lapel pin from the children's section," Angie said. She reached over to straighten Deuce's bow tie.

"Which one, Bashful?" Dom said.

"Grumpy was the only one left," she said.

"Are we going in or not?" Deuce said. He ran his finger around the collar Grumpy held together.

When they came around to the grand entrance, Dom caught the whiff of bad eggs doused in vinegar.

"The grotto stinks," Angie said.

The doormen, outfitted in capes and top hats, herded them inside with several boisterous women who poured out of a luxury party van. Like everyone who first entered the capacious atrium, Dom's eyes were drawn up several stories to the *di sotto in sù* ceiling illustrated with iconic buildings from around the globe. He recognized the Leaning Tower of Pisa, Malaysia's double Petronas Towers, the Chrysler and Empire State Buildings, and Dubai's Burj Khalifa. The artist's skill created an illusion the buildings were suspended around the center skyscraper, One Pepitone Place.

Platoons of cocktail servers armed with trays hustled among dozens of ten-top circular tables set up for the big event. High-speed glass elevators interspersed with luxury retail shops. Two sides of the immense space were all windows.

Men and women sipped drinks and glad-handed on a dais. Behind them a live plant wall soared toward the ceiling.

"Augie's building brochure touts the garden wall for being one of a kind," Angie said.

"With a water bill to match," Deuce said.

"Another reason to jack up the rent," Angie said.

"Which one's Augie?" Dom said.

"The guy in conversation on the stage with his architect and Senator Winther," she said.

A beanstalk with buzzed hair and thick-black-framed glasses, Augie towered above the senator and architect. Well into her eighties, architect Mandisa Hardenberg, with funky, spiky hair, was outfitted in an all-white tuxedo and leaned on a white cane. She surveyed the banquet tables while the senator used her hands when she spoke to the man of the hour. Her form-fitted, full-length red dress had a slit up one side where she displayed an expensive high heel and a bare calf and thigh.

"How do we get at him while he's up there?" Angie said.

"We'll wait for the final curtain. Where'd Winnie put us?" Dom said.

"In the one hundreds with all the trades who worked on his building."

He took a glass of red wine off a waiter's tray and headed toward their table. Three chairs stood open at number 170 with the same rowdy women from the party van who they'd crowded into the building with. Preset salads were already surrounded by empty wine and cocktail glasses. Bold letters under their table number read Genesee Sprinkler, Inc.

"Welcome to the party. Pat Genesee, and these are my girls." A thickset woman with hive-styled hair labored out of her chair and gripped Dom's hand. The plunge in her plus-size dress would make a cliff diver proud.

"Ladies," Dom said.

Pat pushed back the chair next to her for him, then signaled a waiter to bring another round of Blue Hawaiians. One of her girls, who used a putty knife to apply her makeup, held a napkin to cover her mouth while she talked under her breath to her seat-mate. Both couldn't take their eyes off Deuce.

The woman beside Pat wore rings on eight fingers and shoveled blue-cheese dressing onto her salad. "Who're you with?" Rings said.

Dom wasn't sure whose tickets Winnie rustled up for them.

"Friends of a friend," he said.

"Mr. Pepitone's?" Pat said.

"One of his employees. What's your connection?" he said.

"We installed his building sprinklers and custom designed the wall's irrigation system. I'm proud to say, we were the only women-owned and -staffed contractor on the job," Pat said.

A waiter appeared with shot glasses. "Bruised Heart table?" he said.

The one next to Angie, with earrings the size of cherry tomatoes, shot up her hand. Red-liquid-filled shot glasses came off the tray one at a time. Angie shook her head no but was handed a Bruised Heart anyway.

"How complicated is a sprinkler job for a wood building?" Dom said.

"The city took eighteen months to decide what specs they would require," Pat said.

"We thought Mr. Pepitone would never get the go-ahead." Rings said.

"See those tables up front by the platform?" Pat said. "They're higher-ups with city code enforcement and fire department who gave Mr. Pepitone the go-ahead. Fire Chief Penelope Williams is in uniform. Pass the bread, Bobbi."

Bobbi, tangerine readers perched on the tip of her nose, took a roll and handed off the breadbasket. Waiters started to stream through doors with covered dish-stacked trays.

"Skyscraper sprinkler jobs must pay well," Dom said.

"Honey, after what Mr. Pepitone and those fire and city people put us through, we earned every penny. To keep all his garden wall plants alive, Mr. Pepitone wanted a one-of-a-kind mister, which he plans to turn on once the program starts. My team worked seven days a week to get those nozzle heads right. A computer program regulates the moisture content," Pat said.

A Cornish hen nestled on a mound of off-color rice mixed with broccoli and carrots appeared in front of Dom. Angie and Deuce were each given rare prime rib. She leaned toward Dom. "Want to trade?" she said.

They switched plates. A jangle of silverware joined the conversation cacophony. Pat asked the waiter for mayonnaise.

"A major reason for tonight is the company those people work for." She pointed with her buttered bread toward a table by a service bar. "IQ Buildings, a building-intelligence company funded by Mr. Pepitone."

"They're the geeks who turned Mr. Pepitone's building into the brainiest skyscraper anywhere on the planet," Rings said.

"What Cady means, Mr. Pepitone wanted the capability to monitor every building system. The HVAC, elevators, sprinklers, and our pride and joy, the wall's water content. All are tied into IQ's software. An IPO is scheduled for the company next month," Pat said.

"Mr. Pepitone will make another fortune," Bobbi said.

The Blue Hawaiians server distributed highball glasses garnished with pineapple and cherries.

"How does One Pepitone Place compare with Babe Tussey's building?" Angie said.

"Never mention her name around Mr. Pepitone," Pat said. "They can't stand each other. The bad blood goes back to when One Pepitone Place's site was put up for auction. Babe wanted to build her corporate headquarters here, but Mr. Pepitone outbid her."

Pat layered ramekin mayonnaise across her bloody prime rib.

"Have you heard about the grotto situation?" Bobbi said, her hen already shredded.

"Babe's convinced she owns the grotto." Pat chewed the pineapple wedge. "Alberta Mavis, Mr. Pepitone's secretary, told me on the sly, problems started when Babe decided to publish an illustrated coffee-table book about her family's long history in the shampoo and real estate business. She hired a college intern to research all the properties grandfather Benny II bought and sold with his shampoo money. A journalism major, the intern created a scandal when she uncovered a fraud Benny II's live-in girlfriend caregiver perpetrated on him."

"A gold digger twenty-five years his junior," Bobbi said.

"The girlfriend forged grandpa's signature and sold off several of his properties to pay for her Christmas tree farm. Family lawyers tracked down every scammed buyer and negotiated settlement."

"Except for one they missed," Bobbi said.

"A sliver with the Lost Souls Grotto inside Mr. Pepitone's driveway. How does Mr. Pepitone respond when Babe hits him with a lawsuit for the grotto she says belongs to her? He poaches her head leasing agent and largest tenant," Pat said.

Dom watched Augie take his seat at the tip of the V-shaped head table flanked by the senator and Hardenberg.

Up first was the World Green Building Council's chairman, a Taiwanese guy with a hard-to-understand accent. From the little Dom could make out, Augie was receiving the council's top award for his Platinum Green office tower. Next up, a flashy guy with a suitcoat handkerchief. The top person for a national building managers' association, he heaped praise on Augie for all the awards his organization had bestowed on One Pepitone Place.

Servers brought around dessert plates with chocolate-dipped strawberries and white-frosted cupcakes. The Charlotte Chamber of Commerce's top person spoke last. A severe woman who oversaw the governmental compliance department of an Uptown financial institution, she droned on about the city's retail sales numbers, volume dollars of new construction, population in-flow statistics, and total number of new apartment-unit starts in the last twelve months. Her pitch came at the end when she urged everyone to fill out chamber invite cards located in the center of every table.

Everyone stood and clapped while Augie was introduced and made his way to center stage. He launched into his hardscrabble youth, raised by grandparents on a rural North Carolina hog farm, then launched into how One Pepitone Place came to be.

"Here we go," Pat said.

Her mister system came to life, and lights embedded in the vegetation wall projected an enormous shield with Augie's paladin logo in the spray.

The lobby erupted in applause.

Augie was in the middle of how skyscraper construction can sustain forests when Dom noticed the volume of water behind him increased.

"What's up with the water flow?" Bobbie said.

Water volume continued to rise. The chamber of commerce woman used a dinner napkin to wipe water off her forehead.

A popped-off nozzle head made the sound of a nail gun. A jet of water pressure washed plates, glasses, and silverware off the fire department's table. A cupcake beamed Chief Penelope in the forehead. Augie looked behind him and was met by a cataract geyser from more blown nozzle heads.

The Taiwanese architect somersaulted backward in his chair, and the guy with the suitcoat handkerchief upended his entire table when he lost his balance. Senator Winther scrambled to escape being sprayed off the dais, but tripped on her dress and tumbled headlong onto a waiter's tray overloaded with dirty dishes. Her naked leg minus a high heel swung like a pendulum. If Augie never stepped away from the podium, he wouldn't have been flung backward from the impact of four converged sprays. He landed hard and took out the entire code enforcement table. Only a confused and drenched Mandisa Hardenberg remained seated. The entire IQ table sprinted toward Augie. Pat Genesee looked lost for words.

"There goes our chance to speak with Augie," Angie said.

CHAPTER 33

THE NEXT NIGHT Deuce and Angie stopped by Dom's carriage house.

"Blame me for the interruption," Angie said. "Brenda Wick said Jerry was not a New Dawn client." She followed Dom inside. Deuce left to fill up the SUV.

"And you couldn't wait until tomorrow?"

He gave her a soda from the refrigerator.

"I thought we might be able to catch JoJo after the match tonight."

"What match?"

"Roller derby, she rolls with the Queen City Bruisers every Sunday night. They start at seven against the Orangeburg Rage. I figure she might be open to a few questions afterward." Angie popped her soda.

"I'll be a minute," he said. He went to change out of his boots and work clothes.

She called after him. "Have you seen Augie's headlines? *Deluge Ruins Developer's Extravaganza.*"

He came back and found her in front of his jazz CD collection.

"We'll take another run at Augie next week," he said.

"I can only imagine how bad a hangover Pat Genesee has today."

"The shakes set in after she realized the banquet wasn't a dream," he said.

"She and the IQ people whose software controlled the wall have some hard questions to answer," she said.

❧

Deuce turned at the only corner store for miles around and headed toward Highway 16.

"Genesee Sprinkler girls were right about the grotto brouhaha," Angie said. "An internet article I found references Augie picked up the postage-stamp parcel where the grotto sits from a Dutch insurance syndicate that repossessed the entire block after a parking lot operator went into foreclosure."

"Pat mentioned a swindled Tussey, not a parking lot operator?" Dom said.

"Babe's grandfather was ripped off by his much younger flamenco dancer girlfriend who he left his third wife for. The dancer forged his signature to off-load pieces of his property empire. One was the grotto she sold to her own church."

"Duped her minister?" Deuce said.

"The girlfriend was a piece of work. Benny II came to possess the grotto from Portuguese immigrants who first recognized the warm spring's healing properties. They put up the shell structure and renamed it the Lost Souls Grotto. The church used the geothermal spring for their baptisms."

Lourdes in Charlotte owned by a scammed church thanks to a flamenco dancer.

"Where does Augie factor in?" Dom said.

They slowed behind a stock hauler populated with sheep being pulled by an eight-wheel tractor.

"A new pastor comes on board and decides to cash out all the church's Uptown properties and move to the suburbs. Along comes the parking lot operator financed by Dutch bankers. He assembles all the parcels on the block, but before he can pave over the grotto the economy sours. The Dutch repossess all the properties and put them on the market. The highest bidders who each want the site for their skyscrapers are Augie, flush with his Dever Multifamily payday, and Babe Tussey."

"How much did Augie cough up?" Dom said.

"Thirty-two million. Babe takes the corporate jet to Amsterdam to urge the executive committee to drop Augie's bid because a guy from Buncombe County will never be able to close. Augie shows the tulip lenders all the zeros and commas in his checkbook and walks away the winner."

"Thank you, dormitories," Deuce said.

"Now he owns an entire Uptown block that includes a grotto with a suspect history," Dom said.

"Fast-forward a few years and Babe sits up in Tussey Center on the block across from Augie's half-completed lumber tower when the intern stumbles into Benny II's girlfriend problems. Babe lets Jefferson Wallach off his leash, who sends stop-work orders to Augie's lawyers. They maintain, Augie doesn't own the grotto."

"What's Augie's response?" Dom said.

"The lumber trucks never stop. By the time he hammers in his last helicopter-pad nail, he's the litigation winner," she said.

Dom watched a distant searchlight rove above Uptown's polychromatic towers where a lumber wonder in flames twisted across from a snow cone globe.

⁊

They drove along Uptown's periphery on North Kings Drive toward the searchlight at the Grady Cole Center. The arena's billboard read *Uptown Rumble, Queen City Bruisers vs The Orangeburg Rage, 7 PM Sunday.* Deuce found a parking spot near the American Legion Memorial football stadium.

They were about to walk across Armory Drive when a jacked-up eight-seat Navigator with darkened windows blocked their way. Bass-heavy music pulsated from inside and the paint job color matched the underbody's lavender glow.

"Nice light job," Angie said.

Three guys climbed out followed by the sweet smell of reefer. The driver pulled away toward VIP parking.

Once inside, Deuce went to the concession stand and Angie and Dom found their seats. Helmeted women in knee and elbow pads rolled around a rink set up on the basketball court. Disco music blared from the sound system. Coaches, trainers, and referees milled about the rink's open-space center. A pack of Rage skaters circled the oval, their black helmets and red uniforms adorned with yellow lightning bolt logos. The Queen City Bruiser uniforms were on the color spectrum between Charlotte Hornets teal and Carolina Panthers blue.

"She's 00 in the curve," Angie said.

With a slingshot move a teammate whipped JoJo—a stout Bruiser with 00 on her jersey and a helmet star—forward. Dom read the back of her jersey when she shot past in a crouch.

"Smash Rican?" he said.

"A play on her Puerto Rican heritage," Angie said.

"Why the star?" Dom said.

"No idea," she said.

"First-timers?" came a voice behind them.

Dom turned to a grandmother in a Bruisers fan Afro wig. "Never been before," he said.

She steadied a container of nachos smothered with melted cheese and jalapenos on her knees and held an eighteen-ounce draft beer. "Jammers have stars because they're scorers." The nacho she was about to eat dripped onto a paper napkin tucked into her Bruiser jersey. "You picked a good night. The girls from Orangeburg and the Bruisers are big rivals."

Deuce rejoined them with a vacuum cleaner bag of popcorn. He gave Dom his water bottle and Angie her grape Airheads. The three men from the Navigator strode down the aisle to commandeer several seats up front. Dom ate a handful of Deuce's overbuttered, undersalted popcorn. He watched the one in a fur-collared knee-length leather coat, wire-rimmed glasses, and cool temple fade hair continue to the rink's padded guardrail. If he inserted lifts in his untied brand-new high-tops, he'd go maybe five six. JoJo reined-up with a smile and spoke with him.

Angie shook Airheads like dice. "Look at her expression, they more than know each other," she said.

Dom thought back to what Rocko said: Chico knew how to dress and resembled an accountant. "He look like an accounting major to you?" Dom said.

"The only one I've ever seen with a crew," Angie said.

"I'd say he might be Chico Vega," Dom said.

JoJo skated around to her teammates when the horn sounded.

Another guy with hair over his shoulders came down the aisle. Dom recognized the back-of-the-hand spiderweb tattoo when he fist-bumped the Navigator crew.

"Remember him? Officer Earl Jessup," Dom said.

"Why's a Tussey Center guard here?" she said.

"Earl's a derby fan," Dom said. Dom watched Earl take a seat next to Chico.

Between quaffs of beer and munched nachos, the super-fan behind them gave a steady stream of commentary for two thirty-minute periods and several jams. They heard detailed descriptions of booty blocks, getting a goat, apex jumps, techniques for the perfect snowplow, and what "sausage" meant in roller derby parlance. Deuce thrilled over power jams and suicides.

JoJo sat out with a penalty for the knee she delivered to the lower back of a Momma who was carted off on a stretcher. When she returned to action, a trio of Mommas pulled off a perfect waterfall when one after the other delivered an elbow to JoJo's helmet.

She was tough not to have a concussion after such a barrage.

In the final seconds of the third overtime JoJo leaped a sprawled Rage skater for the win. After the match they found her in an empty hallway outside the women's locker room with her Navigator fans. Office Jessup wasn't with them.

Sweat matted her hair, rink rash appeared above each kneepad, and a fresh berry ripened on her right cheek.

Up close Dom saw Chico's creased tan slacks, high-thread-count pink shirt, and double-breasted leather coat. The pencil-thin mustache and part carved through the side of his scalp gave the impression he was all business, a man of commerce, a guy comfortable with spreadsheets and invoices. The giveaway he didn't settle business disputes with his Montblanc fountain pen was a wicked scar sliced through his left eyebrow behind his wire-rimmed glasses.

"Can you not ask your questions at my office?" JoJo said.

"I'm always up for a good derby." Dom stuck his hand out. "Dominick Mundy."

In slow motion the accountant withdrew his hand from the leather pocket. "Chico Vega," he said.

"Nice to meet you, Mr. Vega," Dom said.

"No need for the Mistah," Chico said.

Dom first wondered how a guy with a soft handshake and countertenor voice controlled the Patriots, then he remembered Rocko's hair-trigger, volcanic temper comment. He looked to JoJo, three inches taller than Chico in her skates.

"We're curious about Jerry Qwain."

Chico's crew sauntered over.

"They be conversing," the one with a gold faux hawk said. He could be the gold-hair guy Palmer's brother Nickolas backed off in the liquor house, Dom thought.

"Let's hear what the man has to say, Jorge," Chico said.

Deuce stepped behind Angie when the muscled-up one with diamond stud earrings and the gaunt one with height whose forehead scars appeared to be the work of an apprentice butcher shifted her way.

"I didn't know Jerry," JoJo said.

"But you met him?"

"Once, in a restaurant. Like I told you before."

"Jerry's dead," Dom said.

Her eyes gave away her surprise.

"Hung like your boyfriend," Angie said.

Chico's expression didn't change.

"From a closet rod in the Welker Street office. Police think he was killed Thursday night," Dom said.

"I said I didn't know him," JoJo said.

"Thursday Smash Rican was Pre…Occ…U…Pied," diamond ears said.

Dom caught the imperceptible sway of Chico's head to silence his crew.

"Ms. Cifuentes was a guest in our VIP suite Thursday evening," Chico said.

"What event?" Dom said.

"DJ I IS's show," Chico said.

"Tell us about your one and only meeting with Jerry," Dom said.

She drank from her water bottle. "We're at the bar in Palmer's favorite Mexican restaurant, Los Mochis, for happy hour when

Jerry crowds in on us. He put his finger in my face and said, 'Your date cost me big, I won't be screwed twice.'"

"How'd Palmer react?" Dom said.

"Confrontational people weren't high on his list of favorites."

"You didn't provoke Jerry?" Angie said.

"What do you mean provoke?" JoJo said. With her pinkie finger in a splint, she switched hands with her helmet and gulped more water.

"Some people turn unpleasant when they drink," Angie said.

"I don't catch your reference," JoJo said.

"After a few highballs, your roller derby temper came out and you popped him," Angie said.

"He made a move for a piña colada on the bar. If he doused Palmer, the silk tie I gave him for his birthday would be ruined."

"You clipped Jerry over a piña colada?" Dom said.

"I only tapped him. Too bad he led with his crystal chin."

Chico shared a laugh with his crew.

Dom thought he'd tweak up the heat in the humid hallway. He looked at Chico.

"Ever meet Jerry?"

"He wouldn't kno—"

Chico interrupted her with a touch to the arm.

"Depends what Mr. Qwain drove," Chico said.

"A Hondo Brio," Dom said.

"We don't do no Brios," diamond ears said.

"What Francisco means, we wouldn't have made Mr. Qwain's acquaintance. Our customers don't own subcompacts. We're exclusive to the luxury motorcar owner," Chico said.

"You're a high-end gearhead?" Dom said.

No sign of the temper yet.

"He ain't no mechanic," Francisco said.

Deuce leaned forward and said to Angie under his breath but loud enough for all of them to hear, "Rembrandt with a wrench."

Chico raised his hand to back down his crew.

"Did you know Palmer?" Dom said.

"Only from what JoJo shared."

"I guess his Volvo wagon didn't fit your customer profile."

"He never inquired," Chico said.

"Perhaps you ran into Jerry or Palmer in your other establishment," Dom said.

"Not sure I follow," Chico said.

"A liquor house, the unlicensed kind," Dom said.

Behind his glasses Chico's eyes drilled into him.

"I have to go," JoJo said.

"Did you know Jerry emailed Palmer a threat?" Angie said.

"We never discussed his emails," JoJo said. She drank the last of her water.

"Before you coldcocked him, did Jerry share what he meant by 'screw me twice'?" Dom said.

"He was in no condition to elaborate."

"Palmer say what Jerry may have meant?" Dom said.

"He said Jerry still carried a grudge about some bakery job he botched." She tossed her empty plastic bottle into a garbage can. "Los Mochis was a year ago. I'm fuzzy about all we talked about. Look, Palmer fretted about work all the time. I told him he concerned himself too much with how his clients felt."

"Were you aware of any hurt client feelings around the time he was murdered?" Dom said.

"I only knew of one job he struggled with."

"Who was the client?" Dom said.

"He never said."

"How about the job's location?" Dom said.

"Uptown, I think."

"Could Augie Pepitone and his mountain resort be the client?" Dom said.

"I've no idea, but I can tell you those snails haunted him." She rolled into the locker room hall. "You know, I do remember he said someone named Coldpepper."

&s;

One vehicle at a time filed out from the rink onto East Seventh Street while the SUV's heater went from refrigerator to convection oven. Ten forty-five shone on the dash clock.

"Chico's guy Francisco was quick with JoJo's Thursday night alibi," Deuce said.

"Your Rembrandt quip almost started another rumble," Dom said.

"He'd have you believe the auto business is his only gig," Deuce said.

"I'll take Rocko's word, he's involved with after-hour liquor houses and might be Uptown's Rushers source," Dom said.

Angie typed in her cell phone's browser. "JoJo has a solid alibi, DJ I IS *was* in town." She slid pictures one at a time across her screen.

A Tesla edged in front of them.

Dom's thoughts were on the electrified third rail in Palmer's life, Chico's hair-trigger temper.

Out on Seventh they headed toward Uptown where One Pepitone Place flared across from Tussey Center's brilliant globe.

"Jerry's 'screw me again' comment sounds like he and Palmer may have run into each other on another job," Angie said.

"Could be drunk talk," Deuce said. He adjusted the heat down.

"Would Jerry be desperate enough to take Palmer out if he was about to take another Laphoon-size financial hit?" she said.

"He did say his divorce ruined his financials," Dom said.

"No way running man with his size took out Giron," Deuce said.

"With help, he could," Angie said.

"Where does a guy with a fishing rod in running shorts find a hit man?" Deuce said.

"I'd ask around an illegal liquor house," Dom said.

Dom wanted another go at Chico Vega and knew where to go—Rocko said he enjoyed YMCA pickup basketball games.

"First impression, Chico's a control freak," Angie said.

"You up for some b-ball?" Dom said.

"I'll need shoes," Deuce said.

"What size?" Angie said.

"14 double-wide."

CHAPTER 34

DOM LEFT CHARLOTTE early to drive up to Ashe County. Before they made another attempt to speak with Augie, he wanted to better understand the snail problems Palmer had created for the five-star luxury mountain resort. Five miles past the county seat, Jefferson, he came to Bufflehead Reserve's main gate security guards.

Once cleared through, he drove parallel to an ice-caked stream into six hundred acres of vacation home cul-de-sacs, luxury condominiums, and outdoor heated courts for bocce ball, paddleball, pickleball, and tennis.

From the amount of construction equipment in the broad, flat-floored valley, it didn't appear Palmer's snails hurt real estate sales. Skaters enjoyed a frozen oxbow lake next to a snowed-in, members-only PGA golf course with a heated driving range where irons and woods clipped balls toward yardage signs. At the aquatic center's fifty-meter outdoor pool, swimmers' legs twisted through steamy flip turns.

He wheeled into a space next to concierge UTVs in the hotel and conference center lot. Past the chalet-mottled valley's smoke-trailed chimneys and roofs of snow, he saw a ghost rainbow grace Augie's snail-maligned gorge.

At the front desk he asked to see the resort manager, who Winnie said Augie hired away from a Gstaad hotel. He waited near windows at a display of timeline pictures of the valley's development.

Predevelopment overheads of pristine forests were followed by roads being carved up with bulldozers and excavators at the fifty-meter pool site. After dump trucks at the golf course sand traps came Grand Opening Day photos.

He looked at another picture and saw Palmer with leasing agent Mercer Worthy behind Augie and local political leaders at a ribbon cutting. Augie wielded a three-foot pair of ceremonial scissors.

Out windows he saw several floors of office space with valley views. Mercer's job would be to find tenants, he thought. Children played with a Siberian Husky. Behind Sky Pencil Hollies a woman in a pink parka slid along the curling pitch in a Manitoba tuck.

He turned when someone tapped his shoulder.

"Can you direct us to the wine club room?" a woman with a man said.

"I'm a visitor, try the front desk," he said.

They started toward the desk where Dom saw a guy being pointed in his direction.

If he's the Swiss hotelier, Augie's in good hands.

At least six feet, with slicked-back hair, a hopsack charcoal suit, an asparagus-green Bufflehead Reserve tie, and the confident walk of someone in charge, the guy projected operational competence. Augie's resort wouldn't have any night audit or food and beverage problems on his watch. "I'm Gordon Hass-Kohler," he said.

"Mr. Hass-Kohler, Dominick Mundy, thanks for the time."

They exchanged firm handshakes.

"Gordy, please."

"OK, Gordy, I wanted to ask you about him?" Dom pointed to Palmer in the grand opening picture.

"Palmer Giron, I enjoyed the brief time we spent together. Please." The Swiss manager took his elbow and directed him into a hallway where bridge players milled around a service bar outside their grand ballroom tournament.

"Business appears brisk," Dom said.

"We've been quite fortunate," Gordy said.

"Palmer's snails haven't set you back?"

"A sixty-three percent spike in sales can be contributed to Palmer's find." Gordy directed a bartender to pick up a lime wedge off the floor.

"We heard wildlife bureaucrats paid you a visit."

"They were satisfied with the thousand-yard buffer zone around the gorge Mr. Pepitone agreed to. We're a well-oiled machine outside the No Construction Zone where our snail tourists need a pass to enter. The conchologists' mailers we've sent out have been a huge success. We have a wait list to get into one of our full-time malacologist gorge tours. Is our valley in some way involved with Palmer's death?" Gordy said.

"We're not sure."

"I can tell you Palmer was well thought of here at Bufflehead Reserve."

A loud bridge tournament woman in an overstuffed chair laughed about a Crocodile Coup.

"Why was he here at Bufflehead Reserve in the first place?" Dom said.

"Mr. Pepitone sent Palmer up to look into the gorge when the property came up for sale. I was a skeptic and shared my opinion with Mr. Pepitone. The net usable acres were minimal and I didn't believe were worth the capital outlay. Why add more acreage when our sales were already tepid thanks to a downturn in the second- and third-home property market."

"I guess Augie ignored your advice."

"You'll never make real money if you take investment suggestions from the help."

Gordy stepped away to tell a crew leader to revacuum the gift shop.

"The purchase still moved forward even after Palmer's surprise find?"

"The Mr. Pepitones of the world see opportunity in disaster."

They pushed through kitchen doors, past banquet chefs with crème brûlée torches, and out the exit into the clear mountain air. Gordy waved up the postcard valley to fleecy clouds stacked up behind the gorge.

"We sold every available lot thanks to Palmer's curiosity about our gorge waterfall. Mr. Pepitone has made millions off those noonday globes." At the highest point on each slope identical chalets faced each other.

"Who owns those monstrosities?" Dom said.

"Sisters who operate a computer game company."

"Let me guess, Roo Woo."

"You must play."

"I stick with board games."

Dom looked up the valley at the chalets and gorge rainbow backdrop. Bufflehead Reserve was an out-of-control ATM thanks to those snails.

CHAPTER 35

His cell phone illuminated with the office number when Shingle Gap Road passed in twilight's blur.

"Where are you?" Winnie said.

"On the way back from Ashe County."

"I'm concerned about Angie. She hasn't answered my calls and Deuce can't get through to her either."

Not again, he thought.

"When I left, she was huddled up with the Giron papers," he said.

"I ordered lunch in and we all ate at the big conference table. She received a call from someone named John Brody, then asked Franco to borrow his SUV. She's been gone almost four hours."

He signed off, scrolled to another number, and hit dial.

"Hold on," John Brody said.

Dom heard him finish up a muffled conversation, then come back on.

"Have you heard?"

"Fill me in," Dom said.

"Timor-Leste national police raided a village and found three women. A Canadian photojournalist and a German are both alive but in bad shape. Sandi Burns wasn't so lucky. Our people are on the way to retrieve her body. We're being told a drug overdose. Triads use the village for a way station to move dope to Australia and New Zealand. How's Angie?"

Dom wasn't about to tell him she disappeared.

"You can imagine," he said.

"Tell her not to blame herself."

"I'll be in touch," Dom said.

Angie's number rang to voicemail. He called Winnie back.

"Text me the watering hole address Deuce hauled her out of," he said.

"You think after what she pulled last time, they'd welcome her back?"

"We have to start somewhere," he said. He accelerated toward the sun dog horizon.

⊷

The Porsche accelerated around Uptown's loop freeway when Winnie rang again. "We still haven't gotten through to her," she said.

"I'm on the way to her apartment now," he said. He made a quick move in front of an appliance delivery truck to make First Ward's exit.

"Want Deuce and Pia to head your way?"

"Hold off until I call you," he said.

She clicked off. At the bottom of the exit ramp, he drove into an incandescent maze of high-rise glass.

Where are you, girl?

At her apartment door he knocked several times. If she was in there, he wouldn't tolerate what she'd pulled the last time Winnie came up here. A building maintenance person happened out of the elevator.

He pointed to Angie's door. "You have a resident here who

might be in a problem. What will it take for you to open her door?" Dom said.

"I don't know you and I can't give you access to any apartments."

He gave the manger his card with a folded hundred. "She works with me. I'll stay in the hallway while you check her apartment."

She considered the card and C-note, then pulled out her key ring and went in to find an empty apartment.

Back in the Porsche he drove to the Eighth Street bar address and saw Franco's SUV several buildings away from Dickie's Thyme, the saloon where Deuce had carried her out of the men's room. Ceiling Christmas lights lit the place along with candles in tabletop perforated-metal containers. The sweet smell of maple chicken wings came from the nearest booth where a grandmother sat with a toddler boy. A guy in a crumpled suit slouched at the bar with a beer mug and an empty shot glass and salted a half-eaten boiled egg.

Dom didn't see Angie.

The young woman bartender brought the guy with the egg another round.

"I'm here to find a friend who ran into problems in your men's room several days ago," Dom said.

"I told her we run a neighborhood place and to get her wolverine temper out," the bartender said. "Try the Froth House up the street."

Outside Dom saw the tavern's red-and-blue OPEN sign flicker from the next block. He found Angie in the back at a small table next to a soft drink cooler with her head in her hands. He scraped out the other chair. She looked up with swollen eyes.

"You OK?" he said.

"Dumb question," she said.

Her cocktail and spiral orange-peel garnish were untouched. Dom waved off the bartender when he approached them.

"Two," he said.

"Two what?" she said.

"You asked if I ever lost any of my people. I've lost two," he said.

"Here in Charlotte?" she said.

"In my Coast Guard days, John Brody and I were partnered up with the Canadian Coast Guard to take down a Haitian gang that smuggled cigarettes from Detroit to Toronto on luxury cabin cruisers. My undercover worked at the marina where the Haitians loaded the cruisers. We got played by the CCG's confidential informant who tipped them off. The undercover and an ICE agent were killed."

She wiped tears away. "You should've told me."

"Does Sandi's husband know?"

"John called him before he rang me. They say she overdosed. Sandi never used drugs in her life. Now because of me, her girls grow up without their mother," Angie said.

"They have you."

She looked at him. "The person responsible for her being dead."

"One way to look at what happened, I guess."

"The only way."

"Or, no one could have prevented the situation from going off the rails."

They sat in silence while she dunked her orange peel with the straw. Billy Idol's "Pumping on Steel" ended and The Jonas Brothers' "Black Keys" started up. A shot of cold air blew in when the barback wheeled an empty keg out the receiving door.

"What did you learn about Palmer's snails?" she said.

"They helped Augie sell out Bufflehead Reserve. Guess who owns two of the resort's largest vacation homes? I'll give you a hint, rhymes with Boo Boo."

"The app game sisters?"

"Their identical chalets face each other across the valley."

"A couple of mountain places on top of Augie's office-lease incentives may have been the sweetener the sisters needed to hopscotch out of Babe's building across the street and into One Pepitone Place," she said.

"Even with Bufflehead Reserve's success, I still want Augie's take on Palmer," he said. "How about we get back to the office?"

<h1 style="text-align:center">CHAPTER 36</h1>

Early Monday, Dom drove toward Uptown with Angie. Through Morehead Street's leafless tree canopy, superstructures loomed against taffy-pulled clouds. They crossed South Boulevard's bridge.

"Given what Jerry said in the liquor house about serious Uptown people, we might want to go over a list of his clients to see if he and Palmer were in the midst of another Laphoon-size situation," Dom said.

"I'll call Jerry's office," Angie said.

They used on-street parking and walked a frosty seventeen degrees toward One Pepitone Place. Steam rose out of the Lost Souls Grotto. Across the street Dom could see Chico Vega's acquaintance Officer Earl Jessup at the guard desk through Tussey Center's thirty-foot lobby windows.

Angie pointed toward a number of sidewalk electric scooters near the intersection. "The slice of land with the grotto Babe Tussey says she still owns runs several feet wide from those scooters, loops around the grotto, and cuts back between the fire hydrant and light post to the street," she said.

Dom looked at how the grotto, Augie's grand entrance centerpiece, lined up with One Pepitone Center's columned portico. A line of HVAC service vans were parked around the driveway.

When they approached the revolving doors a man and woman in Alpine ski jackets exited. The woman wore mittens and carried a briefcase.

"Excuse the inconvenience and our HVAC problems today," a doorman said. "We're a tad chilly inside. The AC kicked on after midnight Saturday, then the entire system crashed at noon yesterday. The temperature drop last night didn't help. Replacement parts from a Wisconsin factory should arrive later today."

A banquet washout, now an arctic building. Augie better reschedule his property management IPO, Dom thought.

"Chilly's being generous—it's an icebox in here," Angie said.

Pepitone Group staff in parkas greeted them at a kiosk with complimentary coffee and hot chocolate. A woman in a white cashmere coat and red concert dress played Frédéric Chopin's Nocturne No. 2 in E-flat major at a grand piano. With no banquet tables Dom saw how Augie's architect extended her blaze window concept inside with a circular floor pattern of flame-blue marble and polished sandalwood planks. Sunbeams streamed through windows whose casing mullions, the size of conjoined four by sixes, ran the full vertical length of the cathedral space.

"Augie didn't fire the sprinkler girls," Angie said. She nodded toward the garden wall.

Pat Genesee, in heather coveralls and pink earmuffs, stood at a makeshift table with plans rolled out. Her all-female staff, with *Genesee Sprinkler* splayed across the back of their coveralls, toiled on every level of steel scaffolding erected against the wall. She slid an architect's scale ruler along the wall's design plans. Dom saw the bags under her eyes from lack of sleep. Pat slid her earmuffs off.

"Figure out what happened?" Dom said.

"My mister went wonky after Augie's building software crashed. Now the whole building's offline. You never mentioned your line of work the other night?" Pat said.

"We're investigators."

"Cops?"

"The corporate side of the street."

"Boss?" her radio crackled.

Pat communicated with an employee eighty feet up. When she finished, she tossed the ruler on the plans. "Investigators interested in who?"

"Palmer Giron, an engineer killed in Freedom Park. Augie Pepitone's on the list of clients he worked for."

"You might want to reschedule. The boss is not in the best mood today."

Dom saw Bobbi, another banquet seatmate, halfway up the wall with a coworker whose arms plunged up to her elbows into the green wall.

"How bad's the damage?" Angie said.

Pat picked up the ruler and started to point around the plans. "We've replaced all but a few of the sprinkler heads, a thousand feet of drip tubes, pressure regulators, half the elbow risers, and a controller with fried circuits. A new jockey pump and flow switch should be here by lunch."

"Augie might want to delay his IPO," Dom said.

"When word leaked of the crash, IQ's phones lit up with skyscraper clients from all over the globe concerned they might be next." Bobbi hopped off the ladder and motioned for Pat. "The timing couldn't come at a worse time for Mr. Pepitone."

The guy behind the concierge desk wore a plum worsted wool suit, brown leather gloves, and a cognac scarf tied with a Parisian knot. *Rodrigo Sandoval Associate since 2016* appeared on his ID. He replaced the receiver. "I'm afraid Mr. Pepitone's engaged. His office suggested you call another time."

"Tell him the subject's Palmer Giron," Dom said.

"You'll have to speak with his assistant. She keeps his calendar." He turned and spoke with a delivery driver.

"Call him," Dom said.

Angie typed the main number for The Pepitone Group Companies into her cell phone. After a short conversation she passed the phone to Sandoval, who listened for a few seconds.

"Right away," he said. He handed Angie her phone and scanned in their temporary ID cards. "Who's Palmer Giron?"

"A guy your boss worked with," Dom said.

"He still on the payroll?"

"He's dead," Dom said.

They crossed the atrium, swiped their passes above the scanner, and glass security turnstiles parted. Two of the twelve glass tube elevators were operable.

Dom watched Angie's reaction when they crowded in with four women dressed for the Iditarod. He held up his thumb OK and she nodded. With her eyes shut, the elevator rose above the atrium.

"Thirty-seven dollars a foot in rent and the heat doesn't work," one of the women said. Her dark-green knit cap matched her full-length down coat.

"Our CEO told Mr. Pepitone we'd break the lease if another day went by without heat," the one with bunny gloves said. She held building-complimentary hot chocolates topped with whipped cream and chocolate sprinkles.

"The property manager's email said replacement parts are being shipped from another state," a third one said.

Angie grabbed Dom's arm when the elevator jerked to a stop between the fifth and sixth floors.

"Now what?" the one with red cheeks and nose said.

The elevator jerked up another inch, stopped, then started again. Angie never let go of his arm.

"I'll take the stairs when we get out," bunny gloves said.

"Eleven stories?" green cap said.

"The exercise will do me good."

They limped up to seven, and the doors stuck halfway open. Dom squeezed out last.

∽

Inside Augie Pepitone's corporate offices, the temperature reminded Dom of a beer cooler. The design of the space resembled a mountain lodge with log walls of dark, cherry oak, timber-beamed ceiling, and hardwood floors.

Augie's receptionist spoke into a headset at the same time she typed on her keyboard through fingerless gloves. Her desk nameplate read *Alberta Mavis,* who Dom remembered Pat Genesee said told her about the grotto debacle. In place of a winter coat, Alberta wore an extra-large Dale Earnhardt Sr. sweatshirt. Her jeep cap read *The Intimidator.*

Angie cleared her throat. Alberta peered up through checkered-flag glasses and motioned toward reclaimed barnwood chairs as she continued her headset conversation.

One of the rustic watercolors on the seating area walls depicted a mountain cabin surrounded by fall foliage with German short-haired puppies under a brilliant American red maple. Angie chose *Yachting* instead of *Waterfowl* to leaf through from magazines arrayed on the elk antler coffee table.

"Do what?" Dom heard Alberta say.

Diecast number-three cars lined her desk return. A space heater glowed at her feet. "Pocono and Watkins Glen because Lonnie wants to see his baby Jane Ellen's little ones in Myrtle Beach. We'll be in Martinsville with the RV." She sipped Cheerwine through a straw. "Champion's Overlook, I have one coming in."

Raised voices came from behind a closed office door.

"Augie might be the rough client Palmer's mother mentioned," Angie said.

The door opened and three men in suits with bankers-in-distress looks on their faces crossed the lobby. Alberta went into Augie's office with a handful of telephone messages. After a few minutes she came back out toward her desk. "Mr. Pepitone can see you now," she said.

Augie's small spartan office surprised Dom. He'd expected they'd walk into a workspace fit for a developer with the muscular ego required to erect a back-to-the-land wood office tower. The spartan space didn't have any chairs, shelves, telephones, lamps, computers, or even wastebaskets, only an empty stand-up antique writing desk.

Augie was banged up from being pressure-washed off his stage.

On crutches he faced toward windows with an up-close view of Tussey Center's revolving-door entrance. He wore sunglasses and held his cell phone up to his close-cropped head. Fern frost from lack of heat caked the bottom of the windows. He wore dry-cleaned faded jeans, camel stockman boots, and an untucked, russet western shirt with shoulders and cuffs of embroidered roses. An orthopedic hinged brace encased his right leg. He finished up his call and read his messages. "Dominick Mundy and Angie who?" he said toward Tussey Center.

"Crete," Angie said.

"Like the island?" Augie said.

"I've never been," Angie said.

He crutched to his desk. "You sell life insurance with a name like Mundy and Associates?"

"Personal coverage is one of our lines," Dom said.

"Was Palmer Giron a policyholder?" He rested his crutches against the tall desk.

"Carter Hillstead asked for our input," Dom said.

"Carter and I belong to the same yacht club. What was Palmer's affiliation with him?"

"His father was Carter's personal driver, and his mother went to him for help to find who killed her boy. We're speaking with his personal and professional contacts."

"To find who killed him?"

"Perfect world, yes."

"We live in an imperfect world, Mr. Mundy."

"Like your Lost Souls Grotto, Babe says she owns?" Angie said.

Dom looked at her. How about we jump right in?

"The courts proved her wrong." Augie pinched off a watch alarm.

"Perhaps she's irritated Roo Woo walked out," Angie said.

"Ms. Crete, what do you know about the office space game?"

"I can spell skyscraper."

"We play by one rule: everything's negotiable."

A flock of pigeons made a sharp change of direction outside the windows behind Augie.

"What was Palmer's first job for you?" Dom said.

"He handled the environmental work when I acquired our site here. The guy was good, so I sent him up to our luxury resort development we have underway in Ashe County."

"Where he uncovered a few snails," Dom said.

Augie considered them through his dark shades. "He kayaked into Dusky Notch gorge and saw a rare Carolina northern flying squirrel glide behind Bloodroot Falls where he found noonday globes. Palmer said snails like these would be good for business. I took his advice and instructed my sales staff to include them in their sales pitch to outdoorsy types who have no interest in our ATP tennis complex or PGA-quality golf course. Home sites flew off the shelf."

"How hard were the US Fish and Wildlife Service inspectors on you?" Dom said.

"They ground our eighty-million-dollar project to a halt until we agreed to an action plan."

"Interest carry on a stalled resort development must be painful," Dom said.

Angie's thumbs worked her cell screen. "I calculate seventeen K a day on eighty million," she said.

"All because Palmer paddled around in his kayak," Dom said.

"The wildlife people came up with a work-around we could live with. The big win, my accountants discovered significant tax breaks for an obscure wildlife sanctuary program we qualified for."

"Then you would've worked with Palmer again?" Dom said.

"I did work with him again."

"On Bufflehead Reserve?" Dom said.

"No, here at One Pepitone Place. Before he died, he investigated odors from our grotto."

"Your Lost Souls was ripe with eggs in vinegar the night of your banquet," Dom said.

"Along with our other water problems Friday, the smell started when the first limos pulled up. We have sulfur odors from the geothermal spring on occasion, but nothing like the spoiled egg we've been exposed to for the last year and a half."

Dom thought about the tax map they found in Palmer's office with Coldpepper arrowed to Tussey Center. The circle with an X on Augie's property marked the source of the grotto smells Augie asked him to look into. Why was Coldpepper arrowed to Babe's building on the same tax map with the Lost Souls? "Palmer figure out the problem?" Dom said.

"He was still after the source when he died." Augie held up his finger to hold a minute while he touched his watch screen. "I have people with me, go ahead."

"I can call back," a male voice said.

"Be quick," Augie said.

"The air handlers are at the airport."

"How long before you're here?"

"Ninety minutes. One's already on the truck."

"Make sure Carlos and his crew are in the dock area when you arrive."

He tapped off the call.

"Tough night Friday," Dom said.

"You were here?"

"At Pat Genesee's table."

"Her people have been downstairs for three days at work on the wall's infrastructure." He looked at the watch screen again. "I need to take this."

They opted for the stairs back down to the lobby over the moody elevators.

CHAPTER 37

Dom surveyed the crowded YMCA gym where a few dozen players warmed up. A red-headed player, a few inches under seven feet with knee-length blue-and-white Kentucky Wildcat shorts, came in and jogged toward the scorer's table to put his name on the list. Another guy in a Saint Anselm College shirt missed a dunk and his ball bounced toward Deuce, who pitched it back to another guy who waited to take a run at the basket. More players loitered behind benches and the scorer's table while they waited for the first game to get underway.

Dom figured the security guard's eyes were on Deuce because he never saw a guy his size attempt to play basketball. "Chico Vega around?" he said.

The guard indicated toward an entrance to another gym where a Zumba class was underway. Chico, the shortest guy in the gym, bounced a ball between his legs with his back to them.

Dom recognized his entourage from JoJo's rumble: the brawny one, Francisco, with iced-up ears; the Goldilocks faux hawk Jorge, who wore basketball goggles; and the tall skinny guy with forehead butcher art. A woman in pencil heels ran silver sparkle nails through her shoulder-length black hair and shared a chuckle with Chico.

Jorge nodded for Chico to take a look behind him when Dom and Deuce walked up.

"*La Policia*?" the girl said. Well-placed ripped holes in her high-waisted ankle jeans exposed a pair of gazelle legs.

"The Keystone kind," Chico said. He handed the ball off to Francisco.

Dom still couldn't marry up the tenor voice with Rocko's hair-trigger comment.

"We came to play some hoops," Dom said.

Chico gave Dom's well-used warm-ups and gym shoes the once-over, then Deuce's leather jacket, long-sleeve white dress shirt, and jeans. He smirked when he came to the tie-dye slip-on sneakers, the only 14 triple-Es Winnie could find. "With cool shoes," he said.

"You're a Rembrandt and a cutup," Deuce said.

Chico's eyebrow scar narrowed when his eyes hardened.

Dom motioned toward a corner away from his crew. "Can we have a moment?"

"Here's fine," Chico said.

"You sure you never met Palmer?" Dom said.

"Like I said, we weren't acquainted."

"Why didn't JoJo's fifth step-cousin rank an introduction?"

"Fourth once removed," Chico said.

"I figure she'd at least bring him around for Vega holidays, maybe a Fourth of July or Three Kings Day barbecue."

"He never made no barbecues," Chico said.

"Memories are funny how they play tricks. Like your liquor house meet and greet with Palmer, his brother, JoJo, and another of your acquaintances, Jerry Qwain."

"Can't help you with liquor houses." His stare didn't waver. "Your canary needs a fact-checker."

A whistle blew and players started to make their way off court.

The scorer table's buzzer called all players to be assigned a team. Dom watched Chico direct his crew toward the game organizers.

"Look who's a baller," Deuce said.

A guy with a white head and wrist bands came onto the court past the guard. Dom saw the ponytail and spiderweb hand tattoo. Officer Earl Jessup jogged up to Chico.

Deuce joined Dom at the end of the farthest bench with the guy in Kentucky shorts.

Chico loitered with Earl and his Patriots around several foldout chairs. When the first game ended, random names were selected for each six-man team for game number two. Earl ran out to join five shirts already at midcourt. His skills were evident once the game started with his underhand pass-offs and Euro-step moves.

For the third game Dom and Deuce happened to be chosen on the same skins side opposite Chico, Jorge, and Francisco. Dom removed his warm-ups and T-shirt, while Deuce slipped off his leather jacket. Silence settled throughout the gym when he unbuttoned his long-sleeve white button-down.

"Damn," the referee said under his breath.

In stark contrast to the other inked-up bodies in the gym, every inch of Deuce's upper torso and arms were covered with exquisite, vivid body art. The comparison would be the difference between a Caravaggio and a paint-by-numbers kit.

"OK, show-off, let's play ball," Dom said.

Deuce jogged after him in his tie-dye slip-ons and jeans. The Kentucky redhead, who said his name was Henry, joined Dom's side along with a barber and an equine chiropractor who bragged he started for his JUCO team thirty years ago. The referee blew his whistle.

"Take diamond ears," Dom said.

Henry threw the ball in to Dom, who dribbled down court

with Chico on him. He pulled up for a quick three, but Chico blocked his shot with a springboard jump.

"Nice move, Irwin Coldpepper," Dom said. Dom saw the look—there one second, gone the next—in Chico's eyes. He knew Irwin or Coldpepper. Palmer's Post-it-Note *cv* was Chico Vega.

Jorge's toss to Chico set him up for a stutter-step layup.

The horse chiropractor put the ball back in play with a bounce pass through Jorge's outstretched legs to Deuce, who dribbled circles around Francisco before he pitched the ball with an under-hand pass across the court. The barber caught it and with a quick sidearm toss fed the ball to Dom in the corner.

Chico was on him in two steps.

A fake dribble, a pull-up hard collision, and Chico landed on his rear end. Dom drilled a twenty-eight footer. Near the end of the last period, with fifteen points scored on Chico, Dom caught him flat-footed again and launched a bridge-span skyhook over his head for a total of eighteen points. Rocko was right about JoJo's cousin. He stormed out of the gym.

CHAPTER 38

Thursday evening, Dom saw her enter The Royal Crown Group's Colony Road hotel bar.

"Hello, Detective," he said. He came off his barstool and gave Detective Nita Lopez a hug.

"Your call was a pleasant surprise," she said.

"Thanks for being here," he said.

"Why wouldn't I be?"

"You're an overworked detective," he said.

"Which never stopped us before," she said.

He helped her with her coat and she took the barstool beside him.

"Gin gimlet?" he said.

"Time hasn't clouded your memory," she said.

"It hasn't been that long since we were together." He ordered her gimlet and a draft beer refill for himself. "How's the new partner?"

"The Marine Corps turns out capable investigators. Can you say the same for the Coast Guard?"

"If you consider what she's been through, Angie does all right."

"What happened to her?"

"An operation cost her team members. One killed and another kidnapped, a mother with two children."

Nita gave the slow nod of someone who knew all about sideways operations.

"You mentioned Dr. Braces didn't work out," he said.

She was the one who ended their relationship for an orthodontist whose picture and phone number graced youth sports venues all over the city.

"Took me way too long to realize we weren't simpatico."

"His four-day workweeks became too much?"

"Didn't care for how he handled money."

"I figured those teenage mouths for cash cows."

"Kevin's a tightwad," Nita said. "Never once in our time together did he leave more than five percent to a waiter. On the subject of money, did Rachel take you for a ride?"

"We broke even."

The bartender put fresh napkins down with their drinks.

"Are personal recaps why you asked me here?" she said.

"I'd like your opinion."

"I'm the last person you should ask about relationships," she said.

"Not Rachel, Rushers," he said.

She fixed those graceful dark eyes on him. "I prefer we go back to our exes," she said.

"Is the rumor true, they're popular with Uptown's younger set?"

"Not all are young and yes, they're trendy."

"Who's behind them?"

She stirred her cocktail pick speared through three olives. "The DEA has interest in a Chiapas-based Mexican cartel."

"We hear production might be local."

"Now who told you Rushers are homegrown, Dominick?"

"You're not the only one with detective smarts."

They waved off the bartender when she held out a menu.

"We'd know if industrial-grade methamphetamines were being manufactured somewhere in the city," she said.

"How about their distributor, any ideas?"

"You have someone in mind?"

"Chico Vega."

Two of the olives disappeared between her lips. "If Vega had something to do with Rushers, we'd know."

"JoJo Cifuentes put Palmer and Chico in the same orbit. We think he could be connected to what went down under the Freedom Park bridge and with Jerry Qwain on Welker Street."

"Chico's alibi held up. He footed the all-inclusive Jamaican resort bill for JoJo and eight family members," Nita said.

"But the Patriots were still in town," Dom said.

"These out-of-the-box ideas are one reason I always liked you, but if all you have are Chico and his crew, you're short on boxes."

She ate the last olive.

"JoJo's dope-trade experience would make her the perfect hire if Chico needed a desk jockey to move product. Keep it all in the family."

"You've wasted Ms. Ruby's time and money."

"Stay with Chico being a player and JoJo's an Uptown Willy Loman. If Palmer attempted to separate her from a Rushers side gig, then Chico's sales could go into a nosedive. Now he's motivated to fix the problem." He motioned for another round.

"South-of-the-border cartel suppliers would never let a small-time hood like Chico Vega anywhere near an Uptown meth operation," she said.

"And if the DEA's wrong?"

"Won't be the first time." She finished her gimlet.

"Nickolas Giron told us he was in town with his family Memorial Day weekend before Palmer was murdered. Palmer rang him after midnight, alarmed he couldn't find JoJo. They drive to an after-hours liquor house near the airport and there she is. Guess who else they run into?"

"I'm sure you'll tell me," she said.

A fresh gimlet and draft beer arrived.

"Chico with Jerry Qwain."

"They're together?" she said.

Dom saw she hadn't considered Chico being with Jerry Qwain.

"Nickolas said JoJo, Chico, and Jerry Qwain were at a blackjack table."

"Care to share the liquor house location?"

"All we have is a dead-end street near a temple close to the airport."

"Can't help you with Jerry Qwain, his case is still active," she said.

She tapped her spear on her napkin.

"How about we speculate?" he said.

"Speculate away."

"We know about a business dispute with Palmer over one of Jerry's clients, the Laphoons. Palmer walked away with their business after Jerry botched a job for them. Jerry returned the favor when he became Babe Tussey's go-to environmental engineer after she showed Palmer the door."

"How close have you looked into Giron Environmental Partners?" she said.

He spoke over the loud table of women with margaritas behind them. "Enough to know his clientele either loved him or hated him."

"The Laphoon dustup happened well before Palmer's murder," she said, half her gimlet now gone.

"Maybe those two tangled over another client again. An Uptown customer we didn't find when we checked Palmer's files."

"Why would you think they're located in Uptown?"

"Nickolas overheard Jerry tell Palmer, 'These Uptown people are serious.'"

"What people?"

"We didn't hear any names."

Her snide smile matched her comment. "You can take your pick of serious Uptown people. They all have poker faces. We haven't seen any indication of another situation between Jerry Qwain and Palmer," she said.

"While we're on Jerry, he was the type after a few cocktails, every watering hole became a jubilee. But why would he be in a liquor house with Chico and JoJo? With the fees he charged, he could afford premium whiskey in any bar he walked into."

"Besides enjoying the colorful conversation, he could be a potential Kueentown Motorworks customer," she said.

"Chico's Kueentown would be a stretch for a guy who tooled around in a subcompact. We think Jerry was in Palmer's house because someone wanted what was in one of his files."

"Who's your someone?"

"For starters, Jerry."

"Anyone else you care to speculate on?"

"Chico Vega. The *cv* from Palmer's missing sticky note."

More of the gimlet disappeared. "By the way, we haven't found Palmer involved with any Coldpeppers. Now let's say you're right, which I'm not, Chico's behind Rushers and Palmer's sweetie is his top sales associate. Palmer would be smart enough to know better than to get between a supplier and his addict customers."

"Love doesn't always trump crazy."

"You don't have to tell me about love and crazy."

He finished off the draft. "Toss me a morsel I can share with Ms. Ruby?" he said.

"We have interest in Palmer's relapse." She finished off her cocktail. "No more shop talk. Have you been here since the property's been renovated?"

"First time back."

"I hear every room's been overhauled," she said.

"They're gut rehabs, the bartender said."

"The food's improved too," Nita said.

"Let's get a table and grade the menu," he said.

He saw her playful smile in the bar mirror and knew a side of the dogged, methodical, homicide detective few people ever saw. The tender beauty she hid so well.

"Room service is now second to none," she said.

Dom motioned for the check.

CHAPTER 39

Deuce drove along Highway 51 past fast-food restaurants with bumper-to-bumper drive-through lanes.

"I met Nita Lopez for a drink and she confirmed Chico's in Jamaica with JoJo and his extended family when Jerry's up the ladder inside Palmer's house."

Angie spoke toward the windshield in the front passenger seat. "Drinks with Detective Lopez?"

"An old friend with an opinion I wanted to hear about Rushers and if they're connected to Chico and his crew."

"How opinionated was she?"

"Chico tied to Rushers might be a reach."

Deuce turned into Raintree's tree-lined entrance.

"You two work through any other scenarios?"

"The DEA likes a south-of-the-border cartel for Rushers."

"So how do we handle Chico Vega?" she said.

"He stays right where he is, at the top of our list."

The Tudor where One Pepitone Center's leasing agent Mercer Worthy lived backed up to a golf cart path and fairway bunkers on Smokerise Hill Drive. A woman with a mop answered the door and gave Dom directions to a nearby park where they could find her. The park's parking lot was three-quarters full of vehicles with stay-at-home parents out to take advantage of a brief thaw before another cold front moved in. Angie pointed to a grandmother and a young woman with caramel hair who wore oversize sunglasses and a knit UVA cap on a bench.

"She could be Mercer."

Deuce waited at the frog and shark spring riders while Dom and Angie went toward the bench. They stopped short of the bench when the leashed short-haired buttermilk buckskin dog growled at them.

"Blondie, shush," she said.

"Are you Mercer Worthy?" Dom said.

She paused and looked at them. "Yes."

"We'd like to speak with you about Palmer Giron."

"See you next week, honey," the older woman said. She got up and went toward triplet girls at the chain swings.

"The woman who answered your door told us we could find you here," Dom said.

"Carmen's my mother-in-law who helps out a few days a week. Excuse me." She stepped around puddles in the rubber mulch with her fur-lined boots toward a girl inside the pirate ship jungle gym.

Angie petted Blondie until Mercer came back with a pair of mittens.

"Cute girl," Dom said.

"Madison's with her brother, Logan Junior." She set the mittens in a patch of sunlight.

They sat perpendicular to her on another bench. With an angular face half obscured by the sunglasses, Dom guessed she was in her mid-thirties. "How close were you to Palmer?" he said.

"Close enough to be invited to his dinner parties and for my husband Logan to be invited to go squirrel hunting. He'd take our dog along and Palmer would bring his."

Madison chased a boy down a slide.

"We didn't know Palmer owned a dog," Angie said.

"His rescue labradoodle, Hunter. They'd spend hours with those dogs. His mother gave Hunter to a new family after Palmer died." Her voice catched from the memory.

"JoJo Cifuentes attend these dinner parties?" he said.

"She never missed one. At first we weren't sure how those two ended up together, but after we spent time around them, you could see how much they cared for one another."

"Ever see her drunk?" Angie said.

"Why would you ask such a question?"

"JoJo has a reputation," Angie said.

"I only ever saw her sip wine.

"We'd like to show you a couple of pictures," Dom said.

Angie unfolded a printout and handed it to her. "Augie Pepitone's Bufflehead Reserve announcement," she said.

In the picture a woman glad-handed Augie in front of a group of people with a valley view backdrop. Mercer stood with Palmer near the chocolate-fondue fountain.

"I attended because of the office space Mr. Pepitone needed to lease in his conference center. Logan came up for the ceremony too." Her finger went to the man who shared a laugh with Palmer. With a powerful build, close-cropped sandy hair, he looked like he once played contact sports. She tapped the woman with Augie. "Jefferson's mayor, who drank too much. Half the town turned out for the after-party."

"Did you know about these snails Palmer found?" Dom said.

"Everyone did. The state came in and stopped work until Mr. Pepitone agreed not to build near the gorge. Palmer raised the idea the snails might result in a few extra condo sales. No one could have predicted they'd sell out. Why are you asking about Bufflehead Reserve?"

"We are interested in jobs Palmer worked on around the time of his death, in particular ones where there may have been problems."

"Those snails were moneymakers."

"Mr. Pepitone brought Palmer back on to work on the Lost Souls Grotto," Angie said.

"I know. He had the task of finding out where the smell came from," Mercer said.

"We caught a whiff Friday night," Dom said.

"Sometimes it's so strong, your eyes burn."

Angie handed her another printout. "The day Tussey Center broke ground," she said.

Mercer looked at the white hard-hat line of VIPs with their silver shovels. Palmer on the far left next to her husband, both with camera-ready smiles. Babe Tussey out front with her shovel in designer boots, beige kettle-brim sun hat, and sappy smile.

"The skyscraper witch whose building I helped lease up and where I first met Palmer." She looked closer at the people gathered in the back and tapped hard on an older guy in a Mardi Gras green seersucker suit, with tapered sideburns and a mane of white hair. "Jefferson Wallach, the Tussey's corporate lawyer. He's the type the family likes to have around."

"Type how?" Angie said.

"Evil person with a capital E."

"We heard Babe sicced him on Augie because she believes the Lost Souls Grotto belongs to her," Dom said.

"She wanted One Pepitone Place's site for Tussey Center. After Augie's bid topped hers she welcomed any reason to go after him." Mercer fished a grape juice box out from her bag. Madison jumped off a grounded balance beam, skipped up with another girl, and asked if she could have one for her new friend.

"When you left Tussey Center for Augie's building, didn't you take Roo Woo with you?" Angie said.

"Mr. Pepitone negotiated one-on-one with the game company's principals. He wanted Roo Woo with their millions of followers in his building because he thought they'd attract other technology tenants."

"We were at his banquet the other night, a real drencher," Angie said.

"I received an invite but couldn't make it. Logan Junior was sick," Mercer said.

"You enjoy working at One Pepitone Place?"

"The collaborative environment is the polar opposite of Babe Tussey's toxic workplace. With her constant employee demands, I almost quit a number of times. Every week another memo circulated on how to save money. Gems like paper clip inventories and both sides of copy paper being used."

Blondie took a dog biscuit Mercer held out to distract her from an attentive beagle.

"She owns a skyscraper, why pinch pennies?" Angie said.

"I know of two occasions where she made capital calls to the shampoo side of the family business to avert Tussey Center being repossessed." Madison waved from the top of a spiderweb rope climb. "I knew I was a short-timer after Babe eliminated wine and dines for prospective tenants to save money. You want to know what cheap means, the day after I made my move to One Pepitone Center, a certified letter on Jefferson Wallach's letterhead shows up at the house to inform me lease commissions I'm still owed won't be paid."

"How much did you get dinged for?" Angie said.

"Not quite four hundred thousand dollars."

"Artwork from world-famous artists in her building lobby doesn't give the impression dollars are being stretched," Dom said.

"Babe has no interest in art. The family's art collection dates back to a long-dead relative. Her main focus is tennis and appearances."

Logan Junior hit the ground on a run from a stand-up merry-go-round and came toward them for his juice box.

"A cut-rate style hasn't affected her globe garden," Dom said.

"The globe only went up so Babe could hotdog Tussey Center would best One Pepitone Place for the tallest Uptown tower. When she saw Augie's executive helicopter and helipad, she added two helipads and rented a helicopter to fly around her building and land on one of the helipads once a month. I wanted to hug Augie after he announced he'd throw up more floors to take back the height title."

"Palmer ever share with you jobs he might be involved with?" Dom said.

"We heard he worked on Babe's Mother Lode development off Morehead Street near the Gold District. I remember because Logan Junior was fascinated when Palmer and JoJo were at the house for a cookout and shared stories about Charlotte's gold rush."

"Babe fired him before anyone struck it rich and brought on Jerry Qwain."

"I know who he is."

"You've met Jerry?" Dom said.

"I knew him from my time at Tussey Center. I'd see him from time to time with one of Babe's security guards he fished with. Earl Jessup, a winner related to Babe and an ex-sheriff fired after he responded to a fraternity party noise complaint in western North Carolina. Sent a frat boy to the hospital with a broken collarbone who happened to be the son of a congresswoman. I couldn't stand the guy."

Mercer snapped Blondie back from a Shih Tzu puppy.

"I left the office late one night and ran into Earl with another guard in the parking garage. Earl has a building tenant pinned to the stairwell with his club and says he caught the guy about to break into a Maserati. The poor guy tries to explain his keys were locked inside and points to a coat hanger on the ground. I diffused the situation when I told Earl his car thief was a partner in a boutique M&A firm on the sixtieth floor. The incident cost Babe a substantial amount of free rent to that firm to soft-pedal the blowback."

"Jerry's dead. Murdered in Palmer's house," Angie said.

"He's the guy on the news?"

"He's the guy," Angie said.

"You know he showed up on Welker Street before," Mercer said. "Palmer invited a number of us to his house for a wine tasting when Jerry and Earl Jessup showed up on his front porch. Palmer went out to deal with them. They'd been drinking and I heard Jerry yell at Palmer. I saw Palmer out his picture window grab Earl by the shirt and hold him against a porch pillar. After they left, I asked Palmer what they wanted. His only comment was some waterway job." Mercer jumped up and ran to Madison, who fell off a seesaw.

⤫

Deuce sped up to make the Providence Road turn arrow.

"Earl and Jerry Qwain were at Palmer's?" Angie said.

"You're sure you don't remember any reference to Irwin Creek in Palmer's notes?" Dom said.

"Irwin Creek or waterways."

"Irwin Creek cuts through half the county," Dom said.

"I can check property owners who abut the creek," Angie said.

"You'll find dozens of them."

"All I have is time," she said.

CHAPTER 40

THE FOLLOWING DAY, wind buffeted Dom's Porsche when he parked in the same spot they'd used on the day they left the SUV and found Jerry Qwain's body. He walked down Welker Street and stood opposite Palmer's white Cape Cod.

The cucumber magnolia shielded any view of the side yard where the extension ladder had been used to access the upstairs window. The pyramidal tree also blocked a portion of the neighbor's Dutch Colonial where a construction dumpster stood in the front yard along with a *Honey, Stop the Car!* For Sale real estate sign. The second-floor windows offered an ideal view down between the houses.

He walked back around toward Baxter Street and cut across a vacant lot to the alley behind Palmer's house. A violin being played carried on the wind. The alley ran behind houses on Welker and the next street over, Waco.

On his immediate left, mountain bikes stood chained to a gate post. Next came Palmer's property enclosed with his privacy fence, then the Dutch Colonial with a cement mixer on wheels secured to a telephone pole. Woods blocked the far side of the alley. A hurricane fence laced with bamboo bordered a Waco Street house. A white vinyl privacy fence bordered the next house and the Baxter Street contemporary to his right.

He went to Palmer's, unlatched the gate, and crunched on the frozen pea gravel into the side yard where the snow was now covered with footprints. The path continued along a row of bare rose bushes against the privacy fence and cut between the impregnable waxy-leaved magnolia and the house corner. He looked at the compressor where the extension ladder lay before the police removed it, then up to the easy access to the second-story window.

Turning to the Dutch Colonial across the way he saw the papered-over second-level windows on either side of the chimney. A temporary debris chute extended out a rear window. No one saw Jerry on the extension ladder from up there. The house was under renovation and vacant. With a magnolia wall to block any street view and a vacant neighbor's house, Jerry and his accomplice could have taken their time on the ladder to jimmy the window open.

Back behind the house, he was about to enter Palmer's garage door when the violin stopped. He happened to glance up to the contemporary's wraparound windows. A woman with the instrument and a bow gazed down at him from her music stand.

&

Each time he rang the security-camera bell, two teenage boys in the front room at a large-screen video game ignored him. On his third attempt, a woman in warm-ups came down the stairs.

He heard her castigate the boys for being too lazy to get off the couch to answer the door. He introduced himself, handed her his card. She invited him out of the wind into the glass entryway and gave her name in accented English: Synnove Moller. Her red-dyed hair was pulled into a Jasmine ponytail.

"Even with the wind, I can tell you're an accomplished violinist," he said.

"The house belongs to your city's symphony for their art-ist-in-residency program. I am here with the boys through the end of the year." Freckles sprinkled her nose and cheeks. He thought she might be Scandinavian.

"Were you aware a man was killed in your neighbor's house?"

"Mrs. Rabasco called with the news while we were in Atlanta. She and her husband live across the alley."

"Did you speak with the police?"

"I told them when I practice I could see Mr. Giron come and go. He often worked late hours. Like me, he wasn't a sound sleeper. Lights burned in his house at odd hours. The police never said who died."

One of her boys interrupted to ask where she put her iPad.

"Another self-employed environmental engineer," Dom said.

"The last time we spoke, Mr. Giron asked what sights to see if he ever went to Norway. When I said the palace, he joked about his lack of royal knowledge. He got along with all the neighbors. His lady friend parked her truck in the alley on the nights she stayed over."

"How do you know it was her truck?"

"She doesn't have a tailgate," she said. "The police were already aware our homeless friends may have seen something. They often walk down the alley to the restaurant dumpsters at the South Kings Drive retail center."

Homeless people were behind Palmer's house?

"Did Palmer interact with them?"

"We all do. The Willoughbys, who owned the house under renovation before they sold to a builder, would even let them use their garden hose to clean up. Kip and Tally are never belligerent. Talley was Kipling's nickname for his friend because he played volleyball at university in Tallahassee, Florida. Mr. Giron's lady friend is the one who could use a lesson in manners. I watched from upstairs as she stumbled out of Palmer's back gate one morning. She surprised Tally, who carried plastic bags of food from his dumpster walk. I thought she was about to attack the poor man when Palmer rushed out in his pajamas. Tally's height might have intimidated her, but he wouldn't hurt anyone."

"How often were these homeless men in the alley?"

"They take daily walks back and forth. Kip is the more talkative one. Tally likes to stay to himself. They haven't been back since the man was killed in Palmer's house."

The one called Tally's volleyball height would allow him to see into Palmer's yard over the privacy fence. Dom wondered if on a dumpster-dive stroll he saw a couple of guys on an extension ladder.

"Do you know where I can find them?"

CHAPTER 41

The homeless camp was situated in a depression among pine trees on the backside of a detention pond, hidden from balconies at a nearby apartment complex. Trees swayed in the wind while Dom worked his way down the backside of the pond toward tents and lean-tos.

The first residents he came to were women at the entrance of an appliance box shelter. Their charcoal fire raged in a cracked ceramic-egg grill. One, with an Oakland Raiders hoodie cinched under her chin, sat on pallets and munched on french fries from a fast-food bag. The other poked coals with a golf umbrella.

"Good afternoon, ladies, can you point me toward Kip and Tally?" Dom said.

The one with the umbrella considered him with suspicion from under her straw hat. Paint blotches stained her too-big herringbone coat. "Who are you?" she said.

"Name's Dominick and I'd like to ask them a few questions."

"I told you he wasn't with the others," hoodie said.

"Don't, Tara," umbrella said.

"Mr. Dominick's cute," Tara said.

"You know better than anyone else how cute leads to trouble," umbrella said.

Cinders danced off coals from her umbrella jab.

"I only want to speak with them," Dom said.

"Other men have come into our upscale subdivision looking for our food foragers," Tara said.

"I'm not with those…" Dom said.

Umbrella cut him off. "Behind the tower." A flame quivered on the end of her umbrella, which she aimed toward the latticework of a five-story-high tension-wire tower farther back in the camp.

Other men?

He passed more fires and tree-strung tarps and tents with duct-tape seams. Razor wire coiled the tower's security fence. Trees grew closer together back here, and the air reeked of an open latrine fortified with chicken noodle soup and burned pine needles.

In a hammock beside a blue plastic wading pool propped up with PVC deck boards and silver wrap insulation, a guy in a goldenrod leisure suit snored. Dom could tell he didn't have the height to be able to look over Palmer's privacy fence. Chicken soup boiled in a coffee can on top of coat hangers supported by H-shaped pavers.

Dom tapped the guy's foot.

He jerked up and four empty peach whiskey miniatures clinked from the hammock. His blurry, bloodshot eyes tried to focus. "Never disturb a man's sleep, Mister."

Dom sensed a British accent. The guy steadied himself with his bare feet planted on the frozen ground.

"You Kip?" Dom said.

Another, shorter guy with his hands on his zipper cursed when he tripped into view from behind the wading pool.

The hammock guy yelled, "Run."

Dom almost caught him but tripped on the corner of a half-buried car battery. They dodged trees down toward a concrete stormwater sewer. Before the guy could disappear into a tunnel,

Dom grabbed his collar and sprawled with him on the ground. His eyes were white with fear, and smokeless tobacco blended with his sweet alcohol breath.

"Only want to talk, partner," Dom said.

"You're one of the space invaders."

The high pitch of his voice reminded Dom of a panicked choirboy.

"Where's Tally, Kip?"

"I'm not stupid, I know who you are. You're from the rainbow ship."

"Let's have a talk back at your place," Dom said.

✧

"Mr. Woodroof, meet Mr. Mundy," Kip said.

Mr. Woodroof hunched in unzipped short cowboy boots under a flamingo-dotted blanket at the fire. He belched while he stirred soup with a plastic salad spoon. Kip reclined on a portable chaise lounge. Dom settled on a cooler with a tree trunk backrest.

"Tell me about the lady with the red truck in the alley," Dom said.

"She should mind her manners," Mr. Woodroof said.

"Anger management is what she needs," Kip said. "Should I tell him about the rainbow ship and travelers?"

"Thrusters, not ship, rainbow thrusters. Remember, they spun like tops," Mr. Woodroof said. He slurped down a spoonful of noodles.

Dom shook his head when Kip offered him a miniature brandy from an airline carry-on bag. "Why were these space people here?" Dom said.

"Travelers, not space people," Kip said. He pawed through the airline bag.

"Because Tally saw the window repairmen on the ladder," Mr. Woodroof said.

"They jumped off the ladder and tried to catch Tally," Kip said.

"No one will catch Tally," Mr. Woodroof said.

"Describe these travelers who showed up here?" Dom said.

"Kip and I were over there at Charlie's place." Mr. Woodroof pointed with his spoon toward a lean-to strung by fallen trees. "We saw a miniature traveler—"

"The same rabbit Tally said who jumped off the ladder and chased after him," Kip said.

"Like I tried to say before the interruption, the rabbit went after Tally but lost him when he entered the tunnel," Mr. Woodroof said.

Kip's tobacco plug hissed when he flipped it into the fire.

"The mean traveler ripped into the rabbit when he came back without Tally."

"Mean one?" Dom said.

"With the white stick, which I figure he was about to hit the rabbit with because he didn't come back with Tally," Mr. Woodroof said.

Earl Jessup carried a white nightstick and Jerry Qwain with all his marathons ran like a rabbit.

"The rabbit have any hair?" Dom said.

"Wore a beanie on a shaved head," Mr. Woodroof said.

"He talked like he ran, real fast," Kip said.

"You only saw two of them?" Dom said.

"The one with a club, the rabbit, and another traveler with golden hair," Mr. Woodroof said.

"His hair styled into one of these?" Dom said. He ran his hand over his head to indicate Jorge's faux hawk.

"A strip of gold," Mr. Woodroof said.

Chico's Jorge, Jerry Qwain, and Earl Jessup.

"Where's Tally now?"

"Somewhere never to be found," Kip said. He twisted open and drained a Kahlúa.

Dom made his way up the detention pond's embankment. They still hadn't found any job Palmer worked on that they could connect to Earl Jessup, Jerry Qwain, or Chico's Jorge.

CHAPTER 42

Dom came into the conference room where Angie sat at the table with her paperwork and laptop computer. "I went to Palmer's house yesterday and met with his neighbor, who said homeless men use the alley to make their way toward restaurant dumpsters. She watched JoJo leave Palmer's early one morning and go off on one of the men when she came out the alley gate to her truck. I found their homeless camp. A dumpster diver told me three men showed up looking for his partner, who told him he saw two guys on Palmer's ladder. Two of the three who turned up at the camp were the ladder men, whose descriptions fit Earl Jessup and Jerry Qwain."

"How about the third guy?" Angie said.

"He sported a gold hair strip."

"Chico's Jorge?"

"His faux hawk fits the description. Being inebriated aside, the campers went on to describe the vehicle their visitors showed up in as a spaceship with rainbow thrusters. Who do we know who rides around in a light show?" Dom said.

"Chico Vega arrived at JoJo's rumble in a tricked-out kaleidoscope. Didn't your detective friend confirm he was in Jamaica when Jerry died?"

"JoJo and her cousin were, but the Patriots weren't. Chico goes under a microscope and we need to find the liquor house."

"Those Clean Water Action Committee fanatics who Babe's guards kicked off the shampoo plant property, I called their office. They didn't express much enthusiasm when I mentioned Palmer's topo. I thought we could take a drive to their office," Angie said.

CHAPTER 43

Deuce drove through housing developments, apartment communities, and retail centers on Iredell County's Highway 150 north of Charlotte.

Angie handed her phone back to Dom from the front seat. "Here's a picture of the client list Jerry kept on his desk. His office manager sent it to me."

Dom took the phone and saw an open notebook with penciled names written in impeccable penmanship. Most were LLCs, limited liability corporations. "Have you checked these clients against Palmer's?" he said.

"Not yet. Look at number four. Do you smell shampoo?"

He saw the initials TBP. "Tussey Beauty Products," Dom said.

"Babe told us she hired Jerry for her Mother Lode after Palmer was fired thanks to the problems he caused down at number four. What Babe called a 'confused situation,'" Angie said.

Dom handed the phone back. The dashboard GPS voice said turn at the next side street.

"Have you looked into these LLCs?"

"I only received Jerry's list before we left."

"Search for who's involved with these LLCs on the secretary of state's website. We might get lucky."

Past a locksmith shop they rolled into the parking of a mul-titenant metal building. C-WAC occupied the last unit next to a garage door company. Inside their empty lobby Angie took a card from the counter business card holder.

"A 501c3 nonprofit, cofounded by Stevie and Gus Radspinner," she said.

A fragile woman in jeans and a work shirt came through the warehouse door. Bobby pins held her argent hair in place. She wiped dirt off a wet spot on her sleeve with a paper towel. "Sorry, I didn't know we had visitors," she said.

"Stevie Radspinner?" Dom said.

"I am."

"We'd like a few minutes to talk with you about the Tusseys' shampoo plant and Palmer Giron," Dom said.

Before she could respond, Deuce opened the door for a man who, like Stevie, was well past his first Social Security check. He carried a backpack and a clear plastic bag with sandwiches.

"Gus, they want to talk about number four and Palmer," Stevie said.

"If you're associated with Jefferson Wallach, get out," he said.

"We're not connected with any lawyers," Dom said.

Gus's angry blue eyes went to Stevie, whose shrug telegraphed *what do you want to do?*

"We can use the worktable," he said.

Chemical-infused wet dirt permeated the warehouse. Shelves contained soil and water samples in small plastic containers with black magic-marker letters and screw-on lids. They sat on fold-out chairs at a gritty table near the utility sink.

"I gather Jefferson's not on your Christmas card list," Dom said.

"We don't mention his name around here," Stevie said.

"Because of number four?" Dom said.

"Because he's devoid of ethics," Gus said.

"Watch your blood pressure," Stevie said. She unrolled her veggie wrap.

"We understand you found environmental problems at number four," Dom said.

"The first family of shampoo played hide-and-seek with fifty-five-gallon drums," Gus said.

"A Tussey family member said we were mistaken when we asked about buried drums on the property," Angie said.

"Which Tussey?" Gus said.

"Babe," she said.

"Consider the source," Gus said. He quartered his Reuben with a plastic knife like a line cook with a bad attitude.

"She faulted a plumber who misread plans and buried a defective valve," Dom said.

"A story Wallach concocted. We wouldn't be here if her plant managers used new drums and not old, rusted ones," Gus said.

"Did you confront Babe?" Angie said.

"In her tennis club parking lot where she took a backswing at us," Stevie said.

"We're curious how you came to possess a topo map out of Palmer's Dever Multifamily report?" Dom said.

Stevie munched a pickle wedge. Sauerkraut splattered on Gus's wax paper.

"Anonymous information comes our way on a regular basis," he said.

"Is number four connected to Palmer being killed?" Stevie said.

"We're not sure, but his offices were burglarized by someone who we believe hoped to find a job file. The possibility exists they may have wanted what he found near the shampoo plant," Dom said.

"Tell them, Gus, the poor man's dead already," Stevie said.

Gus pinched off the last of his mayo on his potato chips, then he pushed back and went into the lobby. He returned with

a manila folder he handed to Dom. Inside, Dom found a pho-
tocopy of a topography map with a Flair pen-circled X between
the village of Wesley Chapel and the township of Sandy Ridge,
not far from a massive roof. "Backflow plus 347" was jotted and
underlined in the margin.

"Someone put the topo into our mailbox. X marks Babe's
buried treasure, three hundred and forty-seven feet from number
four's backflow preventer," Gus said.

Dom slid the topo to Angie. He tapped Dever Multifamily–
Giron Environmental Partners at the bottom of the page and the
circled X. The same mark from Palmer's tax map affixed to Augie's
Lost Souls Grotto with Tussey Center and Coldpepper identified.

"Did you call Palmer's office to tell him the topo showed up
in your mailbox?" Dom said.

Angie snapped a picture of the topo with her phone camera.

"Of course we did. He was irritated someone copied his
work," Gus said.

"Do you think it could be your mailman?" Angie said.

"From his reaction, no," Stevie said.

Gus ate a few mayo chips. "I took a volunteer of ours, Joel,
to walk off the three forty-seven. We ran our GRP, ground-pene-
trating radar, on top of the circled X and picked up a mass, a big
mass. When we were about to dig, Tussey guards with their white
billy clubs pulled up and escorted us off the property," Gus said.

"Tell them, or I will," Stevie said.

"Back at the truck, Joel realized in the guard commotion, he
dropped the topo. The next morning men walked in here and
demanded we turn over any material we had on number four."

"Who were they?" Dom said.

"We have no idea," Stevie said.

"I threw them out," Gus said. He traced more mustard on his
rye bread.

"A week later, our dock door's pried open and the office files are trashed. To our knowledge nothing was taken," Stevie said.

"You call the police? Dom said.

"They came and jotted notes, snapped pictures, dusted for fingerprints, and we've heard zero back from them," Gus said.

"These visitors, can you describe them?" Dom said.

"One talked and acted wired on energy drinks," Gus said.

"A tattoo covered the back of the hand of the one who threatened us with a club," Stevie said.

"What color was it?" Dom said.

"White," Stevie said.

"His tattoo a spiderweb?" Dom said.

"You know him?" Gus said.

"Bring up Jerry's website picture," Dom said.

Angie tapped open her phone screen.

"A third with size and muscles didn't talk. He stayed at the door with his arms crossed,"

Gus said.

"His diamond earrings were worth more than my wedding ring," Stevie said.

Chico's Patriot Francisco from JoJo's rumble and the YMCA gym, Dom thought.

Angie handed Stevie her phone. "He's the guy," she said.

Gus took the phone. "He couldn't keep his mouth shut," he said.

"Jerry Qwain, an environmental engineer like Palmer, who we found dead in Palmer's home office," Dom said.

"Thanks to Wallach, number four's shampoo production never stopped. When Joel snuck back on the property with our GPR, the drums were gone," Gus said.

⌇

They sped south on 77 through snow flurries in light traffic.

"Palmer's topo put Gus's radar on Babe's buried drums," Angie said.

"Enough motivation for her to want any information Palmer uncovered about her shampoo plant," Dom said.

"But the drums were gone when Gus's person went back on the property," Angie said.

"No drums, no problems," Deuce said.

"They'll be in another backhoed pit somewhere," Angie said.

"You don't scale the corporate ladder without being a crisis manager. I'm Babe, I'll call my Mother Lode environmental engineer onto my Bermuda grass carpet and demand to know how his topography map ended up in C-WAC's mailbox," Dom said.

A school bus almost cut them off with a quick lane change.

"And if you don't care for how he responds?" Angie said.

"Fire him," Deuce said.

"Jerry Qwain jumps at the chance to replace Palmer. If Babe asked her new engineer to collect documents Palmer might have in his offices, Jerry wouldn't hesitate to go along," Dom said.

"I have a hard time with a guy Jerry's size on an intimidation job inside Gus and Stevie's office," Angie said.

"With two backups, everyone's a tough guy," Deuce said.

"OK, I get Jerry could meet Earl from Babe's high-rise, but where does he pick up Francisco with the earrings and faux-hawk Jorge, who your homeless guy said was with Jerry in their camp?"

"Jerry's connected to Chico and his Patriots through the liquor house where Nickolas saw him," Dom said.

"Babe shares something in common with construction-equipment-pull-apart guy Manny Appino flush with his rental house money—a distaste for Palmer Giron," Angie said.

"We need to pay her another visit," Dom said.

"Not in her bee globe," Angie said.

"I'm curious how strong her backhand is," Dom said.

CHAPTER 44

Late Tuesday morning Angie came into Dom's office. "Babe's assistant said any further questions should be directed to their associate vice president of corporate communications."

"We've been demoted," Dom said.

"I called the family's tennis center and they said Babe plays every Tuesday and Thursday between eleven thirty and two."

✺

They were past 485's loop into townhouse enclaves, McMansion-lined cul-de-sacs, and apartment complexes with enough faux lakes to form their own lake district when Angie pointed ahead to an iron sign. "Tussey's version of paradise," she said.

On look-alike control tower supports the sign arched across the entrance road Mach Way into the estates of Joystick Hacienda. A Tussey guard with a white nightstick let them pass after Dom said they were here to watch Babe's power game. Every home site came with a hangar and an aviation name like Touch-And-Go, Zulu Time, and Crew Juice.

Through a roundabout they drove up to Serve Master Tennis and Racket's majestic sculpted hedges and frigid manicured grounds. Polar Explorer players braved near-zero temperatures on raised paddleball courts. Farther on, an immense air dome covered twelve tennis courts.

Inside the heated dome Dom saw Babe on a middle court. She grunted every time she crushed an out-of-bounds overhead past her partner's head, who guarded the net with crouched, pile-post-driver legs. Both were outfitted in atomic tangerine skorts, tops, and caps. Their hard court shoes and laces even matched.

"They're not here to hit and giggle," Angie said.

On the metal spectator stands Dom made sure to sit in Babe's line of sight. For a split second her eyes locked on his, then she continued to prowl the baseline like a tennis shop puma, with bent, cut arms and racket gripped and loaded. Her snow-white ponytail twirled through the back of her cap with every smash-and-snap volley.

The unfortunate opponents wore boysenberry tennis dresses with matching head- and wristbands—a tall woman with a condor's wingspan, and a spark plug who shifted from foot to foot with a steady stream of affirmations.

Against Babe's violent double backhands and her collaborator's rocket-launch serves, the Boysenberries never stood a chance. On one frenzied back-and-forth the yappy one contested Babe's dinked sideline shot that Dom thought no question the ball skipped out. The poor woman couldn't get a word in edgewise when Babe unleased her broadside with racket jabs a few inches from her nose. When Dom figured Babe might scale the net, her partner wrapped her arms around her and pulled her back.

Babe's next sledgehammer serve beaned her accuser and brought the game to an abrupt end.

When they approached Babe, Dom caught a whiff of her menthol muscle-relief cream. Babe drank from her water bottle and her partner rolled her bag toward the locker room.

"You have a wicked backhand," Dom said.

"Why are you here?" Babe said. She took two quick gulps.

"We have questions about number four's degreaser drums," Dom said.

"Did you not hear me when I said drums weren't the problem?"

"C-WAC's proprietors came to a different conclusion," Dom said.

"They're zealots with too much time on their hands." She rubbed her hair with towels from the bag.

"Why would someone slip Palmer's Giron's topography map into their mailbox with a bull's-eye on the spot to roll their ground radar?" Dom said.

"I have no interest in radar, deceased environmental engineers, or topo maps."

"The radar picked up a mass," Dom said.

"Think fifty-five-gallon-drum pyramid," Angie said.

Babe tucked a towel around her neck. "They're lucky they weren't arrested when they came onto the property."

"One volunteer came back and found the mass was no longer there," he said.

"After your truncheons hustled them away, your backhoe went into action," Angie said.

"Darling, I don't own a backhoe and my security team doesn't bother me with inconveniences." She fed rackets into her tournament bag. Dom figured she was ready for a strong backhand return.

"Another inconvenient situation took place when unannounced guests showed up at C-WAC with demands Gus and Stevie hand over any shampoo plant information," Dom said.

"Too bad they left empty-handed," Angie said.

Babe focused on the order of her rackets.

"Stranger still, their office is broken into like Palmer's home office where your Mother Lode environmental engineer, Jerry

Qwain, ended up on a closet rod. The description the C-WAC people gave us matches Jerry and your guard Earl Jessup for their unwelcome visitors," Dom said.

"Now I see why you're here." She zipped up her bag. "You think I sent Jerry because he's my environmental engineer."

"Who better than an environmental engineer to rifle through offices of a fellow engineer or a clean water group in order to remove any information about a toxic dump?" Dom said.

"Business must be slow if your focus is on errant topography maps," Babe said. She waved to a guy who entered the dome in a suit with his arm in a sling. Dom looked at his stringy silver hair.

"You know the key to being a successful CEO?" he said.

"I'm sure I'm about to hear."

"Delegation. You have to know how to pick the right people for the right job," Dom said.

The suit crossed the service box.

"We heard your former leasing agent caught a bad break with commissions she's owed from the time she leased Tussey Center. Four hundred grand goes a long way when you have toddlers to educate," Angie said.

"I don't owe Mercer Worthy a dime," Babe said.

Closer now, Dom recognized the hair length and tapered sideburns from Tussey Center's shovel ceremony: the law school-educated hit man Jefferson Wallach who Mercer Worthy called nasty and evil.

"Excuse the interruption," Jefferson said. A baritone voice of authority you could only hope for from your corporate fixer.

"You're not interrupting. We're done here," Babe said.

"I have the papers," Jefferson said.

Veins bulged on Babe's arms when she manhandled her bag over her shoulder and left with Jefferson toward the grill.

"He's the evil piece of work from the picture Mercer ID'd," Angie said.

On the way out, Dom watched Babe and Jefferson at a table near soft drink vending machines. Her eyes followed them out of the dome.

CHAPTER 45

DOM OBSERVED THE liquor house from Pia's minivan behind a vandalized construction trailer. Angie located the illegal after-hours booze joint set up in a model home not far from a Hindu temple on the backside of Charlotte Douglas International Airport. The nondescript split-level stood by itself in Serenity Heights, a bankrupt subdivision. Vehicles angled into vacant lots along Hal Tackenberry Court, named after the busted home builder.

Pia trained her telephoto lens on the house.

Dom watched bodies move to music behind closed blinds and thought about who would hand off Palmer's topo to C-WAC. Did a Dever employee with access to the report? Gus and Stevie said Palmer was irritated someone passed them confidential information. The reaction matched what they knew about Palmer being protective of his clients.

Women in short jackets and shorter skirts stepped out of a lunar blue Mercedes and tapped around patches of ice in their high heels up the driveway.

He could see why Babe let Palmer go. His company name appeared on the topo her security guard picked up after Gus and his volunteer were led away from number four. It nagged at him that Palmer was already off Babe's payroll. Why a circle around

Tussey Center on the tax map with Coldpepper and the Lost Souls Grotto identified? Could there be another one of those "confused situations" Babe mentioned?

Men exited the house to greet the women.

The porch light reflected off Jorge's gold faux hawk and Francisco's diamond ears. Pia squeezed off several pictures. After the women's handbags were checked, they all entered the house.

"Busy for a Thursday," Pia said.

Dom saw the lavender-illuminated underbody slow-roll down Hal Tackenberry Court, followed by four all-terrain vehicles and two dirt bikes. The light show came from Chico's Navigator they'd seen at JoJo's rumble. "Here comes the boss," Dom said.

The Navigator pulled to a stop on the driveway. The ATVs and bikes were left in the rounded cul-de-sac. Dom glanced at the dashboard clock: 1:58 a.m. Right on time for the bar rush. A pickup without a tailgate pulled in behind the Navigator. Angie had confirmed JoJo drove a truck, the same truck the homeless guy described.

"Here's JoJo," Dom said.

Pia pattered off more pictures.

JoJo gave Chico a hug. An older guy left a four-door midsize car parked at an angle and walked up to them. He exchanged greetings with Chico and JoJo like he knew them. With his back turned their way, Dom couldn't make out his face, but he did see shoulder-length hair and an arm in a sling. They disappeared through the front door. Jefferson Wallach had walked into Babe's tennis dome with an arm sling and hair in need of a trim.

If he's Wallach, why would he be in Chico's liquor house?

"I want a better look at the guy with the arm sling," Dom said.

Outside the minivan the early morning air was bone cold. A crescent moon and pinprick stars shone in Uptown's reflected light on the eastern horizon. Music thumped inside the liquor house.

He made his way around the trailer, between parked cars to empty lots across the court. Being careful to avoid infrastructure pipes left exposed when Hal's money ran out, he left the snow and went toward the crushed-stone run-off ditch along the property line. In a crouch, he moved along the crusty ditch to the back of the split-level and stole inside a utility shed in the backyard.

The tight space smelled of small engine oil, wood dust, and cases of empty liquor bottles. He wedged between a wheelbarrow and a lawn mower to see out the only window. Women in winter coats smoked on the patio. Bodies bumped and swayed to strobe-light music in the bonus room. A Patriot on security ambled up and started to chat up the women.

At the kitchen window he saw JoJo throw back a shot glass and enjoy a laugh with the arm-sling guy. He still couldn't get a clear look at the guy's face. A patron stumbled from the sliding glass door with the help of his lady friend and was sick near the garbage cans.

Chico appeared beside JoJo. Dom saw his angry reaction with a pointed finger aimed at the one-arm guy, who motioned with the palm of his good hand for Chico to calm down.

A guy with empty liquor bottle cases exited the mudroom and started toward the shed. He yelled at the security guy on the patio with the women to get a move on. Dom figured in less than a minute he'd be at the shed with his empties.

Dom slipped back out the rear door and prepared to hop into the ditch when the sweet smell hit him. Two guys shared a blunt in a cleared thicket patch across the ditch near the next property's fence line.

"Hey, you."

He took off along the frozen ditch and heard behind him more yells and a crash when the liquor box empties hit the ground. Someone slipped and went down hard in the ditch behind him.

He retraced his way behind the construction trailer and climbed back into the minivan.

"Let's go," he said.

Pia set the camera aside and fingered on a pair of leather gloves. Dom knew from experience a seat belt might be a good idea.

When lights flicked on ATVs and the dirt bikes, Pia punched back out from behind the trailer. They sped onto a country road under a flight pattern while a jet roared overhead. In a straight-away, one of the dirt bikes accelerated toward Pia's door. Bad idea, Dom thought. With a quick jerk of the wheel the minivan smacked the bike and driver into a snowbank. They tore into a blind curve. Out his window Dom saw sets of ATV lights cut through the woods.

"See our friends?" he said.

Pia replied by coaxing the minivan's speedometer higher. He saw where the ATVs were about to exit the woods and braced for impact. An instant before the off-road machines flew off the dirt road, the minivan launched into the construction site of a massive warehouse building.

One of the ATV drivers stomped the passenger side sliding door. Ahead of them Dom saw the trencher's hellish cup-hook chain Pia drove toward. When the driver turned his helmet forward, he slammed on his brakes and somersaulted off the ATV over the trencher and disappeared into a steel caisson-lined pit.

The next ATV came up on Pia's left shoulder and attempted to nose in front of them. With her dexterous wheel and brake work, she whirligigged the ATV into a row of Porta Johns.

Another all-terrain vehicle arched to a position ahead of them. Pia took a direct bead on the machine. The driver panicked and boosted forward out of control toward an asphalt lot paver into a stack of concrete-coated reinforcement bars.

Dom heard the dirt bike's whine when Pia flew up a ramp

into the open-sided 750,000-square-foot cross-dock building. Columns whizzed past them. She accelerated toward a tractor trailer drive-in door at the far end of the building. The bike mirrored them on the other side of the column line.

"Screwdriver," Pia said. She pointed to the canvas tool bag at his feet.

Dom pulled up a standard-size Phillips-head screwdriver.

"The twenty-two-inch if you please."

He came up with a tool used to reach hard-to-get-at engine screws.

"Heave toward the front tire when I say," she said.

Dom rolled down his window. The columns a blur, the building's end fast approached and the bike edged closer.

"Be ready, Dominick," she said.

The minivan accelerated toward the thirty-five-foot tilt-up concrete wall. At the last column she veered hard toward the bike. "Now, thanks."

His sideways toss hit its target. The mohawk-helmeted driver's attention deflected for an instant when the screwdriver clipped around his front spokes. Pia skidded sideways and stopped inches from the wall, reversed, and bulldogged the bike toward unfinished office space. Dom figured she intended to plant the Patriot into the improved space, but her abrupt stop jettisoned the bike and drove into a truck pit. By the time he saw the last ATV race along the length of the building, Pia floored the minivan out the oversize door.

They disappeared on the rear construction road.

"How about a cappuccino?" she said.

"I'll make mine a triple espresso," he said.

CHAPTER 46

T HE P ORSCHE WAS down the block from Kueentown Motorworks, pulled into a maintenance drive on a shipping container lot.

"I couldn't make out his face, but if you saw the hair and arm sling, your first thought would be Jefferson Wallach," Dom said.

"How would Babe's white-collar pit bull know where to find a liquor house?" Angie said.

"Jerry Qwain found the place, didn't he?"

"An arm sling's not much to go on," Angie said.

"JoJo was with him and Chico. She'll know who he is," Dom said.

Chico's showroom salesmen were busy for a Friday morning. One of them raised the hood of a Bugatti for a customer. A technician with a handheld computer revived a BMW inside one of the open service bays.

"How does Chico find a bankrupt subdivision for his liquor house?"

"See whose name is on the house in the tax records. My guess is you won't find Chico billed for property taxes." An Audi's driver parked and went inside the service department. "Make any headway with Jerry's client list?"

"I've started on his LLCs but haven't seen any matches with Palmer's clients," Angie said.

Truck exhaust mixed with breakfast biscuits from a food processing plant flooded in when she cracked her window to let in some fresh air.

A white diesel Super Duty drove onto the property and backed a car hauler trailer through an open bay door. *Kueentown Champion Transport* was advertised on the panel sides of the trailer and magnetic door signs on the truck. Two service technicians unhitched the trailer. The Super Duty rolled away and every roll-up door came down.

"Why advertise your company name without a phone number or website?" Angie said.

"And why close up shop?" Dom said.

The Super Duty's driver's side door opened and out came Jorge with his gold faux hawk. He disappeared inside the building.

"Isn't he the Patriot we saw at JoJo's rumble?" Angie said.

"Jorge, and we saw him at the YMCA basketball game and the liquor house."

"We haven't heard Chico was in the car-hauler business," Angie said.

"The guy's a serial entrepreneur," Dom said.

Ten minutes later, Jorge came out and got into the Super Duty. The roll-up door went up and he reversed so the trailer could be reattached.

Francisco with his diamond ears walked out of the service area and climbed in next to Jorge. The Super Duty drove away.

"Chico must have another garage somewhere," Angie said.

"We're about to find out," Dom said.

The trailer's red LEDs guided them through industrial side streets out to Rozzelles Ferry Road where a freight train thumped and squealed on a parallel track to the road. They followed a tile company's step van, which stayed close to the Super Duty. At South Hoskins Road the van turned. Out from under I-85's overpass, Dom saw the LEDs beyond an elevated railroad crossing whose lights flashed below a crossbuck sign. Candy-striped arms started to lower.

"You won't make it," Angie said.

Dom punched the gas and cleared the arms by a few inches.

The Super Duty disappeared into a snow shower. Before Dom lost visibility, he glimpsed metallic in his rearview mirror. When the snow lessened, they found themselves at Johnson C. Smith University. LEDs a number of blocks up ahead turned into a residential neighborhood.

Dom looked in the rearview mirror. "Check out our friend," he said. He nodded to the mirror. The same Triple Nickel Challenger from the Laphoons' parking lot and the one he'd tried to stop at Tussey Center was behind them.

"How long's he been back there?"

"Since before Johnson C. Smith."

They passed quadplexes where boys engaged in a snowball fight, then a broken-down bus being worked on by transportation department mechanics.

Dom cut across Freedom Drive's outbound traffic and caught the traffic light where the Super Duty turned. Angie glanced behind them. "The Challenger's still there."

When the light changed, Dom sped beneath another freeway bridge past construction sites and refurbished buildings in time to see the Super Duty's trailer disappear in a whirl of snow beside a multistory warehouse office building.

Angie's eyes were on her side mirror. "Our friend's not far behind," she said.

They turned onto the short dead-end street but didn't see the truck or the trailer. Angie pointed across acres of snow-swept gravel surface lot parking to a metal building. The LEDs glowed inside the building's open drive-in door.

At the end of the street, Dom pulled the Porsche into snow-drift ripples out of view of the Challenger between the car transport building's driveway and a less-than-thousand-square-foot one-story building. With the building for cover, they got out and went through shin-deep snow. A sign above the door read *Wick and Brew*.

Dom looked around the building corner and saw the Challenger slow-roll into view. "Go back around and step in front of our friend," he said.

Angie disappeared, and a few seconds later the Challenger's brake lights tapped on.

Dom picked up a half-exposed discarded fence post with a jagged ball of concrete attached to one end and came out at the Triple Nickel's rear end. Angie stood with her hands planted between the hood pins. He swung the post like a bludgeon from the Teutonic War through the Challenger's exhaust smoke and obliterated the brake light with the concrete ball. Next went the rear passenger's side window.

The driver popped open his door to get out. Dom saw the same turquoise ring and Smith & Wesson. An underhand swing brought the concrete into his left knee. The gun flipped out of his hand when he grabbed his knee and he let loose a four-letter-word torrent. Dom roof-planted the pole, retrieved the gun, and hauled the driver up by his flannel shirt. Agarwood beads were braided through his beard and a camo fleece beanie hid his forehead.

"I don't like being followed," Dom said.

The driver skipped with his knee in his cupped hands while he machine-gunned expletives.

Dom backhanded him on the side of the head. Angie started to pat him down. She found his wallet, flipped it open, and showed Dom.

"Jethro Contreras, Julian Ybarra's private investigator," Dom said. "Mr. Julian said his investigator would be brought in only if we dropped the ball."

"We must be butterfingers if we dropped the ball," Angie said.

Dom spread fingers in Jethro's blanched face. "Are we butterfingers?"

The response came back a whisper.

Dom kneed his cupped hands. "Come again?" he said.

Jethro through clenched teeth: "No butterfingers."

"Have we dropped any balls?" Dom said.

The S & W's bullets went into Dom's pocket. Jethro's heavy-lidded eyes followed his gun being tossed through his shattered rear window. "No dropped balls," he said.

"I'm confused then. What's your interest?"

Jethro steadied on one foot. "To find out what you know before Julian tells Mrs. Giron he wants to hold a news conference to level accusations against CMP why her son's killer hasn't been caught."

"When's his televised circus?" Dom said.

"No date yet."

"Tell your boss, we pick up on any more followers, his orthopedic surgeon better be on speed dial."

Dom tossed the fence post through the shattered window after the S & W.

CHAPTER 47

Monday afternoon, Winnie stopped Dom when he came into the building. "She left two hours ago in the SUV and I can't reach her on her cell phone," Winnie said.

Dom stood at her reception desk. "I told Franco not to give her his keys again," Dom said.

"He wouldn't deny Angie," Winnie said.

"We won't be going on any more bar hunts," Dom said. "Let me know if you reach her."

Angie knew the consequences if she went dark on them again.

Dom went in Jock's office to talk about the architect Jock selected to design the additional offices he planned to add onto the building. When he came back into the reception area, he saw Angie.

"Her phone was dead," Winnie said.

He looked at Angie's dark screen she held up, relieved he wouldn't have to ask her to pack up and leave. "Remember the parking lot receipt from Palmer's pants?"

"Bill Eversole showed us," Dom said.

"You'll want to see where the lot's located."

She used the Porsche's charger to juice up her phone while she guided Dom through the city onto Morehead Street near the NFL stadium, under the light at South Cedar Street, and down past the short street with Wick and Brew's small building where Jethro met the fence post. "Turn here, those are my tracks," she said.

He made an immediate right past the several-story renovated warehouse onto a surface lot for hundreds of game day cars. Two sets of tire tracks, one in, one out, traced through the vast snow-field. The control arm angled up after he retrieved the ticket, and he followed her SUV tire tracks to where they stopped out in the middle. Wind sandblasted snow around them. Straight ahead, on the adjacent property, stood the car transport building.

She handed him her phone with the charger cord still attached. "The receipt Palmer's dry cleaner found," she said.

Dom saw fifty-three minutes stamped beside the date, twelve-dollar amount, and the lot's partial West Morehead Street address.

"Check the time and date."

"June fourteenth," he said.

"Palmer was here two and a half weeks before his murder. Irwin Creek runs along the freeway embankment behind Chico's building. Irwin Creek's the Irwin from his sticky note and the waterway we've heard he stressed about," she said.

Dom looked over his shoulder to the warehouse and the Office Space for Lease sign. "He may have been here to meet with one of those office tenants."

"Why pay to park out here when the building has free park-ing?" she said.

"We don't know of a customer in the area from Ms. Ruby's bag?"

"Only Babe's Mother Lode, which is back past the bridge among all those buildings."

"But she fired Palmer," he said.

"Which leaves us with a torn receipt and Irwin Creek fifty yards away."

He plowed forward toward a limestone-boulder property barrier. "Let's look around," he said.

They trudged onto the car hauler's property. Wind howls competed with freeway traffic. Dom figured the metal building measured fifteen-thousand square feet under a twenty-foot-high roof.

"Not much advertising," Angie said.

On the front locked door, Kueentown Champion Transport's dime-size stick-on letters weren't in line. They looked inside through the only window. Dom saw a single desk in an empty office with a few potted plants in one corner.

"I see the trailer," Angie said.

Through an open interior door, the car hauler trailer sat in the warehouse-skylight gloom.

They tracked through drifted snow around to the drive-in door tall enough to handle a semitruck rig. On the backside Angie found another personnel door locked. Landscaped railroad ties separated the next property, a narrow lot used for more parking. At the overgrown creek embankment, Dom looked down the steep slope through naked bushes and scrubs. Ice-crusted riffles covered Irwin Creek.

Now why would you be on a Morehead Street lot near a building Chico Vega used?

The downshift from a freeway tractor trailer reverberated off the metal building. Snow blew sideways along the impassable creek toward a tunnel dozens of yards away under Morehead Street where the freeway crossed overhead.

"Do you smell that?" Angie said.

Dom caught a brief whiff of bad eggs soaked in vinegar, gone now on the wind. "May have come from the industrial area upstream past Third Ward."

"What's Palmer's interest in a public waterway?" Angie said.

"Something brought him over here. Let's go meet the neighbors."

Back in the Porsche, headlights swept across them from Wick and Brew. A woman in a fur-lined parka came out of a pickup truck and unlocked the building, followed by man with a ball cap under a sweatshirt hoodie.

Dom parked next to the pickup and happened to glance up as he stepped out. Strapped ten feet up a telephone pole was a game camera. Angie saw the box too. "Not the place I'd expect wild turkeys," she said.

The interior's aroma was a curious mix of coconut lilac and fresh-brewed butterscotch coffee. The guy in the ball cap stood from his fold-out chair, and a few white-chocolate-covered coffee beans spilled from his plastic snack bag and bounced on the polished cement floor. "We're closed," he said.

His cheeks and neck were matted gray stubble. *Panama City* in light coral on the cap. Behind him were shelves of bagged coffee, an elaborate coffee maker, and clear-wrapped glass candle containers. The woman came out of the bathroom, her oversize sweater adorned with green Christmas trees.

"I told them we were closed," the guy said.

"Don't be rude, Layton. I'm Franky Sparkman. Would you like a fresh coffee?"

They accepted her offer and Dom gave her his card. "We'd like to ask about your neighbor," Dom said.

"Is Arlo in trouble?" Layton said.

"No trouble, we're curious about his deliveries," Dom said.

"We've never met the man," Layton said.

"He doesn't put in many hours," Frankie said.

"I'd like to have his job," Layton said.

"A few times a month we see his truck and one of his two trailers comes and goes."

"He has another trailer besides the car hauler?" Dom said.

"An elliptical tank he pulls with weed killer in the summer and snow removal chemicals in the winter," Frankie said.

Butterscotch floated from their coffee mugs.

"Tell them the odd part," Layton said.

"The transparent tank is always a quarter full whether they come or go. The amount never varies," Frankie said.

"How long has your business been here?" Dom said.

"We purchased the property three years ago," Frankie said.

The phone rang and Frankie told a customer they opened at 1 p.m.

"Arlo's been your neighbor ever since?" Dom said.

"His building was here when we bought our place," she said.

"Have you seen what's inside the car hauler?" Dom said.

"No idea, the dock door's always closed," Layton said.

Dom sipped his coffee. Too much butterscotch. "Have you met a guy named Chico Vega?"

"Who's he?" Layton said.

"Someone Arlo works with," Dom said.

"The only person we've spoken with is one of the drivers. He rolled down his window to tell us to get our garbage can off their property. A big guy with earrings," Layton said.

Francisco drives too.

"If he's your Chico, he's a nice neighbor," Layton said.

"Why a game camera on your pole?" Angie said.

"If punks try to break in again, we have them on camera," Layton said.

"We saw a guy last week take our discarded fence post," Frankie said.

Dom picked up on Angie's grin. "Your camera view take in Arlo's driveway?" Dom said.

"All the way to the other parking lot," Layton said.

"Mind if we scroll through your images?" Dom said.

Layton shook his head no to Frankie.

"Of course, you can. Layton planned to climb up and check the batteries anyway," Frankie said.

"Won't be until tomorrow," Layton said.

Frankie looked at Dom's business card.

"We can drop them off at your office when we take Layton's son and daughter to their mother's."

"Have you ever picked up any odd smells?" Angie said.

"We stopped being surprised what blows on the wind through here," Frankie said.

"The worst was the cat pee when I fished last summer," Layton said.

CHAPTER 48

A WEATHER GLAZE event covered the city for the next seventy-two hours. Out-of-state utility trucks joined local crews to restore power in every enameled zip code. Once the cloister's power came back on and Dom confirmed the Sisters didn't need any food or supplies, he made his way to the office.

His building was still without power, but a gas-powered generator ran next to Deuce's tiny rear building. A bouquet of sauteed onions, peppers, and garlic flooded out when he opened the door. Deuce stabbed at the potbelly stove with a poker, and in the kitchen Angie swayed with a spatula to the clock radio's "Ain't Too Proud To Beg" by the Temptations.

"In time to eat," Deuce said.

"Lucky someone stocked the refrigerator before the ice show," Angie said.

"We have a generator now?" Dom said.

"Got the last one," Deuce said.

"Make sure Winnie reimburses you. What's on the menu?" Dom said.

Dom settled into one of the leather club chairs and took the glass of white wine Deuce offered him.

"Korean skillet chicken bulgogi," Deuce said.

Angie lowered the flame and the Temptations, and joined them.

"Tell him the good news," Deuce said.

"I found our Coldpepper before the tax office was knocked offline. Chico's liquor house is held in an entity called Coldpepper I 2784 LLC, which happens to be the Hal Tackenberry Court street number. The secretary of state lists a Sally Meagers for the only name attached to the LLC. She's a notary with a print, copy, and fax mailbox shop in a building lobby near Uptown. When I clicked her name, several more LLCs appeared where she's the sole member agent. One is a Coldpepper II 815. Ring any bells?"

"Jog my memory."

"Eight fifteen's the address for Chico's car lot. Kueentown Motorworks sits on a property owned by Coldpepper II 815 LLC."

"The notary's on both Chico's LLCs?" Dom said.

Deuce poked at the fire, then settled back into his recliner with his wine glass.

"On both of them," Angie said. "I also found she's the contact for Kloudcatcher LLCs I, II, III, and IV. Those entities were put together for Babe Tussey when she assembled Tussey Center's site. Palmer may have written Coldpepper with a question mark next to Babe's circled skyscraper on the tax map because he came to the same conclusion about Sally Meagers."

"And the X'd off and circled Lost Souls Grotto on the same tax map?" Dom said.

"I'm not sure why he identified Augie's geothermal spring," Angie said.

"Maybe for a point of reference," Deuce said.

"I do know those LLCs have mail sent to PO boxes in Sally's shop. Her address is the same office building with a reinsurance company, an ad agency, a payroll outfit, a couple of technology start-ups, and a number of law firms," Angie said.

She went back to stir the skillet.

"Ready for the kicker?" Deuce said.

"On the top floor with the best city view sits the esteemed Stoll, Chatham, Ostrow, Wallach and Lacfold," Angie said.

"Jefferson Wallach's outfit?" Dom said.

"The same PLLP where he runs herd over dozens of Juris Doctor degrees. I asked myself, would Sally have occasion to meet a silver-haired member of the bar with a bum arm?"

Deuce topped off her wine glass when she came back.

"And what answer did you give yourself?" Dom said.

"I gave SCOWL a call."

"SCOWL?" Dom said.

"My wordplay for Stoll, Chatham, Ostrow, Wallach and Lacfold. I figured like truck stops, Big Law never sleeps, ice storms or no ice storms. I was right. When I asked the receptionist to connect me to Coldpepper and Kloudcatcher's contact person, she put me on hold. The jolt came after a long wait when the word-slinger himself boomed on the line."

"She jolted," Deuce said.

Wood popped and cracked in the fire.

"I thought superlawyers like Jefferson Wallach never answered their own phones," Angie said.

"You think he's tied into Chico and Babe's properties?" Dom said.

"Why else would he make the effort to lift up the receiver and bark, 'who are you?' I hung up before he could bark again. I'm no expert on law firms, but I thought upper-echelon legal talent only punched the clock when a gravy train pulled into the station with an IPO or headline business merger. Why would Jefferson Wallach stoop to second-rate LLC work a trainee could handle?"

"Billable hours are billable hours," Deuce said.

She went back to the skillet. "I get why he's attached to Babe

Tussey's Kloudcatcher. He's her corporate lawyer. But how does a northside hood with a car lot and an after-hours illegal liquor joint end up on the billable worksheet of a seven-hundred-dollar-an-hour attorney?" Angie said.

"Perhaps they share the same lunch club," Deuce said.

"Say I'm Chico out to expand my business footprint and settle on two new lines of business not dependent on high-maintenance car owners," Dom said.

"Money streams like Rushers and nontaxed whiskey?" Angie said.

"Smart operators know how to cross-pollinate customers. Every business needs sharp lawyer work. Chico asks a high-net-worth car client who their legal rope-a-dope pro is and hello Jefferson Wallach," Dom said.

Deuce took the wine bottle and topped off both his and Dom's glass. "Lawyers aren't picky," he said.

"Explain how Jefferson puts Chico into a piece of property in a bankrupt subdivision under a flight path?" Dom said.

"All bankruptcies have what in common?" Angie said.

"Sleepless nights," Deuce said.

"Sympathetic lawyers who hand-hold business owners about to go under. You know who babysat Hal through his liquidation? SCOWL's bankruptcy department. Jefferson would have firsthand knowledge about a smart real estate play near the airport that could be scooped up for pennies on the dollar. Let's eat." She started to remove plates from the cupboard.

CHAPTER 49

A DAY AND a half later, with the power back on in his building, Dom read on JoJo's Tabberson and Associates profile how she prided herself in being an early riser. He thought before sunrise might be the ideal time for some answers.

Six fifty-eight the next morning, he came out the second-floor elevator into her employer's darkened lobby. Through the glass door behind the empty reception desk, he saw lights burning in the cubicle farm.

The other elevator's doors pinged open, and a man stepped out with a grande coffee who considered Dom through wire-rimmed glasses. "We're open at eight thirty," he said. His Stormy Kromer plaid cap pushed up on his forehead.

"Tell JoJo Chico's here," Dom said. He didn't wait for a reply and went into the guest telephone room.

Moments later, JoJo opened the door in her burgundy pantsuit with a short-lived smile. The spiky hair replaced with a slicked-back look. Heavy liner under her eyes. Dom at the small room's telephone side table.

"You people need to stop with the harassment."

"You a big fan of *Jeopardy*?" he said.

"What?"

She looked down at him from halfway out the door.

"You know, the game show where players rack up easy money being quick with an answer."

"I'm in the middle of a project."

"Here's an easy one. What rose do an AutoCAD operator and Brenda Wick have in common?"

JoJo looked at him with no answer.

"New Dawn, where you met Palmer," he said.

"Her organization helped me through a rough period. Palmer was part of Brenda's business outreach team. We started up after I left."

"You mean after Brenda showed you the door for prescription pills."

"The staff knew they weren't mine."

"We also know about your corrections department staycation."

"Staycation is a reach."

"Did Palmer know?"

"Of course, I told him. He knew I had a job here thanks to someone I met in the reading program."

He could hear New Dawn's Brenda Wick say truth wasn't JoJo's strong suit.

"Be ready quick. What's another name for Hal Tackenberry's model?"

She flinched when he slapped the table.

"What's a liquor house?" Dom said.

From the look she gave him, he knew JoJo didn't know whether to stay or leave.

"Habitat questions always trip me up. Like, what nocturnal creatures can be found under flight paths?"

He snapped the lamp on and slid an unfolded printout toward her. She glanced in the circle of light to Pia's photograph of her with Chico out front of the liquor house.

"What are party animals? Chico's Twenty-Eighth Street Patriots."

"They work security." She pulled the door closed when people exited the elevators behind her.

"Palmer turns up on Hal Tackenberry with his brother Nickolas because you haven't responded to his calls or text messages."

"They found me, we left, big deal."

"But we were told you never met Nickolas."

"Call it too much to drink in the liquor house."

"Like another boozy night in a Mexican food place where you tagged Jerry Qwain. We were told the only time you two ever saw each other. Nickolas noticed a guy who fit Jerry's description in the liquor house with you and Chico."

"He was at the blackjack table. Jerry was addicted to booze and card games."

"Remember he's dead, we found him in Palmer's closet. What did Jerry mean in the liquor house basement?"

She leaned both hands on the chair back. Tape bound her pinkie and fourth finger together under her LOVE knuckles. "I didn't hear him. The music was loud and the game tables were crowded."

Being smooth was another reason Brother Rocko and Brenda weren't JoJo fans.

"I thought he was beside you when he referenced 'serious Uptown people.'"

"I have no idea who his serious people were. Jerry was a creep, always edged in on your personal space. Palmer couldn't stand him."

"How about the elbow he gave Chico after he made the comment? An elbow like they were in on a secret?"

"Chico doesn't like being touched."

"Jerry happen to bring up Welker Street?"

"If he did, I didn't hear him. I have no idea why he was in Palmer's house."

"Was the liquor house Jerry and Chico's only involvement, or did they have another business arrangement?"

"Chico never talks work with me. Look, I'm sorry I forgot to mention I saw Jerry in the liquor house."

"And forgot about being in New Dawn and prison. Next I'll hear you're clueless how Chico makes his money."

"The after-hours club and Kueentown Motorworks are all I'm familiar with."

"You left out Rushers."

Without hesitation, she said, "Chico into go-go juice… no way."

Dom sensed her being genuine. Maybe genuine was a prison-honed skill. "Then you've heard of Rushers?"

"Work around these buildings long enough, you'll hear about Uptown Rushers."

"Chico surrounds himself with people he can trust. People with dope sales on their résumé who could move high-octane ice into skyscrapers."

"I would never jeopardize the second chance my boss gave me."

"You know Palmer went to New Dawn thanks to Rushers?"

"You don't have to tell me." She pulled the chair back and sat.

"Work pressures kick him off the wagon, or being in a JoJo yo-yo relationship too much to handle?"

"He needed help. What else mattered?"

"Chico might get testy if someone tried to get between his product and a top producer saleswoman."

"Palmer would have told me if Chico ever paid him a visit. The liquor house was the one and only time they ever met. Don't you think I would know if my cousin had something to do with methamphetamines?"

He unfolded the printout Mercer Worthy had looked at on the playground and pushed it toward JoJo's knuckle-art hand. Babe Tussey was front and center in a silver-shovel line of white hard hats at Tussey Center's groundbreaking. With a soft show of affection, JoJo ran her taped fingers next to the crease on Palmer. If she was being real, Dom thought her thespian chops were on full display.

"See tapered sideburns in the seersucker suit?"

"Him?" She tapped a guy with sterling hair at the portable bar. The same one who Mercer called evil.

"Ever see him before?"

Dom pushed a second printout Pia snapped at the liquor house of JoJo, Chico, and the same guy, only now with a bum arm and his head turned from the camera.

"He looks like Mr. Dobbins, who Chico said made his money in the paper business," JoJo said.

"Paper baron Mr. Dobbins is Jefferson Wallach. Babe Tussey's corporate hatchet man who set up LLCs for Chico's car lot and liquor house," Dom said.

She picked up the printout for a closer look. "Babe Tussey and Chico share the same lawyer? The only legal reference Chico ever made was good lawyering came at a price."

Dom felt his cell phone vibrate.

"On the subject of Babe, ever have the occasion to meet her?"

"No, but Palmer worked for her once before she fired him."

He slid a third printout, a picture of Dever Multifamily's phase one topo Gus and Stevie came to possess. "Ever see this Dever topo before?"

She looked at the topo and avoided his eyes.

"Tussey guards chased environmental activists off their shampoo plant property and found Palmer's topo. The circle and X indicate where Palmer thought degreaser drums were buried."

"He didn't think, he knew what the Tusseys were up to." Her eyes never left the topo.

"We're curious how a phase one topo ends up in C-WAC's mailbox. We figure Palmer for a professional who'd never share clients' work."

"Typical Tussey move, find the cheapest solutions, use rusted drums to bury their problem. They never thought they'd get caught. Palmer had an assignment for another of Babe's high-profile developments at the time…"

"The Mother Lode?" Dom said.

"The golden girl of real estate's with a Gold District development. Palmer told Babe what he found on number four's property. He thought she might want to know her plant managers may have hidden a problem they didn't want her or her family to know about. She gave Palmer her all-concerned look and thanked him and said she'd look into the situation. When she didn't lift a finger, Palmer knew Babe ignored him. He felt his hands were tied because of his Mother Lode work. So I decided I would slip a copy of the unfinished report's topo into the Radspinners' mailbox with a note to check out what the Tusseys were up to. I was familiar with their work from another job my firm collaborated on where they stopped a regional mall development after they found the project manager bulldozed a bog turtle habitat."

She ran her fingers with affection along Palmer's image again. "Babe confronted Palmer with the topo. She didn't believe him when he said he wouldn't share client information like a document out of Dever's phase one. She let him go anyway."

"Was he aware you delivered the topo?"

"He thanked me."

"Your postal delivery got him fired."

"It ate at him that Babe never lifted a finger, those drums stayed put and leaked degreaser. Typical of Palmer, do right over money."

"Jerry Qwain picked up the Mother Lode work after Palmer was shown the door."

"There's a guy who never shied away from a paycheck or compromised situation."

Dom reached over and tapped Wallach on the liquor house picture. "Weren't you in the kitchen with them?"

"How do you know? Were you on the patio?"

"The toolshed beside the weed whacker. I saw the tension between Wallach and Chico."

"Chico said Mr. Dobb… Jefferson shorted him on his last payment."

"Payment for what?"

"Merchandise Jefferson said his client would make up for with an overpayment on the next delivery."

"The client mentioned?"

"A disturbance outside cut their conversation short."

Dom figured his drainage ditch run for the ruckus.

A thought bothered him: did CEO Babe know her legal counsel associated with an after-hours illegal liquor house operator?

"Did Palmer ever mention Irwin Creek or Coldpepper?"

"The confidentiality reasons, he could never tell me who he worked for or what he worked on."

"How about the argument the night you took off for the liquor house?"

She rubbed Palmer at Tussey Center's grand opening and looked at him through swimming-pool eyes. "We fought because I wouldn't commit to a date." She pulled a gold chain and a diamond tension engagement ring out from around her neck and handed it to him. "Our wedding."

Dom saw engraved inside *PG Always*.

Mascara smeared when she wiped away tears with the palm

of her hand. He went into the lobby and brought back a box of tissues from the reception desk.

"I said yes every time he asked but couldn't commit to a date. Not only did we fight over our wedding date the night of the liquor house, but we argued about my fear he'd walk out on me because of my lifelong obsession with bad decisions. Now I live with his ring around my neck and regret I hurt such a wonderful man." She folded the tissue into a rectangle. "You want to hear what type of man he was? One night I found him at his computer with the home page up for a neighborhood soccer team. He said the team would be perfect for our son or daughter."

"Ms. Ruby know you were engaged?"

"He wanted to tell her, but we agreed to wait until we figured out a date." She used the rectangle on her eyes and cheeks. "I called him before he left his office the night he was murdered to tell him Easter Sunday was the perfect day for a wedding."

CHAPTER 50

Dom looked up to Tabberson's second-floor windows before he drove off. Brenda Wick and Rocko's opinion of JoJo's rubbery sense of the truth aside, he accepted she didn't have anything to do with Rushers. Chico, he thought, might be another story.

He remembered his cell phone had vibrated and saw the voice message and hit play. "Mr. Mundy, Bill Eversole from Palmer Giron's building. A fax came in I thought you might want to see."

The time was 8:16 in the morning. He could swing by East Boulevard on his way to the office.

❧

Bill Eversole came down the hallway when Dom rapped on the glass door. "You're fast," Bill said.

"I was close by when I got your message," Dom said.

Bill took several papers from the lobby copy/fax machine. "These were here when I came in. A data analytical report for samples Palmer sent for evaluation. The company misplaced his order."

Dom saw the letterhead: *Environmental Structured Research Labs, Columbia, Missouri.* "How late are they?" he said.

Bill showed him the request-for-service date on the front page. "He placed his order June twentieth last year."

A little over a week before he was murdered.

"Palmer would never stand for such a late response. He was too impatient to put up with tardy people."

Dom leafed through the test sample results of chemical hieroglyphics, graphs, and charts only an environmental engineer would understand. When he came to the second-to-last page, he stopped at the name near the bottom of the page. "Can I have a copy?" Dom said.

"Take that one," Bill said.

CHAPTER 51

DOM SAW THE photographs Angie displayed on the wall-mounted conference room flat screen.

"From the Sparkmans' game camera," she said.

"They took their time," Dom said.

"Medical emergency with Layton's father at the beach set them back several days."

Dom saw Wick and Brew's windows, snow-blanketed parking spaces, and partial tire tracks on Chico's car transport driveway.

"Been through them twice. No pictures of the Super Duty or car hauler."

"I stopped by Tabberson Associates on my way in and spent a few minutes with JoJo. She said Chico didn't involve her with his businesses."

"Brenda Wick and Brother Rocko wouldn't believe a word she says," Angie said.

"I believed her. She's not connected to Rushers. When I asked her if Palmer told her about Irwin Creek or Coldpepper, she said he respected his clients' confidentiality and never shared their names or jobs."

"I can't wait to hear what she said about the night Palmer was in the liquor house with his brother." She clicked the pictures off the screen.

"Between too much to drink and the basement noise she didn't recall an 'Uptown serious people' comment."

"Did you ask her about the argument with Palmer?"

"It had to do with their wedding date."

"He popped the question to her?"

"I saw the engagement ring with his inscription she wears around her neck."

"What's there to argue about a wedding date?"

"The problem she said was her not being able to commit. Her fear about the poor choices she's made held her back. On the night Palmer was murdered, she rang him before his bike commute to tell him Easter Sunday's a great day for a wedding."

"And you believe her?"

"JoJo was being up front with me. I saw the vulnerable side Palmer fell for."

"You realize without JoJo, we can't get to her cousin?"

"With or without her, we stay on Chico Vega." He handed her the fax. "Insurance man Bill Eversole rang me. Palmer received these water sample results eight months after he sent them in, less than two weeks before he died."

She flipped between the pages. "I don't see a client name."

"Because there isn't one. Check the bottom of the second-to-last page."

She skimmed down the page, then looked up at him. "Irwin Creek?"

"Look at the sample collection site," Dom said.

Exhibit A's map was marked up with arrows where Palmer drew his samples.

She set the fax aside and typed on her keyboard. A Mecklenburg County tax office map came up on the flat screen. She scrolled to the junction of Morehead Street, I-77 South, and Irwin Creek. "The arrows are here," she said. Her cursor circled next to a street called Radio.

"Scroll right," he said.

The creek emerged out from under Morehead into a dense tree canopy. With her next sideways move, he saw Irwin snake along expansive gravel lots and the steep freeway embankment. He went to the screen and put his finger on the only rooftop, Chico's metal building. "Here," he said.

With a cursor click, county property tax information populated the screen. The property owner: Coldpepper 914 LLC.

"I don't know how I missed another Coldpepper," she said.

"A Chico Coldpepper papered up by Jefferson Wallach a hundred yards from Palmer's sample site," he said.

⚜

They drove away from his building into Thursday's late afternoon gloom and flurries. Angie held Palmer's fax report open to the results section.

"I told the testing lab contact person about the eggy vinegar odor and cat pee the Wick and Brew guy smelled. She said these chemicals are what you would find in marine fuel; sodium peroxide goes by another name, lye; the traces of red phosphorous can be used to manufacture road flares; and salt is, well, salt. Combine them with the odors, and the lab said you might have a meth lab in the area."

"She have a client name?" he said.

"Palmer never shared who he worked for."

"Suspicious odors downstream from Chico's warehouse. We need access to his building. He may have more than a car trailer and elliptical tank in there."

He came out from under Highway 77's bridge and made an

immediate left alongside Irwin Creek onto Radio Street next to a building. They stood above the waterway at a county Adopt-a-Stream sign with the name of a volunteer group. Freeway traffic loud along here, he thought. A cast iron pipe on supports spanned the river and disappeared into each embankment. Wind howled out of the tunnel.

"The arrows are there," Angie said. She aimed the rolled-up fax pages to Palmer's sample site between the pipe and tunnel entrance.

"And we have no idea who hired him?" Dom said.

"Before we left, I checked again and didn't see any mention of an Irwin Creek assignment in what Ms. Ruby gave us."

Dom watched snow channel along the ice. Did Palmer know methamphetamines were being produced nearby?

CHAPTER 52

THEY PASSED THROUGH streetlight pools on South Summit Avenue into Third Ward on Fourth Street. Blocks away, charcoal-ash clouds smothered sky lobbies and penthouses in Uptown's high-rent district.

They left the Porsche near townhouses close to Frazier Park and with turned-up collars leaned into lateral snow on Irwin Creek's greenway. The wind was fresh and clean with no hint of vinegar, eggs, or cat urine.

Around a curve near Chico's building, Dom saw another Adopt-a-Stream sign posted with Piedmont Cloggers, the same volunteer group from two hundred yards downstream through the tunnel. Vehicle lights raced along the freeway above them.

"Give these stream volunteers a call. See if they're aware of any smells or chemicals being dumped along here," Dom said.

Angie snapped a picture of the sign with her cell phone. They picked their way up a short incline onto a narrow rectangular lot under fresh snow next to Chico's building. Railroad ties and unkept shrubs separated the two properties. They tried Chico's front door again with no luck.

"How do we get inside?" Angie said.

"Retired cat burglar Franco might have some ideas," Dom said.

They retraced their steps back onto the rectangular lot when a metal chain rattled and the drive-in door started to rise. Dom and Angie took cover behind tall shrubs. Twin mufflers rumbled to life and powerful high beams blazed from inside the warehouse. The Super Duty nosed out into view with another magnetic door sign with no phone number or website, *Kueentown Champion Ice and Snow Removal.* Blue LEDs glowed from the bed rim, cargo box, and underbody. Darkened windows hid the driver. Hooked up to the truck, a two-axle trailer loaded with a snow sweeper, dual-stage snow blower, several snow shovels, and a three-quarters-empty transparent white elliptical tank with a hose wheel mounted on a skid assembly.

"Chico changes companies like lunch specials," Angie said.

"Frankie and Layton Sparkman said they never saw any change to the amount of liquid in the tank," he said.

The mechanical drive-in door came down. The blue lights disappeared behind a row of buildings. In dusk's snow-blurred distance, high beams and multicolor roof running lights on another pickup truck cut across a street near the stadium.

Dom was about to turn to go back to the Porsche when the Super Duty reemerged on the same cross street. The two trucks were about to pass when whoever was inside the Super Duty popped on the rest of the light package. Rainbows dazzled from the wheel wells. The other truck flicked high beams in acknowledgment. Once they passed, the rainbows went off.

⁂

Angie braced herself when Dom's Porsche rooster-tailed away from the townhouses.

"Those look like rainbow thrusters to you?"

"I thought Chico's Navigator lavender underbody was the homeless camp spaceship?" she said.

"His wheel wells don't glow rainbows. The Super Duty was in the camp."

They shot up Victoria Avenue. At Johnson and Wales University they scanned for blue lights through the snowstorm.

"Which way?" Angie said.

Straight took them past the baseball stadium into Uptown where they saw no sign of the Super Duty. He cut left between a block-long condo building and an office complex. At Fifth Street, they still didn't see the LEDs. He swung right underneath a viaduct and went past Old Settlers' Cemetery populated with three-hundred-year-old graves. Next, they were into Uptown's glass-and-steel canyons.

He accelerated through Tryon Street's yellow-to-red lights and rounded Spectrum Stadium.

"There," Angie said.

Dom saw a blue flash disappear when an express bus pulled out. His tires gripped when he sped past the bus, only to find the blue lights disappeared again. He slowed and they searched hotel properties, church parking lots, and new apartment buildings. Snow raged around them. Out of the corner of his eye, he caught blue with red trailer brake lights disappear down a skyscraper's parking garage ramp.

"There," he said.

The garage stood across from One Pepitone Place below Tussey Center.

"Babe Tussey's a Chico customer?" Angie said.

"Her sidewalks need snow removal too," Dom said.

They entered the garage, retrieved a machine-generated ticket, and started down. With the Porsche's lights off, they passed fewer and fewer cars the deeper they went. Levels eleven and twelve were devoid of vehicles altogether. No Super Duty.

"Where's the truck and trailer?" Angie said.

Dom inched around a column onto a short ramp where dozens of overflow parking rows spread out before them. At the far side of the empty space, the Super Duty was inside a fenced-off area and the trailer was backed into a portable garage shelter with the flaps closed. Babe's guard Earl Jessup stood outside the shelter. Chico's Jorge and Francisco climbed down from the Super Duty and disappeared with Earl into the shelter with the trailer.

"Those three get around, don't they?" Angie said.

Dom drove up and exited the garage. He found an on-street parking spot near Augie's U-shaped drive and Lost Souls Grotto across from Tussey Center's elevated revolving door entrance.

"We'll wait for the Super Duty," he said. He could see Babe's garage entrance and exit in his side mirror. The Porsche idled in park with the heat on low. They were there for only a few minutes when the interior started to fill with an eggy vinegar odor.

"Are we back on Irwin Creek?" Angie said.

"Power down your window." The smell intensified with the frigid air. "Augie paid Palmer to find the source of his grotto odors," Dom said.

"The tax map we found on East Boulevard with Tussey Center circled, the Coldpepper note, and an X inside Augie's entrance drive may have been because Palmer found out about the grotto's ownership squabble between Augie and Babe," Angie said.

"Or he found what you did, the same notary connected to the Coldpeppers and Babe's Kloudcatcher LLCs. We don't know of any association between One Pepitone Place and Sally Meagers?"

"I haven't seen one. Augie uses a different law firm."

The Super Duty came up and out of the garage. When the truck and trailer passed them, Dom saw no change to the elliptical's liquid level. He pulled out and followed a number of car lengths behind. Liquid sloshed around inside the tank through Uptown along the stadium cross street and back into Chico's metal building.

CHAPTER 53

Franco stood with Dom at the flat screen. From her laptop Angie manipulated an aerial map on top of Chico's roof.

"Can you work with those?" Dom said.

"Domed skylights are a personal favorite," Franco said.

Handyman Hector de Losa walked in.

"Hector, glad you came," Dom said. "Here's the building I told you about."

Hector walked up to the screen and looked closer at the area behind the building. "Move closer here, por favor?" he said.

Angie's enhancement brought a telephone pole's transformer into view.

"Excelente. I will kill the power from here," Hector said.

Dom handed Franco a slip of paper with the building's address.

"Hector, care to join me for a drive?" Franco said.

"Of course," the Cuban said.

Angie populated the screen with a current weather report. "A once-in-a-decade Siberian Express is on the way," she said. "Stores can't keep eggs and milk stocked."

CHAPTER 54

The Piedmont Cloggers' studio stood among several look-alike brick buildings an orphanage once owned. Tap-shoe cadence with Earl Scruggs's voice and banjo came from the building they approached. Inside, a guy in satin pants and a candy-apple-red ballroom shirt put senior citizen cloggers through double-step exercises. A woman in dark warm-ups tapped up to them. She noticed they were empty-handed. "No shoes?" she said.

"We're here for your president, not to clog," Angie said.

A woman named Harper had told Angie on the ride over she'd be here.

"Check studio B."

They went along mirrored walls into a backroom studio to find a woman whose footwork to fiddle music was a white-shoe and steel-plate dazzle. She saw them and turned off her portable music box. "Can I help you?" Black roots anchored her short, bleached hair. She dabbed her face with a towel.

"Harper?" Angie said.

"Yes," she said.

"We spoke on the phone."

"Angie Crete?"

"And Dominick Mundy," Angie said.

They sat on fold-out chairs near a wall-mounted balance bar. Angie gave her Dom's card with her name penciled above his. Harper took out a pair of readers and read the card. "Why the interest with our volunteer cleanup crew?"

Angie gave her the fax with Palmer's Irwin Creek arrows.

"Did your volunteers come into contact with an environmental engineer named Palmer Giron while they picked up trash along Irwin Creek? He collected water samples indicated on the fax near the Morehead Street tunnel," Dom said.

"We saw your organization on a county Adopt-a-Stream sign," Angie said.

"Last May we were on the creek for our annual volunteer pitch-in. We've been responsible for our section for fifteen years, but the smell was so bad, we called off the cleanup at noon."

"Vinegar-infused eggs?" Angie said.

"More like cat pee," Harper said.

"Did you call the city?" Dom said.

"Twice, and each time they said inspectors couldn't detect any odors. One of our instructors said she lived across the street from an environmental engineer who she could ask what he thought we should do. Palmer told her he was covered up with work but would take a look into our concerns. He reported back there were no odors, but he drew water samples and would let us know the results."

"Did you have any further contact with him?" Dom said.

"He was murdered a week later. Does the fax mean you have the results?" Harper said.

"Someone is using your volunteer cleanup waterway for a methamphetamine chemical dump," Dom said.

᷑

They were halfway out of the parking lot when Harper clogged after them. "Sorry, I remembered Palmer told our sergeant at arms he ran into someone while he drew his samples, a guy who came down the embankment and warned him to stay off their property."

"He say where he came from?" Dom said.

"A metal building with a drive-in door."

CHAPTER 55

The dashboard clock flicked to 3:17 in the morning at the same time another powder keg from the Siberian Express rocked the Porsche.

"Those lights should be out by now," Dom said.

Across the parking lot floodlights burned along the roofline of Chico's metal building. Hector was supposed to be up the telephone pole at the transformer by now. Franco waited in his SUV behind the building ready to scale up to the domed skylights.

At 3:22, the building went dark. Twelve and a half minutes later, a text appeared on Dom's phone of a lampshade-mustached smiley-face emoji in a beret.

"He's in," Dom said.

Franco met them at the open front door. "Bonsoir," he said.

"Better late than never," Dom said.

Hector emerged with a frosty goatee dressed like an Arctic explorer. With flashlights they moved into the warehouse and found the Super Duty with the car-hauler trailer up against a mechanic's pit with the rear doors open.

Another trailer with landscaping tools, stand-up riding mower, and an elliptical sat toward the rear of the warehouse.

"Check the office," Dom said.

Franco's light moved back into the lobby, Angie started for the car-hauler trailer, and Hector with his flashlight looked through the grate inside the pit.

Dom shined his light around the empty warehouse and went to the landscaping trailer. Odd for a car hauler, snow removal, and landscape company building not to smell of tire rubber, grease, or even gas and not have any workbenches, tools, chains, or even a trolley jack. The warehouse looked like the day of the final inspection—unused.

The trailer displayed another set of magnetic door signs for *Kueentown Champion Lawn and Garden* with no phone number or website.

Hector opened the grate and climbed down. A roof ventilation fan rattled in the storm.

"Dominick," Angie said. She stood at the hauler's open doors.

He joined her and looked at the brilliant Petra Gold Rolls-Royce Phantom secured inside. She pressed the button on a well-engineered rectangle box from the luxury car company inside the trunk. The box opened to reveal a table, silverware, linen napkins, champagne flutes, and two bottle chillers cradled on either side.

"Someone parties in style," she said.

Franco joined them.

"What about the office?" Dom said

"Never been used," Franco said.

"Down here," Hector said.

Dom took the rungs into the pit. A hollow sound followed each metallic tap of his flashlight on one of the smooth cement walls. He pressed the wall and it hinged. Damp moldy air filled the pit from a tunnel with wet-rot wood supports. "An abandoned gold mine shaft," Dom said.

Somewhere he heard water rush. Hector stooped and went in. Dom followed him. A dozen and a half feet inside they came to where the ceiling collapsed. A rusted lantern from the 1800s still hung in place on a roof-support member. Dom could feel the rush of air and hear water through a space created by the downed rotted support beams and boulders. Hector bent sideways and looked through the opening with his flashlight.

"A stream," he said.

He moved aside and Dom put his light inside. A few feet away, water flowed toward Irwin Creek.

⁂

They stood around the mechanics pit.

"Gold in Charlotte?" Franco said.

"Abandoned mine shafts crisscross around here from the city's gold rush," Dom said.

"You're sure these cloggers smelled cat piss?" Hector said.

"They canceled their annual cleanup, the smell was so intense," Angie said.

"Palmer's water sample results indicated meth lab chemicals are being dumped in the creek," Dom said.

"But I smell no odor," Franco said.

"Perhaps we're in the wrong building," Hector said.

"Palmer's focus was on Chico's building. We know the car trailer disappeared into Kueentown Motorworks, then came back here, and an elliptical tank left the building for Tussey Center," Dom said.

Hector pointed inside the trunk to the champagne chest. "They take the party box to Kueentown Motorworks?" Hector said.

"We don't know what was inside the trailer," Dom said.

"A conversation with Mr. Chico might be called for," Hector said.

"Or at least a return trip to Ms. Tussey's garage to see why the need to hide the other elliptical tank," Dom said.

"Have you seen the number of guards she employs?" Angie said.

"Every building has challenges," Franco said.

"Like skylights?" Angie said.

"An underground stream would be perfect to siphon off chemicals from Rushers production," Dom said.

"Then where's your lab?" Franco said.

"You're a creative guy. Could you pull off a meth lab in a high-rise office tower?" Dom said.

"Vertical logistics are my strong suit," Franco said.

CHAPTER 56

Pia wound the rented Executive Suburban deeper into Tussey Center's parking garage. Vehicles crowded every level from a valve convention in Babe's exposition hall. She went down the ramp to the overflow level where most every space was occupied. In the back-row seat with Angie, Dom looked out the tinted windows above the glossy roofs and saw, on the far side of the low ceiling space, the second rented Executive Deuce had pulled alongside the fenced-off area yesterday. The Super Duty sat behind the fence with the trailer inside the flaps.

Franco had made the suggestion to use Suburbans to block guards at security camera monitors because they wouldn't attract attention. Pia maneuvered toward the fence and turned off the interior light. She stopped with a few inches of overlap to the front end of the second Executive, then climbed out and went to the front left tire. When she crouched for a closer look at a perceived tire problem, Dom and Angie slid out, and with the Executive's height for cover, hustled past the Super Duty through the canvas flaps. Only a pair of double metal doors and the trailer with no elliptical occupied the space.

When Dom tried the handles, one of the doors opened to a storeroom and freight elevator, and a heavy brew of bleach enhanced with Lysol with a witch hazel kicker. He turned on the light to shelves stocked with bathroom cleaning supplies, pressure washers, riding scrubbers, and a parking lot striper. Another single door behind the shelves opened to a floor mop sink. His eyes started to water from the smell of rotten eggs in vinegar doused with cat urine, the same smell from Augie's grotto and Irwin Creek.

"Rushers come out of Tussey Center," Angie said.

Voices came from outside.

"Tire problems, lady?"

Pia's reply inaudible.

"How about we take a look?" a different voice said.

"Guards with Pia," Dom said.

"You sure now?" one of them said.

Another Pia reply Dom couldn't make out. He heard the Executive door close and Pia roll away.

"Get the striper, Lenny."

"The elevator," Dom said.

He pressed the call button and saw the elevator dread in Angie's eyes. Shaft mechanisms engaged, gears shifted, and air swooshed, then open doors parted to a padded cab. Inside, Angie grabbed his elbow when the floor gave way an inch. He hit the top floor button. The doors came together.

He heard the storeroom guard. "Who left the light on?"

Their cab slow-hoisted, then gained speed. Angie stood tense, her eyes closed at the doors. A padded elevator, the last place she wanted to be, Dom thought.

Red electronic numbers ticked away on the display screen, LL 11, LL 10, LL 9. They passed the lobby with the guard station and hurtled up through tens of thousands of square feet. At thirty-three they slowed, then a couple of floors later the doors parted.

"You OK?" he said.

Angie didn't respond and quick-stepped into another wide-aisle storeroom on thirty-five stocked with more skyscraper supplies.

"Let Pia know where we are," he said.

Angie took out her phone and thumbed off a text. As in the storeroom hundreds of feet below, there was no elliptical.

"Wait here," he said.

Out in the carpeted hallway a sign indicated another freight elevator behind double doors across the hall. Two freight elevators, he thought—one lower bank, one upper bank. He tried the upper-bank storeroom door's handles. They opened to racks of hand sanitizer, carpet cleaner, and an elliptical tank cradled on a skid assembly. He went back for Angie.

The two-hundred-gallon white plastic tank, a quarter filled with liquid, rested on the skid assembly. When Dom turned the drain valve nozzle, liquid dripped out. He touched and smelled it with his fingers. "Water."

"Why go to all the trouble to transport water?" she said.

"Give me your cell phone flashlight," he said.

He tilted the elliptical toward her. She gripped the top waffle-size lid and steadied the tank and assembly. The liquid waved back and forth. Dom moved her light and only saw solid-gray industrial plastic.

"Let me have the light," she said.

They brought the tank back down. She rotated the lid off and through the hole looked at the bottom of the tank. The translucent plastic lit up from her light. "I can see another tank down there," she said.

Dom saw the second tank when he looked inside. "At least fifty gallons," he said.

She looked along her side of the assembly and reached down at the corner.

Dom heard a click.

"Here's another drain nozzle," she said.

He came around to a smaller valve in a space she'd exposed. She twisted the small red handle and liquid dribbled out followed by the same acrid smell from the mop sink, Irwin Creek, and the Lost Souls Grotto. She continued along the assembly with the light. Dom watched her release another flap to a hollowed-out concealed space under the tank.

"Rushers lab is somewhere above us," he said.

"We don't have time to check thirty-five floors."

"We'll be back," he said.

They made it back down to the lower-level storeroom with no stops. Pia had returned to her place with the Executive when they came through the flaps. They rounded up each level in silence until a group of valve expo goers with lanyard name badges and brochures blocked their way on level three. A pair of lights came up behind them.

"The Super Duty," Pia said.

Dom glanced back when they cornered onto the next level. The Super Duty was tight behind them. He couldn't make out the driver.

"Are we being followed?" Angie said.

"We're about to find out," he said.

Pia paid the booth attendant and exited left.

"We're not in a hurry," Dom said.

At the next intersection the light turned red and the Super Duty with no trailer came alongside. Dom saw Earl Jessup behind the wheel with Jorge in the passenger seat. Earl smoked a cigarette and tapped his thumbs on the steering wheel while Jorge talked on his cell phone. Earl gunned the Super Duty when the light changed.

CHAPTER 57

SITTING BETWEEN DEUCE and Franco, Angie clicked the conference table mouse twice and a copy of the tax map they'd found on East Boulevard appeared on the wall flat screen. Coldpepper was noted next to a circled Tussey Center with the grotto X'd off and circled inside Augie's U drive.

"From Palmer's office," Dom said, "he made the connection between Chico's real estate entities and Tussey Center. The same notary handled the paperwork with Jefferson Wallach, a corporate lawyer on Babe's payroll," Angie said.

"Did Giron know about tanks, Tussey Center, and Chico's warehouse?" Pia said.

'We're not sure," Dom said.

"Why an X and a circle?" Franco said.

"They're on Augie's grotto. We've confirmed an underground stream runs down gradient from Tussey Center under One Pepitone Place. Bring up Babe's stacking plan," Dom said.

Seventy stories of multicolored tenant space appeared on top of twelve levels of below-grade parking. A global insurance-company anchor tenant occupied all lower-bank floors, one through thirty-five, and full- and partial-floor tenants rented space on thirty-six up to fifty.

Dom went to the screen and pointed to the parking garage storeroom.

"The mop sink's here, where discarded Rushers chemicals are being dumped," he said.

"You need nose plugs to go in there. The sink must not be hooked up to city water or sewer," Angie said.

"Show them where we found the elliptical," Dom said.

A close-up of thirty-five appeared, and she ran the cursor around the upper-bank freight-elevator storeroom.

"Earl Jessup, a building security guard, is in the Rushers meth business with Chico Vega and his crew somewhere above thirty-five. If you're an ambitious chemist, where do you set up shop?" Dom said.

"In another storeroom," Pia said.

"I've searched every floor plan and only found storerooms on parking level twelve and the two on thirty-five," Angie said.

"I'd use vacant space," Deuce said.

Besides the three crown floors, a few white vacant spaces dotted the upper bank. Dom looked toward the room's only building expert. "Any ideas?" he said.

"Don't focus on vacancies," Franco said.

"Why not?" Angie said.

"The lab needs to be vented," Franco said.

"Drill window holes," Angie said.

"Too obvious. Find the mechanical rooms," Franco said.

The cursor traced under the lower of the top two floors.

"Here's one," Angie said.

"Zoom in on the main page's top floors," Dom said.

The skyscraper's photograph with a brilliant green globe under the top setback floors appeared. Safety mesh for exhaust fans lined along the north side of the sixty-ninth floor.

Franco motioned Angie for the mouse. He clicked on the

menu tab. Under Building Specifications, below links for high-speed elevators and LEED-certification qualifications, he opened Tenant Experience. After more links for services like concierge desk and valet, he hovered and tapped on TLD for the skyscraper's tuned liquid damper. A medium-size pool of water with baffle separators appeared on seventy.

Dom's first thought was Babe installed a vanity swimming pool.

"The enemy of all skyscrapers is what?" Franco said.

"Movie star gorillas," Angie said.

"Lateral deflection. Towers sway in high wind. Motion-sick tenants at a million bucks a year in rent is not good. The water moves in counterbalance to the sway to lessen the movement. Look on the TLD floor for your Rushers. They could vent down one floor to the exhaust fans. You have many challenges, Dominick," Franco said.

"You mean we," Dom said.

"Nous?" Franco said.

Dom walked them through how he planned to find where Rushers were produced in a trophy skyscraper.

CHAPTER 58

Dom watched Tussey Center's entrance from the front seat of Franco's SUV as Pia pulled into a metered street space. The Lost Souls Grotto was across from Babe's cavernous lobby.

When he'd asked around his building for skyscraper-assault volunteers, everyone signed on. First up were the Mexican marines who leased office space from him, who now walked into Tussey Center with facade inspector gear.

Dom saw Earl Jessup at the guard desk.

After a brief conversation, another guard appeared to escort the marines toward the elevators with their safety ropes, vests, and helmets.

"Our janitors have arrived," Pia said.

Janitorial company executives Jock and Hector strode in from the parking garage elevators, there to tour the building to prepare a cleaning quote. Hector carried the tower map Angie had marked up with vacant spaces. Their job was to include all non-occupied space below the top few floors on their pre-quote building walk-through. If Rushers were being churned out in unleased space, they'd find it. A property manager met them and led them away.

Dom scratched his salt-and-pepper bushman beard, which one of his former tenants, a sometime-employed makeup artist, had applied to his face. Her scissor cut, magic silver hair dust, and eight-inch beard put ten years on him. Winnie insisted on a pair of round, black glasses.

Angie, in the back next to Franco, had also received the full Hollywood treatment. With her outfit and blond wig with bangs, she looked like an executive on the hunt for office space.

Dom saw a woman walk up the sidewalk toward them. Winnie had arranged for her friend, office space broker Georgie, to escort them on their bogus Tussey Center space showing where they planned to access the mechanical and TLD floors. When Winnie explained the situation, Georgie said she was all in because Babe came after her commission on a lease she had arranged in Tussey Center.

"Here she is," he said.

Pia stayed at the wheel when they all got out, and Dom introduced everyone on the sidewalk.

"OK, we're a fake French company on the hunt for office space. Are you the Frenchman?" Georgie said. Her set jaw told Dom if he ever needed office space, he knew who to call.

"I'm the interior space planner," he said.

Georgie's finger aimed at Angie, who held up her leather padfolio. "The company in-house counsel," Angie said.

Her hard brown eyes went to Franco. "Igor de la Croix from Lyons," Franco said.

"You sound French, good."

"Not French, Parisian," Franco said.

"Before we head in, let's review what I told Winnie. What cities are in contention for your corporate headquarters?"

"Richmond, Tampa, and Nashville," Dom said.

"Never forget Atlanta. Charlotte always competes with Atlanta. Now, how do you make your money?"

"Crème contre les éruptions cutanées," Franco said.

"Rash cream, right?" Georgie said.

"Why would Babe Tussey allow a beauty products competitor in her building?" Angie said.

"She would never let ambiguity get between her and a crown multifloor tenant. Her nephew leasing agent, Benny Tussey the Fourth, only knows we're Project Gatepost in town to look at space for a possible corporate headquarters move."

"Should we expect to see Babe?" Angie said.

"For a crown prospect, count on it. Remember, I do all the talking, but if they ask, your financials are strong," Georgie said.

She hustled them across the marble expanse toward Benny Four at the guard desk.

"We're on?" Dom said.

Angie showed him her smartphone face down against the padfolio. A tiny green light blinked with an open conference call app. The marines, janitorial executives, and Pia right outside the main entrance in the SUV, and Deuce in the Porsche on parking garage level twelve at the fence enclosure would all monitor their progress on Bluetooth earpieces.

Benny Four waited, armed with glossy brochures and a glad-hand smile ready to move office space. With a post-college paunch and apricot comb-over, he looked relaxed in his khakis, open-collar lemon golf shirt, and smallish sport jacket.

Dom thought he looked more beach house Sunday brunch than Uptown space hustler. He guessed only a guy with his name on a skyscraper could pull off pink argyle socks and handmade pomegranate slip-ons.

Earl fish-eyed Angie.

"We're always glad when Georgie includes Tussey Center on her tours," Benny said, his voice scratchy from a head cold.

Georgie introduced Project Gatepost. "We're tight for time," she said.

"Let's walk and talk," Benny said. "Does the company have a name?"

"Nice try, Benny. The name will be on the RFP if you make the cut," Georgie said.

"Who are we up against?" Benny said.

"Nashville, Richmond, Atlanta, and one of your Uptown competitors," Georgie said.

"Pepitone's Tinkertoy building?"

Earl winked at Angie.

"Augie wants the business too," Georgie said.

Benny passed out clip-on Visitor badges.

"Hold on, partner," Earl said. "Have you been in the building before?"

"First time," Dom said.

"They flew in for the tour, Earl," Benny said.

"Let's see the bag," Earl said.

"Good grief, Benny, not a building prospect," Georgie said.

"Spot checks are one of our many security measures," Benny said.

Dom handed Chester his man bag that Winnie had stocked with architecture supplies. Earl made a show of the items he removed. A few were the T-square, adjustable triangle, handheld laser, and a drafting brush Dom thought Winnie went overboard with. Earl made Frisbee motions with the clear plastic French curve. The last four items he pulled out were razor cut-out knives.

"These weapons?" Earl said.

Dom made an educated guess. "Floor plan model equipment."

"Can we start already, Benny?" Georgie said.

The cutters disappeared into Earl's oversize clasp envelope. "Pick them up on your way out," Earl said.

Dom reshouldered the bag. Benny led them away.

"Gestapo," Franco said.

"We have a secure building thanks to Earl and his fellow offi-cers," Benny said.

"Those white clubs must do the trick," Angie said.

"They're for show only," Benny said.

At the elevators Benny passed out his brochures. Dom sensed Angie's unease being surrounded by all these elevator doors.

"You'll find interior and exterior photos along with our build-ing amenities, specifications, and floor plans."

Franco tapped an open page in his brochure. A fire truck siren blared beyond the windows and blocked out what he said to Georgie.

"He's curious why you don't have a stated rental rate?" Georgie said.

"Depends on your build-out, term, and credit," Benny said.

"He asked for a ballpark," Georgie said.

"Crown floors figure forty-five a foot. We might have some wiggle room if their financials hold up."

Franco played up his part with an exaggerated accent. "Our numbers are superb."

Dom thought now was the time to act like a space planner. "How many floor feet in the crown?"

"You mean our floor plate size?" Benny said.

Georgie mouthed yes behind Benny.

"Of course, crown plates."

Benny flipped brochure pages and his finger landed on an obvious number in the center of a light-orange floor plan. "Twenty thousand square feet of unobstructed views."

"And the load factor?" Georgie said.

"Fifteen percent," Benny said.

"A facteur?" Franco said.

Georgie was quick to explain.

"A percentage difference between what you pay rent on and your carpetable usable area."

"My Persian rugs?" Franco said.

"Sure, where you throw your rugs," Georgie said. Georgie's expression told Dom, *what's up with Franco and all these comments?*

"Load factors come off your rent to reimburse for common areas," Benny said.

"But you own the common areas," Franco said.

"And tenants use the hallways, elevator lobbies, and bathrooms we have to maintain," Benny said.

Franco rubbed his fingers like money. "Larceny, fifteen percent of forty-five."

Benny was fluent in the universal dialect of office space leasing agents and knew how to respond when confronted with a prospect's objections. "With full-floor takedowns we might consider load factor recalculations."

Doors parted when Benny pressed an elevator call button. Angie hung back, came in behind Dom, and faced the closed doors. A news reader discussed recent OPEC moves on a miniature screen above the control panel.

Benny touched thirty-five, the crossover floor with the storeroom elliptical tank. They lifted off.

"Our elevators are the most efficient in the city with the shortest tenant wait times," he said.

Franco curled his arms like a weightlifter. "Gymnasium?"

"Do we have a gym?" Benny said.

"Oui."

"Our fitness facility is one of a kind," Benny said.

"With dumbbells?" Franco said.

Georgie looked at Dom again.

"No free weights, but we have next-generation machines," said Benny.

"I prefer dumbbells," Franco said.

Benny with another quick comeback. "The fitness center's free of charge to building tenants."

Angie spoke to the doors. "*Libre*, no cost," she said.

Benny appeared relieved when they started to slow. The doors opened to the property manager and make-believe janitorial executives Jock and Hector in their Sunday suits. Jock motioned with his head toward Dom, no Rushers. Benny crossed to and pressed the upper-tower elevator call button.

"Can you share what industry they're in?" he said.

Georgie nodded go ahead to Franco.

"Rash cream," he said.

A set of guards emerged from a lower back elevator. "Mind if we catch a ride?" one said.

"By all means," Benny said.

Their doors swooshed open. Inside a mutual fund advertisement played on another screen.

"Where to?" Benny said.

"Fifty-eight," one guard said.

Benny touched fifty-eight and seventy.

Dom saw the mechanical and tuned-damper floors were locked off on the control panel. Angie, crowded into the corner by the warehouse-dock-worker-size guard, took long slow breaths. One of guards had lathered on too much Old Spice.

The uniforms left on fifty-eight. At seventy they came out onto an unimproved floor with a view into the clouds. Dom thought Angie looked pale. He pulled her aside. "You good?" he said.

"Get on with it," she said.

Benny led them toward sample floor plan displays on easels. Franco inquired about building signage.

Dom saw ropes the Mexican marine facade inspectors would rappel down to look for the Rushers clandestine production facility on the two floors below them. "We'll have to take the stairs, the floors are locked off," he said.

Angie nodded and they stepped behind the center core. At the exit door Dom heard Benny say, "We lost two of your party."

"We can start," Georgie said.

Dom and Angie hurried into the stairwell up to the first set-back floor. Dom waited for Angie to continue up to the tuned-damper floor.

She called down. "I'm in."

He turned lights on inside the mechanical room. The high-sheen gray floor was half the size of the unimproved floor below where Benny made his presentation. White tape-wrapped pipes wedged between ceiling HVAC returns. Gauges and valves protruded from larger pipes that arched down one wall through watermelon-size filter containers into the floor. A number of generators stood at beige electrical panel boxes whose steel tube connections could handle dozens of wires.

On the north side, Dom saw the ventilation mesh below windows Franco had identified as ideal to vent vapors, but he only smelled machine grease laced with lemon floor disinfectant. He checked doors on either side of the freight elevator. One opened to an empty closet and the other to vacant expansion space where he didn't see an elliptical tank or Rushers lab.

Were they off base to think Earl and Chico could pull off a drug production up in Tussey Center's apex?

Back in the stairwell he called to Angie. "Any luck?"

She didn't answer.

"Angie?"

Silence.

He took the steps two at a time and went into another half-size floor with the baffled pool of water Franco said counteracted building high-wind movement.

She wasn't there.

Did she rejoin Georgie and Franco? Why wouldn't she tell him on her way back down?

His call to her cell went to voicemail. She didn't answer his text. Back on the tour floor he came around the building's core. Benny pointed out landmarks on an Uptown aerial. Angie wasn't with them.

"Where's your company counsel?" Benny said.

Good question, Dom thought. "She needed to use the bathroom," he said.

"Is she OK?" Benny said.

"She's fine and will be back in a few minutes," Dom said.

"We are going to inspect the fitness facility," Georgie said.

Dom held up his cell phone. "I'll snap a few pictures and join you when she gets back."

On the way to the elevators, Benny asked Franco if he played golf.

"Where is she?" Georgie said.

"I thought she was with you," Dom said.

"Do you need my help?" Georgie said.

"Stay with Franco."

Once their elevator descended, he raced back up to the damper floor. Only the freight elevator offered another way down, but it was locked off at the control panel. He couldn't see her stepping foot inside the padded cab anyway. To be sure, he pressed the call button. No response. The only other way out was down the stairs, seventy stories to the lobby. How far could she have gone?

Before he went back to the stairwell and started down, he rescanned the floor. He saw the freight door, solid walls, and pool of crystal-clear water. He didn't see how she could… then he saw the carve-out he'd missed beyond the pool. He circled the water to the opening and found they weren't wrong about these top floors.

An elliptical tank in an assembly stood there next to a coiled hose attached to a pipe nozzle. A bank drive through a pneumatic tube carrier station was on the wall alongside the nozzle. The tube and pipe disappeared into the ceiling next to another door. The door was unlocked and led out to metal stairs up to a roof access door.

Why would she go up to the roof?

At the top of the stairs, he pushed out into a vestibule with double doors, one solid and one half glass. Through the glass he saw Babe's rented helicopter on one of her helipads and no tracks out in the snow. Angie must've used the other door. He pushed through the solid door and found himself next to garden tools in a vertical storage shed inside Babe's humid greenhouse globe. The odor overlay was troweled peat moss and manure. Glass panes sweated with moisture. Wood benches were lined with plant trays. The few identification labels he could read told him Babe's killer instinct didn't stop with office space or tennis courts. All the plants were carnivores. Rows of Venus flytraps interspersed with rosy-pink sundews. A colony of cobra lilies looked hungry. Food for these killers were dried bloodworms in glass containers.

The pipe and the pneumatic tube came up through holes drilled into a bench of monkey cup plants. A hose ran off the pipe into a glass partition that separated the other half of the greenhouse. A thermal champagne bottle cooler like one of the ones he saw inside the Phantom trunk in Chico's building rested next to another pneumatic tube station. He picked up the cooler. Both ends were screwed shut. When he twisted off one of the lids, ammonia cat pee flushed his nostrils.

His phone vibrated with a text from Pia, who copied every-one. "Where's Angie?"

Jock on the property management tour added, "I heard her walk on gravel."

Dom saw the garden globe was covered with pea gravel.

Pia again. "I heard her speak with a woman."

What woman?

He stepped around a makeshift pond's yellow bladderworts to the partition. When he pulled it open, the intense smell hit him, the Rushers lab. Bags of fertilizer were stacked with pet store cat litter and five-gallon containers with chemical labels. Discarded cheesecloth, red-colored coffee liners, generic pill bottles, and empty twenty-ounce soda bottles overflowed from a garbage can. Hazmat suits hung on a coat stand.

The hose came through the partition to connect with a steel whirlpool filled with phosphorous chemicals and large enough to accommodate a three-hundred-pound offensive lineman. Above a luxury home's four-burner range, a vent hood dispersed by-product a thousand feet over Uptown. He lifted the lid on a one-hundred-fifty-quart marine chest full of ice.

Rushers were sent down to the ellipticals through the pneumatic tube inside the champagne bottle coolers. The discarded chemicals were hosed down. Once in Chico's building, Rushers in the coolers were transferred into the champagne chest to be delivered to Kueentown Motorworks. The chemicals were dumped in Irwin Creek through the gold mine stream and into Augie's grotto via the mop sink.

He blast-texted, "Rushers superlab in globe."

Past the toolshed he crunched out of the greenhouse through the Amazon growth. Next to the private elevator he stepped onto the Bermuda grass and found Tussey Center's developer in full beekeeper mode. A shaft of sunlight cut between her and Angie, who stood frozen with her eyes squeezed shut. Bees massed around her neck and upper torso.

"My bees follow their queen anywhere," Babe said.

"Get them off her," Dom said.

He saw Angie's cell phone on the grass under the garden

table. The tiny green speaker light for the open conference call app blipped.

"She'll be fine if she doesn't twitch," Babe said.

Through guava tree leaves Dom saw the Mexican marines hurry around the globe.

"You left Rushers off building amenities in your brochure. You might want to give your distributor Chico Vega a credit too," Dom said.

"Mr. Vega is quite well compensated," Babe said.

"You caught a bad break when Palmer waded into Irwin Creek," he said.

"He was warned off," Babe said.

A bee tributary started to form up the side of Angie's head.

"Jerry Qwain warned off too when you sent him and Earl to retrieve what Palmer may have determined put the stink in Augie's grotto," Dom said.

"Jerry's run-on sentences could be hard to take."

"His chatter didn't bother Chico in his liquor house."

"Mr. Vega's a people person," Babe said.

The sound of broken glass came from the greenhouse, and the marines pushed through passion flower vines. Deuce came out of the private elevator like a rodeo bull.

Babe held her concealed carry pistol inches from Angie's head. Outside the globe, Dom heard a helicopter somewhere in the clouds. Babe backed up with Angie and disappeared through banana leaves.

In the white-out clouds the helicopter roared overhead.

Dom went after Babe through thick vegetation and came out at the curved glass where a section of panes stood ajar. Babe was out on the roof with Angie, headed toward her rented helicopter. He ran through drifts up to his knees toward them. The marines and Deuce fanned out behind him.

The engine whine of the unseen helicopter circled the rooftop.

At the helipad's ladder Dom saw the bees start to swarm. Babe raised her purple-handled pistol toward him when the other helicopter came in hard on the unoccupied helipad. Rotor downwash blew every bee off Angie and ripped Babe's bee veil from her head. Through the whirlwind he made out a tail-boom paladin and Augie Pepitone with the pilot's headset on. Babe stood beside her helicopter now with a wild white mane. She fired.

Hit, Angie spun off the helipad into his arms.

A flash from Augie's Sikorsky's open passenger door shattered Babe's helicopter windshield. Two sparks came from Babe's extended arm toward the corporate helicopter. Babe moved around her whirlybird's rotor blade for a better angle at whoever was inside Augie's machine. She brought her pistol up for another shot. A white burst from the Sikorsky knocked her back off balance. Another quick pop reeled her over the roof's edge into skyscraper oblivion. Pia jumped out with her Hellcat and ran toward Dom.

CHAPTER 59

Sɪsᴛᴇʀ Mᴀʀɪᴀ Cᴏɴᴄᴇᴛᴛᴀ Pucci stood framed in the cloister's doorway with her hockey coat pulled tight around her.

"No change from when we spoke last week," she said.

"How's her shoulder?"

"Lucky only grazed. Every morning after four o'clock prayers, she joins us in the bakery. I understand Sister Eli has taught her how to play cribbage."

"The Sisters play card games?" Dom said.

"Raucous has been used to describe our poker nights. Give Angie time, Dominick, she's only been with us for a month. Our routine and solitude are what she needs."

He noticed the low firewood supply.

"I'll cut more wood for you."

She handed him a twine-tied brown paper package.

"An Armenian gata cake for your sweet tooth."

CHAPTER 60

SNOWMELT FROM MID-FIFTY-DEGREE temperatures glistened off cars and asphalt outside Dom and Nita Lopez's diner booth.

"She still with your Sisters?"

"Their cloister is the perfect place for her," Dom said.

"Tranquility in a chaotic world."

"Spoken like a true homicide detective."

Nita palmed her café Americano.

"Lucky Augie's helicopter was on hand," she said.

"He broke a few rules when he dropped from the clouds onto Carolina Medical Center's heliport with Angie inside."

"How does a former taxi driver sharpshooter in her golden years convince Augie Pepitone to fly across Uptown?"

Steam rose off his black coffee.

"Pia figured if Angie was in trouble, the Sikorsky would be the quickest way to the top of Tussey Center. When Augie's secretary put Pia through to him, Pia asked Augie if he wanted some high-rise payback for the trouble Babe and her lawyer unleashed over his grotto ownership."

"How'd she get to his building so fast?"

"You haven't seen her drive."

"Where do you find these people?"

"They find me."

A slab of ice slid off the diner's awning and shattered on pavers.

"Babe's lawyer, Jefferson Wallach, was picked up yesterday while he attempted to cross from Maine into New Brunswick, Canada, with his girlfriend."

"Is she a notary?"

"How did you know?"

"An educated guess," he said.

"Chico and Babe Tussey made quite the pair."

"We heard her skyscraper is a money pit," he said.

"Tussey Center burns through money like a prairie fire. Her family cut Babe off from the shampoo money when she refused to sell the property. With personal guaranteed loans she turned to Jefferson, desperate for creative ways to generate cash flow. Jefferson recommended a guy he knew on the hunt for new business opportunities."

"Jefferson should be lawyer of the year if he recommended Chico Vega."

"Chico suggests the solution to her financial dilemma might be a niche product with broad market appeal and a catchy name," she said.

"Rushers," Dom said. He waved to the barista for another round.

"A product with unlimited customers. Jefferson came up with the idea of a greenhouse globe for the perfect location for a super lab."

"And here we thought the globe went up to win back the height title from One Pepitone Place," he said.

"True, Babe can't stand her rival across the street, but the globe was all Jefferson Wallach. He made sure reporters played up the One Pepitone Place and Tussey Center competition angle. Who doesn't like to read about skyscraper wars?"

A floor mat delivery truck splashed to a stop.

"Babe handed off the day-to-day production to a relative, a building security guard."

"Earl Jessup," Don said.

"We have him in custody too. He churned out Rushers in the clouds while Chico and his crew moved them up and down the East Coast. The partnership staved off Babe's financial ruin. She washed millions through tenant improvement contractors she paid off in cash."

"Palmer being in Irwin Creek for the cloggers was the wrong place at the wrong time."

"Earl saw him and alerted Babe, who was smart enough to know it was only a matter of time before Palmer zeroed in on Chico's metal building for one of their chemical dump sites. When Augie brought Palmer on to look into his grotto smell, he suspected the waterway under Tussey Center."

The delivery driver wheeled rolls of mats into the shop.

"Babe sent Earl to Freedom Park, didn't she?" he said.

"With Jorge and Francisco from Chico's crew. Babe's a micromanager, doesn't care for loose ends. She sends Jerry Qwain to Palmer's offices to remove all he has on Irwin Creek and the grotto. Earl understood she only wanted one of them to come back down the Welker Street ladder. Your girl Friday had her timber hitch job descriptions right. Before Babe brought Earl to the big city and dressed him in a security guard uniform, he did right-of-way tree work in the mountains."

She sipped her fresh Americano from the server.

"Why didn't I rate a call when you suspected the lab in Tussey Center?"

"I seem to remember from a prior conversation when Babe Tussey came up you said we might want to focus our attention elsewhere."

"Do you have any other subjects your attention is focused on?"

"Like skyscrapers and garden globes?"

"Or gut rehabs."

A NOTE FROM THE AUTHOR

Thank you so much for joining Dom, Angie, and the rest of the gang at Mundy and Associates on this adventure. Reviews are the lifeblood of independent authors, and if you have the time and inclination I would greatly appreciate your honest opinion, wherever you prefer to review books. I truly value candid feedback. If you prefer not to review, though, that's perfectly okay. Either way, I sincerely hope you enjoyed the book.

I. James Bertolina

https://ijamesbertolina.com/

https://www.facebook.com/IJamesBertolina

www.ingramcontent.com/pod-product-compliance
Lightning Source LLC
Chambersburg PA
CBHW060651190726
48289CB00002B/358